Buckle Up Buttercup

Copyright

No AI was used in the creation of any part of this book or art. It was 100% written by an insane human (me) and the art was crafted by real humans (not me) who I'm so grateful to work with!

Paperback ISBN: 978-1-957873-65-7
Hardcover ISBN: 978-1-957873-66-4
eBook ISBN: 978-1-957873-73-2

Map - Ink & Laurel Design & Anna Fury
Editing - Mountains Wanted Editing
Cover Art - Linda Noeran
Cover Design - MiblArt
Comics - MisutoreKunArt on VGen

Contents

The Haven System

Monsters live among us in hidden towns called havens. Camouflaged from the broader human world despite sometimes being located in big cities, these havens are connected through a series of portals originating from a headquarters location called Hearth HQ.

Each haven is run by a Keeper, something like a human mayor, who's both the Hearth HQ representative and the local authority in advocating for the haven's needs. The Keeper also works with the town herself, where every building is sentient and has... opinions.

Keepers can invite outside humans into the haven via a magical homing beacon object, which varies by location. Havens are protected from prying human eyes by magically spelled wards, and time passes more quickly inside monster havens than outside. Within this world, monsters live lives of peace and happiness, finding love, community, and family. It's not without challenges, though. Thralls—monsters bewitched by those who don't believe in the sanctity of the haven system—are attracted to haven magic and always looking for a way in.

We visited the darling haven of Ever, Massachusetts in the Haven Ever After series. Now we're venturing to Montana and wild west territory. You don't need to have read the HEA series to understand this one, but if you love my crazy world, there's plenty more for you there. Nine books worth, in fact.

Welcome to the haven system, human reader!

Buckle Up, Buttercup

PINE GULCH EVER AFTER BOOK TWO

HAZEL MACK

Hadrian

Swooping between a giant minotaur's horns, I push off his head and execute a 720 turn, then land on the turf. Skyball tucked firmly beneath my left arm, I bullet for the end zone with wings lifted high at my back, even as the opposing team's defense bunches together to stop me.

The Hearth HQ Hellions are a kickass team—I was their star quarterback just last year—but the Punishers are better this season. Especially since I joined.

"Al-ka-zar! Al-ka-zar!" The crowd screams my last name as my offense gets into formation. Dipping to the left, my right-side defense barrels into the opposing team's, and I duck and roll beneath the fray. The Hellions weren't expecting that. It'd be far more common for a gargoyle player to leap up and over or take up into the sky as high as the rules legally allow.

Never stopping, I rise and keep sprinting fast as hells to the end zone, where I dive and roll again.

Safe. The skyball ref declares a touchdown, and the crowd goes wild. My teammates crowd around me, lifting me high as the entire arena chants my house name on repeat.

My eyes drift to the sidelines where my former academy coach, Manorin Longhorn, sits with his new mate, Catherine Evrien.

Someone else coaches the Hearth HQ Hellions these days, so I know Nor and Cath came to watch *me*. He tried to recruit me to the small monster haven of Ever, in Massachusetts, but my heart led me home to Pine Gulch and the Punishers. In a perfect world, he'd have taken over the Punishers, and I'd have gotten my dream monster town, dream team and dream coach all at the same time.

I'll settle for two out of three, though.

A horn blows, and the game ends. Most of my team heads for the lockers, but I head to the sidelines to sign a few t-shirts and more than one pair of boobs.

Nor waits patiently until I reach him, then pulls me in for a firm handshake and a clap on the shoulder, red eyes sparkling. "Great game, kid."

I resist the urge to remind him that, at thirty-four, I'm not a kid. But if I hadn't left the Protector Academy partway through my senior year last year, I'd still be there, so I suppose he has a point. To him I *am* a kid.

He shoots me a wry look. "Still wish you'd come to Ever."

I laugh. "Building year for you, huh?"

"Or three," he grumbles. "Give me three years, and we'll be ready to kick anyone's asses."

We part, and Catherine pulls me in for a hug next, gray eyes wrinkling in the corners. She smells like fancy French perfume as her elegant gray waves tickle my face.

"We're so proud of you," she says quietly. "Awesome game, Hadrian..."

"I can't wait to get home," I whisper with a little laugh.

Catherine and Nor bounce back and forth between the tiny monster towns of Ever and Pine Gulch, where I've just moved, and I'm a regular at their place for dinner at least a few times a month. We're all a touch homebody-ish, and I think that tendency bonded our little trio. Not to mention Nor's like a second father to me, and Catherine is my cool auntie who's wholly unrelated but absolutely there if I need something.

I'd have followed Nor when he left the Hellions to build

Ever's team, but Pine Gulch called me in a way nothing else ever really has. There were so many reasons to come back to the Montana-based monster haven.

My best friend, Jasper, is in town. His family. And I love his family more than my own.

Nor, Catherine, and I catch up for a moment before I sense Coach's eyes on me. Turning, I jog across the field and head to the locker room for the post-game rundown. After the analysis and a quick shower, I'm dressing when one of the other gargoyle players claps me on the shoulder.

"Hey, Alk, we're headed out to Cattedrale for a little fun." He waggles his bushy brows. "You wanna come this time?"

Cattedrale. I've had a few sexy experiences there, but these days, it's not for me.

Laughing, I shake my head as I grab my bag and shut the locker. "Nah. You guys have fun."

He cocks his head to the side. "If I didn't know you better, I'd assume you have a sweetie, as much as you refuse to come out with us." He groans. "Or don't tell me, you're going to the gods-damned library again for some *book.*"

"No mate," I confirm. "No girlfriend. No guy friend. No books this time. I'm just gonna visit some *friend* friends while we're here. I promise I'll come next time, though."

All lies.

"Liar," he says with a snort, slapping my back with the spade-shaped tip of his long purple tail. "You never come."

"Not true," I correct. "I went to that whiskey tasting event."

He groans again and slaps a hand over his face, running it up and over one long, curved horn. "That was, like, eight games ago, dude. I'm not gonna bug you about tonight, but come with us sometime, please? We kinda like you. And it'll be good for you."

I doubt it. I wasn't a party animal at the Protector Academy, and I'm not a party animal now. Give me a nice whiskey, a library, a roaring fire and a great view, and I'm happy.

I promise again that I will, but the reality is that I can't wait to get back to Pine Gulch. It's where I feel the most like myself. It's where I feel at home. And even though the big old ranch house I bought is in terrible shape and needs a lot of work, I'd still rather be there dealing with that than here in a sex club dungeon watching my teammates enjoy the perks of being famous skyball players.

Sex dungeon could be fun with the right person, my brain helpfully supplies.

But I don't *have* the right person, so I'd rather not go.

Not that I wouldn't take someone special if the chance arose.

After grabbing my bag, I head out the players' exit and pull a hoodie up over my head, slotting my curved horns through dual holes in the top of it. My black hair is knotted at the base of my neck, and if I keep my head down, I can mostly walk through monster headquarters without getting stopped a ton of times for autographs. Of course, my size alone makes other monsters look, but that can't be helped. I've learned to hunch my shoulders and shuffle a bit.

Hearth HQ's black sky opens up and dumps out snow, slicking up the streets. I love it because it means most monsters will be consumed with getting inside.

Dipping into an alleyway, I walk until I reach Sembin Jewelers, a small shop owned by a family friend. Inside, I head directly to the back display case and glance at a specific piece I've seen before. Breathing a sigh of relief, I smile at the sales clerk as I point to a delicate chain necklace.

"I'll take that necklace, please, and can you ship it in a gift box for me?"

I'll see Bluebell tomorrow but I love sending her things in the mail. It's become a tradition of ours.

The pixie clerk smiles as she removes the dainty necklace from its velvet tray. "Of course, Hadrian. This is absolutely gorgeous. Girlfriend?"

Shaking my head, I fish around in my pocket for my credit card, then slap it onto the counter. "Just a friend."

Friend.

That word's never really fit the complicated maelstrom of my emotions toward Bluebell Tucker. But, per usual, I keep it friendly out of my respect for her brother and our friendship.

Completing the transaction, I scribble a little note to be included with the shipment. It's perfect for her and while she doesn't wear a ton of jewelry, I know she'll love this.

A snowy half hour later, I make my way inside the Grand Portal Station on the Protector Academy grounds. The school might be my old haunt, but as I think about home, my feet move faster.

Stalking through the wide arched entryway, I head for the Higher Grounds coffee shop at the far end of the station. Glowing green doorways situated around the room form a network of magical portals connecting all fifty-plus hidden monster havens. The bright doors emit faint green light into the oval-shaped, cavernous room. It's busy with monsters of all species hurrying across the space, traveling between havens.

It used to be that each monster haven was only connected to one other, making it a real pain in the ass to travel between them. Away games were a nightmare to get to when that was the case.

The new Grand Portal Station has been open six months, and I can't imagine life before it. Traveling with the Academy team to other havens sometimes took us the better part of a day, making multiple stops.

This late, there's no line at Higher Grounds. I order, returning the gargoyle worker's soft smile when she recognizes me. She tucks her hair behind one long, delicate ear, and I take a moment to admire how pretty she is. It's something I've done for the better part of five years since I went to the Academy.

I examine the females who seem interested in me, and I wait to see if they produce any sort of physical reaction in my chest. My heart's silent, and it will be until I find my mate. When I bite and claim her, it'll start beating. It's a sensation all gargoyle males are obsessed with. I can't wait to feel it.

But like every other time I focus on it, everything inside me is quiet and cool, despite her smile growing flirtatious.

And then there's the other part of my brain that reminds me how this female stands a head higher than someone else I know. How the gargoyle's hair is a long, silky black, whereas another's is always brilliantly royal blue—except for Punishers' game days when the little human female uses a spell to change her locks to match my team's colors, black and gold.

She's on the sidelines for every home game, screaming my last name like a banshee. She's practically my sister, although that's never been right.

Even thinking about Bluebell's hair makes something inside me simultaneously clench and unfurl. It's an unpleasant sensation because what I really want right now is to be at the Tucker dinner table, spending time with my favorite people, winking at her dad while I poke fun at Jasper.

Jasper and Jack are the oldest Tucker kids…twins.

Jace is the middle Tucker, the bookish one.

And Bluebell is the only daughter and the youngest one, although she wears first daughter energy like a cloak.

Bill and Elena are the kindest humans I've ever met and they've done more for me in the last two decades than my real parents have.

Tucker Ranch is my favorite place in the whole world.

I take my drink without flirting with the gargoyle female, heading across the station to the Pine Gulch portal. Just as I enter, another gargoyle male exits with a beautiful blond human riding him piggyback. They're both in hysterics as she kisses her way up his neck, snickering and laughing.

"Not now, Thea," he says, slapping her ass with his tail spade. The smile on his face is huge. He's in love. They must be mated….and then I hear it. His heartbeat. It's synced to hers.

"C'mon, baby," she whispers in his ear as they pass me. "Now that this is open, we could go anywhere at any time! You've been promising to show me every haven for a while now, and we only did, like, two hours in Pine Gulch."

"Later," he gruffs, pretending to be serious, but it's easy to see from his teasing tone that they're just playing.

Their connection is joyful, easy, and I crave that so much, my fangs ache.

Halting in place, I watch as she bites her way up his neck until they're both laughing so hard he nearly drops her. Just before she hits the ground he catches her smoothly in one wing. When he lifts her up and curls his wing around them to make things private, I nearly let out a groan. I'd do that in a heartbeat with... someone.

It feels wrong to keep watching the couple, though, so I force my gaze away.

Above the portal, a guardian gargoyle sits perfectly still on a platform, watching the station's interior with glittering amethyst eyes. I'm glad I didn't pursue the more common gargoyle career in security and guardianship. He's guarding against any sort of breach, but given how protected this haven is, I can't imagine he sees much action. I couldn't do it.

Stalking beneath him, I dip my head low as I pass through the portal's glowing green surface. It's cool on my already chilly skin, and I don't breathe easy as I walk down the bright green tunnel connecting the portal station with Pine Gulch.

When I emerge into the Pine Gulch portal room, it's quiet and empty save for the minotaur female manning the ticket counter across the room. She nods at me, then returns her snout to a copy of the *Gulch Gossip* paper. I managed to get myself in that a couple times when I first moved, but the ancient pixie twins who write the articles seem to have moved on to other stories. Thank gods.

Reaching into my bag, I grab my communication watch and strap it around my wrist. Now that I'm back home in Pine Gulch, I can actually use it.

"Call Jasper Tucker," I command into the face.

Jasper's name hovers over the watch's flat surface, and he picks up on the first ring. "Hay, you comin' to dinner or what?"

No "hello," no "how are you; how was the game?" Every time Jasper and I talk, it's like we pick up mid-conversation. There's never a hello or goodbye from him.

"If you think your folks won't mind," I say, knowing they've never said no a single time in the thirty years I've known the Tuckers.

"Don't be stupid," he says with a snort. "Gotta go." He signs off without another word as I walk out of the portal station. Outside, a row of trucks waits for monsters who need rides, but this is when it's nice to have wings. I get to fly everywhere. The scents of home fill my senses and wrap me up like a hug. Wheat, grass, dirt, wide-open space. Maybe even a hint of incoming snow. Bulleting up into the sky with my bag clutched to my chest, I claw into the air and head toward downtown.

The discomfort I felt being away from Pine Gulch fades as I fly over the gulch itself. Soft nickering bounces off its steep rock walls as the mustangs who live in the gulch move along the riverbank, eating grass and drinking from the river.

Swooping low, I admire their freedom as I glide over the herd, then up out of the natural space. I catch current after current, spinning up into the sky as I follow Mabel the train's tracks along the gulch and toward downtown. Winking lights in the distance seem to welcome me home and I push my wings harder despite a leftover ache from the game.

I glide over the Dance Hall and High Moon Tattoo Parlor first, then swoop along Main Street. This late at night there's a crowd tumbling out of every bar on Main. Gulchers know how to throw a party. A few monsters look up and wave at me but unlike other havens, no one's snapping photos. There are no gasps of awe, no one pointing or whispering about me.

I love that so much. Here I'm just Hadrian.

As I reach the end of Main Street I angle north toward the foothills where the Tuckers' ranch is located. Brisk wind blows my hair back and I tuck my ears tighter against my head, warding against the chill.

When their place comes into view, excitement builds into butterflies in my chest. I circle over their barn and drop into their front yard, admiring the rustic rock garden and the pebbled walkway leading to double front doors. You'd think a family of mostly green witches would have a kickass, verdant garden everywhere, but the Tuckers aren't like others of their kind.

Rumbling echoes from behind me, and I turn to see the youngest Tucker—Bluebell—pulling into the driveway. When she sees me standing in front of the house, she grins and puts the truck in park.

She opens the door and hops out of the truck. There's paint across her left cheek and in one of the bright blue space buns on top of her head. Like always, she seems to have just rolled out of one project or another. She can't keep still. "Heard you demolished the Hellions, Alk."

"Twenty-six to four," I say with a smirk, slipping my hands into my jeans pockets. It's a tight fit, and I make a mental note to order new clothing. The Punishers workout routine is packing the pounds on me, and nothing fits like it used to.

She gives me a quick glance, smiling as she crosses to me and hops into my arms. It's easy to pull her up close as her arms slide around my neck and she hugs me tight.

"Missed my Tuckers, though," I say with a little laugh. "Nobody's as funny as you."

"Or as good-lookin'," shouts Jasper from the porch. "Get your hands off my damn sister! You know the rules!"

As I set Bluebell down, we share a playful eye roll. We've been friends since the twins and I were twelve and she was seven. I've hugged her about fifty million times at this point.

Snickering, she reaches out and wiggles her fingers all over my stomach and side. It tickles and I arch away from the touch, but she's fully focused on Jasper.

"Oh no! I'm touching your best friend!" she shouts at him.

When she grabs my leg and humps it like a chihuahua, I roll my eyes again.

"Stop that right now!" Jasper shouts. "I'm supposed to protect you from men, not men from you!"

Glancing down, I thump Bluebell on the tip of the nose. "You done fuckin' with your brother yet?"

She releases my thigh and shrugs and I try not to notice the pretty blush across her high cheekbones.

"Get in here, Hay!" shouts Jasper's twin from somewhere inside the house.

Gesturing for Bluebell to go ahead of me, I smile as I follow her through the Tuckers' front door. Inside, a tall ceiling soars above us as we dump into their living room in a tight group. The twins, Jasper and Jack, talk over one another, Bluebell shouts for her mother, and Jace paces quietly past us to the kitchen where the scents of beef and onion saturate the air.

Elena and Bill Tucker stand at the stove, ignoring the raucous shouts of three of their children as they discuss the dinner seasoning.

"Alk's here!" announces Bluebell.

Elena turns, wrinkled face breaking into a huge smile as she pulls Bluebell in for a hug. I wait patiently for Bluebell to untangle herself from her mama, then I dip low and haul Elena into my arms. She kisses my cheek as she squeezes my neck.

"Saw that win, Hay. You kicked ass, son," says Bill from his spot at the stove.

Son.

"You look hungry," Elena says. "Help Bluebell set the table, and we'll get you fed. Lord, you've packed on some muscle, honey. Need to feed you less, or more, depending on how one looks at it."

"Shouldn't his parents do that?" Jack snarks. He loves to remind everyone how the Tuckers more or less adopted me since my folks are always traveling for work.

"Hard to feed me when they're on a long-term expedition in

Brazil," I say back, setting Elena down and slapping Jack on the head with my tail spade. "Not to mention I'm a grown-ass man and can feed myself. You might wanna try it sometime, Jackhole."

He rolls his eyes and disappears toward the dining room back behind the kitchen. Bluebell's nowhere to be seen, but the fast beat of her heart thuds somewhere behind him, so I trail it to the dining room. She's there, up on her tiptoes as she grabs a stack of plates from the giant wooden armoire where they keep everything.

Stacks of receipts and files.

Two dozen mismatched coffee cups.

Tons of frames filled with pictures of all of us. I'm in pretty much every photograph and that makes me smile.

"Allow me." I reach over her, grab the stack, and hand them to her as she rolls her eyes.

"Must be nice to be seven feet tall."

"I do get to see the top of your space buns," I say with a snort. "Cute from way up here, although there's paint on both of 'em."

She elbows me in the gut, then turns and deposits the plates in my hands. "Do this, would ya? I've got to go send a couple invoices before dinner 'cause I'm ninety-nine percent sure the boys didn't do it."

"We didn't," Jasper says as he comes into the room with a tray covered tall with biscuits and toasted bread.

She and I share an eye roll before she disappears down the long hall behind the dining room. She'll be gone a solid half hour, I'd bet, missing the first part of dinner like usual. I wish I could help, but I don't know how the Tuckers do their invoicing for Tucker Greens, their green witch services business.

Jasper and Jack sit at their usual seats. Jace comes in from the kitchen with a tray of lasagna balanced in each hand. Elena and Bill follow him, Elena carrying an enormous salad bowl and Bill with two pitchers of beer.

Stalking back into the kitchen, I grab three pitchers of ice water and follow them back into the tall, round dining room.

"Where's Bluebell?" Elena asks, glancing at Jack.

He shrugs, snagging a piece of bread from the tray in front of him. "Doing some shit we said we'd do but haven't gotten around to doing yet, I imagine."

Bill groans. "Your sister doesn't even work for Tucker Greens, Jack Clinton Tucker. She ain't even a green witch!"

Jack shrugs again. "And yet she does a better job than I'd ever do. I'd probably fuck up the invoices and—"

"Language!" shout Bill and Elena at the same time.

Snickering, I dip into the back hall and trail Bluebell's scent again until I find her in the cramped under-stair office she's claimed as her working area. A laptop illuminates her upturned nose and the current bright blue of her freckles.

"I'm comin'," she barks, waving me away. "Just get started without me, Alk. If I don't get this done now, it'll never get done 'cause I'll forget."

"Lies." I poke her in the side with one of my pointed wing tips. "We both know you got a to-do list in your back pocket right this second."

She shoots me a harsh look. "And I'd like to check something off it today. Sooner you give me a second, the sooner I can get this done."

Laughing, I poke her again, loving how she squirms away from me. Her citrusy scent fills the small space, soaking into my senses. I always try to ignore how it starts a heat burning low in my core, but that's harder since I'm around her so much more often these days.

"You take more than two minutes, and I'll show back up with a plate for you."

"Mhm 'kay," she says, absorbed in her work and paying me no mind.

Turning, I head back up the hallway and find my place at the table. The lasagna trays are going around, and I wait for my turn to pile my plate high. At a demanding look from Elena, I put a second piece of lasagna on top of the first.

"Good boy," she says. "You need plenty of calories to power those wings."

I cut a piece of lasagna and put it on Bluebell's plate. As the rest of the food makes its way around, I make a whole plate for her so it's ready when she reappears. If I don't, Jasper'll eat all the lasagna and totally forget she hasn't even sat down yet.

I'm just about to grab tin foil to cover it when she stomps down the hallway and joins us, flopping into the seat next to mine. "Thanks, Alk," she says as she shovels the lasagna into her mouth, rolling her eyes and moaning. "Damn, this is good. Ma, what'd you add this time?"

"Pesto," Bill says with a grin. "Was my idea. Your ma didn't want to do it."

Elena laughs. "He says it's the human way to make lasagna, as if we aren't all human. Minus you, Alk." She waves her fork at me.

Bill snorts. "Yeah, but I'm, like, fully human. You're all witches, so I know more about regular humans, plus I lived in the human world for twenty-two years, I'll have you remember."

Ma Tucker drags her knuckles along Bill's angular jawline and into his salt-and-pepper chocolate hair. "But ain't you glad I summoned you here all those decades ago? You could be wasting away in Cincinnati, but instead you get to live in a little hidden monster town with me."

"Cincinnati's got nothin' on you, honey." He leans forward to peck the tip of her nose.

Jack makes a barfing sound, Jace looks away, and Jasper covers Bluebell's eyes with his free hand, shoveling lasagna with the other.

"Get your hand away from my face," Bluebell snaps, swatting at him. "I'm twenty-nine, for gods' sake, and you're almost thirty-five. Our parents had sex. Here we are. You should be so lucky to have what they have. On top of which I'm not a virgin, so..."

A chorus of groans rises from the boys again, but all I can do is choke down a bite of food. The Tuckers don't do anything quietly. There's not a poker face to be had in this entire household. But they love fiercely, they use their green magic for good, and they're diehard Gulchers, not to mention diehard Punishers fanatics.

That comment about her not being a virgin, though...

"Hey!" Bill shouts. "We need to toast Bluebell for signing the Bodice paperwork, right? Blue, that happened this morning, if I remember correctly?"

She keeps eating without looking up from her plate. "Tomorrow," she mutters. "It got rescheduled for tomorrow."

I turn to look at her. "Hey, that's a huge deal, right? Are you excited?"

She looks up at me, and a range of emotions flits across her delicate features. I can't say "excited" seems to be one of them, though.

"Yeah," she says in a neutral tone, dark lashes fluttering against her heart-shaped cheeks. "Yeah! I mean, big day. I've been wanting this for a while." She finally smiles, and the rest of the Tuckers burst into raucous cheering and clapping. They're so loud, I resist the urge to flatten my hands over my ears.

It wouldn't help. The Tucker family has one volume, and that's all the way up.

Glancing around the love-filled room, I smile as I spear another bite of lasagna and shove it into my mouth. It's good to be home.

Bluebell

"Congratulations, Bluebell," says the bespectacled female minotaur behind the desk at the Titles & Deeds Office the morning after family dinner. She slides a stack of papers in my direction with a friendly smile. "Can't believe you need another business to manage, but I know you'll do right by the Buxom Bodice."

I take the finalized sales contract with slightly trembling hands. Minerva's right—I don't really need another business to keep track of. I already run Buttercup Rental Agency for my parents, and I help them and my brothers with the scheduling for Tucker Greens, too. Sitting still just isn't in my wheelhouse, so to speak.

Plus, I've always wanted to build something from scratch, something that's entirely *mine*. Not to mention I was *past* ready to move off my folks' ranch and into downtown Pine Gulch, where I can be closer to my responsibilities and get a little distance from my crazy family.

It's not that living with a bunch of witches and one human is tiresome, but it means their work surrounds me twenty-four-seven.

"Thanks, Minerva." I stick the paperwork under an arm.

"Everything okay out at your place?" She's my newest long-term resident, having just signed a two-year contract for one of our small cottages at the far end of Main Street.

"Still adjusting," she says with a shrug that shimmies the gold ring through her snout. "Being single at two hundred wasn't in the cards, but the cottage has a cute little personality, and I think we'll get on just fine." She winks at me. "Mead Cute Festival's coming up soon. I'm thinking perhaps I'll meet some young hot thang while I'm there. Whaddya think?"

I reach across the desk and squeeze her heavily bejeweled fingers. "Love life is not something I can assist with but if you need a single thing out at your property, you holler at me, alright?"

Her fuzzy brows lift, and she raises both hands as if in shock. "Oh! I nearly forgot the dadgum key, Bluebell. You'd have gotten all the way to the Buxom Bodice and not been able to get in." She spins on her swivel chair and rummages around in a drawer I can't see from this angle.

I consider her comment as she looks for the wayward key. Shit, I hadn't necessarily expected to still be single at twenty-nine either, but here we are. Truly, I don't know when I'd have time for a love life, and it's plenty of fun watching my friends fall in love. Lotta that in Pine Gulch lately, and I'm fine being on the sidelines of it.

Who has time, anyway?

Minerva spins back around with a beautiful vintage-looking key in hand. She slides it over the countertop while she beams at me. "Go get yer girl, Bluebell Tucker."

I should be excited. I *am* excited. But my to do list for today is also a million items long.

"Can I ask you somethin'?"

I bet I can guess before she even gets the question out of her mouth, and so I lift the key. "You wanna know why I have so many jobs?"

Minerva's mouth drops open as she nods. "Yeah, girl. Tucker

Greens, Buttercup Rental Agency, shifts at Whiskey Business and sometimes Lizard Lick Saloon. I swear there ain't a business on Main I ain't seen you in a time or two. I don't know how you do it."

I shove the key in my pocket with a wry laugh. "I can't keep still. Mama says I was even that way in the womb—kicking her all day and night so she couldn't get any sleep. Now I exist on carbs, coffee, and colored pens."

Minerva shakes her head, the ring through her nose shimmying against her snout. "You young things have more energy than the gods, I swear. Been decades since I could roust myself for more than this *one* job."

We share a laugh at that before I tell her goodbye.

Leaving the office, I head down the long hallway that houses most of Pine Gulch's government offices. These are small, so we use an unneeded hallway in the Auction House. Pine Gulch isn't as populated as most of the other hidden monster havens, and we don't like a lotta...overhead. If you end up in PG, or the Gulch, as we local Gulchers call it, it's 'cause you wanted wide-open spaces and a little bit of lawlessness.

Outside, I turn toward Main Street's straightaway, passing Glimmer Potions House on my left and the abandoned Keeper's mansion on the right. Although, these days, the mansion's a little friendlier than she used to be. I blame my friend Lemon, who seems to have broken through the prickly home's rough exterior.

I chuckle as I muse how Lemon, she of the sparkly pink, definitely-doesn't-fit-in-here cowboy boots came to the Gulch and immediately rocked everyone's worlds. Now she's practically the unofficial mayor, and there ain't a monster in town who doesn't know and love her.

Good thing she loves me the most. And our friend Oz. I'd call us the Three Musketeers if we lived out in the human world instead of a haven.

Main Street's busy this time of day, gargoyles, minotaurs, pixies and various other monsters walking up and down the street in groups. Giant flower pots are full to the brim with yellow yarrow and purple wildflowers that hang over the edge like colorful waterfalls.

A woman wearing a black V-neck tee stands from behind one of the pots, smiling at me. "Hey, Bloob, you headed to the Bodice?"

I laugh at Shadow's nickname for me. She's a human witch like me, although we grew up in different monster towns. Lifting the ornate key, I wave it side to side with a pleased grin. "Signed, sealed, and delivered!" The beautiful pots catch my eye again as the yarrow waves in the breeze. "This your doing? Surely my brothers didn't take it upon themselves to do up ornamental flower pots."

Shadow huffs out a laugh, eyeing the pots with obvious love as she strokes one of the yarrow's spiky heads. "Fully my doing; it was one of the original keeper's projects that never got completed so I'm doing it now. I did ask Jasper if he was interested in helping. His green magic is so *strong*, ya know? But he said, and I quote, 'what a ridiculous waste of time. There's already a garden behind the shops.'" She looks at me. "Can you imagine a *green* witch saying that?! I know he's prepping for his level-three mastery test, but damn."

I sigh as sunshine filters through the haven's protective ward above us, warming my skin after a long morning dealing with paperwork and resident requests. "*Any* green witch? No. Jasper? Absolutely."

Shadow sucks at her teeth. "Well, Dain and I are back to Rainbow this week to wrap up some stuff with my job before we move back here. Mind keeping an eye on the pots? They shouldn't need much, but I bet Jace would fix them up even if Jasper won't."

My youngest brother is the quietest Tucker, and that suits him fine. He's observant and actually *thinks* before he speaks, a character trait the rest of us didn't inherit. Of my three brothers, he's the most likely to help with this project of Shadow's to brighten up downtown Pine Gulch's main drag.

Personally, I think it's already perfect despite the dirt street and railroad tracks running up the middle of it. It's home. But if Shadow wants to make it a little brighter, that's fine, too.

"You got it," I promise, flashing her a final smile before turning to face the building to my right. I let out a sigh of excitement at seeing the Buxom Bodice Outfitter in a new light, knowing she's all mine.

The building's gorgeous with dark paneled siding and red window trim. A door on the right side leads to the Whiskey Business Saloon. But the left and the two apartments on the second story? Those belong to me now.

A deer with giant boobs winks down from a wooden sign that announces the shop as the Buxom Bodice. Bright cowboy boots, turquoise jewelry and trappings, and silver belt buckles shine from the huge singular front window. The building's quiet as I stand there, but her longtime owner just sold her to me, so it'll be an adjustment, I'm sure. Like all the buildings in Pine Gulch, she's got a big, saucy personality.

"Hey, sweet girl," I say softly, stepping forward to run my fingertips up the front door admiringly. My black magic pings and twitches, and tiny sparks fly from my fingers. The front door creaks and groans, an angry sound that has me cocking my head to the side as a warning sensation fills my chest. My magic shouldn't hurt her—it's meant for healing.

Shadow joins me. "She snapping at you, Bloob?"

I stick the key in the door and unlock it. Yet when I push on the glossy red surface, it doesn't open. Frowning, I push a little harder. It gives way quickly, and I stumble forward, falling onto matte rust-colored entry tiles.

Shadow jumps to my side and grabs me by the elbow, helping me upright. When I stand, wincing at the pain in my kneecaps, she gives me a concerned look. "You okay?"

I nod. "Guess that door's a little bit stuck. I'll have to work on that. Thank gods I can fix her right up."

"Yeah," Shadow murmurs, glancing up at the ceiling as the Bodice lets out a grumbly, unhappy-sounding groan. Shadow turns to me with a forced smile. "Okay, I'm gonna leave you to it because I'm off to meet Dain. Comm me if you need me?"

A thumbs-up is my answer, and she heads back out the door, which opens easily, the bell above it dinging to announce her departure.

Looking around the store, I admire how beautiful she is. Shoe boxes are stacked floor to ceiling on the left-hand side. Displays of jewelry, shoes, and western-style clothing fill the space in long rows leading to the checkout counter and changing rooms toward the back. I haven't been in the storage section yet, but that's where all the extra product sits, and I purchased everything in stock from Rebekah, the prior owner.

"Hey, Bodice," I say softly. "We've met many times over the years, of course, but I'm so proud to be in partnership with you going forward."

Silence.

I frown.

The Buxom Bodice has always been such a friendly building, greeting me warmly every time I've entered, and I've lived in Pine Gulch my entire life. This silence seems almost hostile. But then I consider how the woman who literally started this business sold it and left, and I don't know how the building might be feeling. Left behind, perhaps. Of course, if Rebekah didn't have a brand new grandbaby I'm sure she'd never have left PG. Sometimes plans change depending on what life throws at you.

Walking to the nearest wall, I rest my hand on the wooden planks. They shudder beneath my fingertips, and my magic sparks again.

She's unhappy. Deeply unhappy. But that's not a thing I can fix with my black magic like I can other building ailments—termites, foundation issues, stuff like that. This is emotional, and that's as complicated for haven buildings as it is for humans and monsters.

The heart is a prickly, noncompliant patient on the best of days.

I'm about to attempt reassuring her when the door swings open again, and my three brothers burst through with hoots and hollers. Jasper and Jack raise the roof as they come in like twin bulldozers—black hair, green eyes, that same olive skin we all got from our mother, Elena. Jace comes in quietly behind them, as observant as ever with his arms crossed. His upturned nose is covered in freckles, his hair a paler shade of brown like mine. Well, when I don't use my magic to recolor it to royal blue, my favorite color in the literal entire world.

"So?!" Jasper yanks me to his chest for a hug. "You did it? The Bodice is yours?!"

"Mmph, yeah..." I manage with my face smashed into his broad, muscular chest. My older twin brothers stand two heads taller than me. Even for humans, they're big. But Jace? Jace is normal-sized like me—he barely breaks six feet.

When the building lets out a series of angry squeaks, all three brothers look up and around.

Jack turns to me with a surprised look. "Okayyyy then. Was gonna say congrats to you both, but it seems like maybe I should just say, 'Hey, girls, it's gonna be fine'?"

The Bodice falls into silence, and I shrug. "Big changes for everyone. I walked in the door sixty seconds ago."

"You mean fell through," Jack says with a playful wink. "We were across the street watching."

I resist the urge to slap any brother I can reach. Jace rolls his eyes at the older two but then smirks at me.

When I'm released from the prison of my brother's overexuberant embrace, I pull back and smile wryly. "Aren't you three supposed to be at the Rhubarb Ranch right now? You had an appointment and—"

"Don't worry," Jace says softly, smiling. "They're running

behind from grabbing stuff at the Feed Shop. We figured we had enough time to come congratulate you two." He looks up and around the quiet ceiling of the Bodice. "So…umm, congratulations?"

Nobody says anything, and the building doesn't respond to his polite comment.

I spin Jasper and shove him toward the door. "Okay, you guys, get going. You've got a full afternoon of appointments, and if you leave one late, the whole day will be fucked."

"We knowwwww," Jack says in an exasperated tone. "We're not noobs, Bluebell. Tucker Greens won't fall apart if we're half an hour late."

It's my turn to roll my eyes. "And yet if I don't keep you three on schedule, everything goes tits up, and I have to make a bunch of apology phone calls."

"We'll do better," promises Jace.

The twins snort but don't agree. They *know* they won't do better. If I didn't tell them where to go, I honestly don't know what they'd do with themselves all day. Thank gods Tucker Greens is the only company of green witches in Pine Gulch, meaning we've got a bit of a monopoly on green magic jobs. Being a farming and ranching community, there's always a need for green witches to grow and support farmers' crops and land.

When the twins leave first, Jace pulls me in for a quiet, gentle hug. "Proud of you," he whispers against the side of my head. "It's all gonna work out in the end, sis, you'll see."

"I know," I say brightly, squeezing him hard. "Love you."

"Love you too," he says in that quiet, thoughtful tone I love so much. Jack and Jasper are loud and brash. Jace is so understated, and I love that about him. But when the wit comes out, it's darkly sarcastic. I can't get enough of him.

"Git," I say after a few long huggy moments. "You promised not to be late."

He follows the other knuckleheads out, and I step to the door's single round window to watch them. Jack and Jasper hop into the truck like the dudes they are, and Jace slips gracefully into the back seat on his preferred side. I sigh as they motor up Main Street toward the edge of town.

Slipping a hand into my back pocket, I retrieve my daily to-do list and my pocket calendar. It's got my entire family's schedule for the day plus mine.

While I signed the purchase paperwork today, I actually don't have time to hang with the Bodice until I officially move into one of the upstairs apartments this weekend.

I open the front door and step out, locking the place up behind me. Detaching a red sheet of paper from my to-do list, I tape it up on the front window. It's a Closed sign, letting folks know we won't be open until next week while I get everything up and running and figure out the register, et cetera.

Patting the door one final time, I force a smile up at the beautiful building. "We're gonna be fine, honey, I promise, okay?"

Silence.

I wasn't expecting the vibe to be different now that I own the building, but that's a problem for another day, unfortunately. But as a black witch with the power to heal buildings and many monster and animal ailments, I'm certain I'll figure it out. My power is unique in my family and unique in Pine Gulch—black magic work keeps me plenty busy.

Heading left along Main Street, I pass Whiskey Business, the alleyway to the hidden pumpkin garden and then the Welcome Inn. After that, I dip into the post office to check for the first shipments of items I've ordered for the Bodice. My hope is to expand into more home and ranch decor and some fancier clothing like Lemon's partial to. Now that I've seen her sparkly pink cowboy boots—despite how impractical they are—I kinda want some blue ones. Or black and gold to wear to the Punishers skyball games.

That would totally rock.

Behind the post office's rustic wooden counter, a giant minotaur male smiles at me as he leans onto his beefy forearms. "Bluebell Tucker, just the woman I need to see. You got a few packages back here, girly. And the rest of the Tucker clan is taking up my back storage room. Those brothers of yours got a shopping habit lately, it seems."

I chuckle at that. "They're prepping for the spring harvest season, so yeah, Tucker Ranch could be its own post office right now. You should see the dining table. Covered in seed starting trays and packets of seeds and invoices."

He snorts, his nose ring jiggling as he jerks his head toward a tall stack of packages at his back. "You bring a party wagon to haul these? 'Cause this is more than you can do with those tiny lil' human hands." He waggles fuzzy brown brows at me.

Groaning, I eye the stack. "Party wagon's in my truck. Let me grab it, and I'll be right back."

He nods, so I turn and head out the door and back up Main. I wasn't expecting my brothers to have gone that crazy with the ordering, but if I leave it up to them, the packages will sit at the post for ages. At least half are probably plants or seeds, so it would be best to get them into the greenhouse behind our parents' place. Many of the local ranches rely on us to get their annual plantings started—we can't risk fucking it up.

Opening my truck's bed, I pull out the foldable wagon I resort to when the Tuckers get *real* crazy with their credit cards. Sighing, I unfold it then head back to the post office.

"Bluebell Tucker, I gotta talk to you."

I squeeze my eyes shut for a moment before I turn to face Bishop Rygold, the big grumpy sheriff. When I do, he's got both hands on his hips, wearing his usual glare. It highlights the scar that bisects one side of his face. An old war wound.

Plastering a smile on, I wave. "Hey, Sheriff Rygold. What can I do you for?"

He shakes his head, lashing his big tail at his back. "The pixie twins are throwin' a fit and callin' me every two seconds about the changes y'all made to the Mead Cute shindig this year and I am plum wore out over it."

I cross my arms. "The changes were needed, Bishop, and I'm not gonna ask the committee to meet again just to make things the way they used to be. We're...modernizin'. Or something."

He spreads his big purple wings wide. "Tell 'em to stop callin' *me* about it."

"You're the sheriff!" I say as a belly laugh bursts from me. "Tell 'em I'm not breaking a single law. I'm literally doing my *volunteer* job and it's not my fault they're outnumbered so they didn't get their way when we voted on the changes. It's a democracy, as you know."

"Don't know and don't care," he snips, lifting lightly off the ground. Hovering like he is, it's easy to see a smattering of pinprick holes in his left wing. Poor guy.

I do believe a change of subject is in order, so I smirk at him. "A little birdie told me you were thinkin' about getting one of those mail order mates. That true?"

He rolls his eyes and lifts up higher. "Somebody or somebodies needs to leave my nonexistent love life alone. Goodbye, Bluebell."

"Bye now," I say softly as he shoots up into the clouds and disappears from view.

Back inside the post office, Luther helps me load the party wagon, and it takes three trips to get everything into my truck. As we place the final few boxes, a smaller one tumbles to the dirt road. Luther bends to pick it up, handing it to me with a wry smile.

"You got a boyfriend I don't know about, Bluebell? This looks adorable."

I take the box, look at the return label, then smile. "Just a friend," I assure Luther. Although that doesn't feel quite right. Never has.

He snorts again. "If you say so, Tucker."

"I do." I tuck the box into my pocket and thank him for his help.

Once he goes, I hop in the front seat and withdraw the box.

It's from a fancy little jeweler at the headquarters monster haven, Hearth HQ. Opening it, I grin at finding a delicate golden link necklace inside. Each link is a western emblem like a cowboy boot or lasso or sheriff's badge. But they're so small that from afar they just look like miniature ovals. Picking it carefully up out of the box, I admire how stunning it is. A folded slip of paper pops up, and I smile at that too.

Opening the note, my smile grows bigger.

Happy Birthday, Blue. I know you'd never buy this for yourself, so it was my sworn duty to fulfill that need for you, per our arrangement.

-Hay

My smile is so big, it practically hurts. Hadrian gives the best gifts. He must have bought this while on the road with the team. Perks of being the team's newest player and a general all-star to boot. I love how he always sends my gifts so I get fun stuff in the mail. He could have just given this to me last night, but he's been mailing gifts to me for like, ten years at this point. My birthday's not for a few weeks, but he's always early with the presents.

Per our arrangement.

I chuckle thinking about the marriage promise we made to one another when I was at the ripe age of nine.

Sighing, I put the truck into gear just as the blue-banded watch around my wrist pings, my father's name hovering above it. Lord knows what he needs, but it's bound to be something ridiculous. Bill Tucker can't find the salt on a shelf in front of his face. His talents lie elsewhere—namely finding and negotiating the purchase of our real estate empire—but even though I'm the baby, I'm blessed with that first daughter energy, for better or worse.

Directing the watch to answer him, I pull into the street and head for home.

"Bluebell Delia, where y'at, girl?" My father's rough, tinny voice echoes through the leather surface.

"Downtown."

"Listen. I'm puttin' in an offer on a little cottage out by 234. I need you to come take a look, tell me if anything's wrong with it before I finalize my number. You got a minute? I could use your magic, girl."

A minute means an hour, and I really don't. But instead, I grit my teeth and agree to meet him there. I blame him and my mother for passing along the monstrepreneurial instinct.

And gods know, when the Tuckers smell money and opportunity, we jump.

Hadrian

"Why the hells did you even try to live in that place?" Jasper asks as he hikes a box of skyballs up in his arms, glaring at me. "I coulda told you your new ranch was a shitheap, and it needed work before you moved in, asshole."

"I was overly optimistic," I grumble, shoving him against the wall so he drops the box. Two of the skyballs bounce down the stairs. "You dropped something, Jazzy! Better go grab it."

"Ugh," he complains. "I hate you sometimes."

"You do not," I call up the stairs as I descend, bypassing the wayward skyballs and emerging into the alleyway between the Buxom Bodice Outfitter and the next shop over.

Outside, Bluebell grabs a smaller box from the back of my truck. "Hey, neighbor!"

I grin, bumping her hip with mine as I pass. "You don't need to move my shit, Bluebell. Jasper's here."

She snorts, rolling her eyes. "I was across the street for a quarter hour having coffee with a friend, and in that entire time, I saw you make ten trips while he made one. So, it seems like he's about as much help as I'd expect." She looks down at the box in her hands. "Although, knowing him, he'll open them all up and poke through your shit."

That produces an uncomfortable heat that spreads along my neck, shoulders, and cheeks. There are a couple boxes I would decidedly *not* like any of the Tuckers looking into—Bluebell 'cause it would be embarrassing, and Jasper 'cause he'd never let me hear the end of it.

Which leads me to the box she's currently holding. It's nondescript, small, and fuck me, I'm pretty sure it's the box with all my sex toys in it.

I take it from her, but she scoffs and grabs it back. The toys roll around inside it, and I swear to gods, if one of them turns on, I'll sink into Main Street and die of mortification.

She slaps me with one hand. "Hadrian Alkazar, why are you being weird about this box?" Blue brows lift into a mischievous vee, and she lifts it high, shaking it again. The toys rock and roll inside.

"Bluebell," I warn. "Stop that."

Her mouth drops open. "Oh my gods, Alk, is there something spicy in here? I was kidding, but..."

I snatch it from her with a harsh look. "Don't ask questions you don't want the answer to." It's the best comeback I can summon as I haul the box high and grab another, piling it on top of the first.

"Well, well, well," she says as she grabs another box and follows me into the alleyway. "Good thing I'm your landlord, technically, since I own the building now. I could just let myself in and poke around in all your things, you know. That idea is sorta appealing, if I'm honest." She winks at me. "Shame you're only here until you get your place fixed up."

"Invasion of privacy." I poke at her with my tail spade as I ascend the stairs. "I can't be held liable for you being scarred by what you see in my apartment, and you gave me no limitations on behavior. I can have parties or whatever I want, I'm sure."

She barks out a loud laugh. "You? Parties? Yeah, okay, big guy. That'll be the day."

"Called out." Jasper appears in the doorway at the top, still holding the box of skyballs.

"Your sister's right," I mutter, "you're the fucking worst at helping me move."

"She's a menace," Jasper says, scrunching his nose up. "You sure you wanna live across the hall from her?"

"Don't be jelly, Jazzy." She sticks her tongue out at him as she brushes roughly past. Heading down the hallway, she disappears inside my apartment.

I follow with the other boxes, entering the tall, bright studio space and tucking the boxes into the corner of the kitchen where I hope she won't go.

"I was kidding about snooping, Alk," she calls out as she disappears back out the door.

Jasper joins me in the kitchen, eyeing the boxes. "Oooo, what are we snooping about, though? You got a hidden box of cool shit?"

I slap a hand over my face, then run it up over my right horn. "You Tuckers need to mind your own business. Can't you help me move without examining all of my belongings?"

Jasper barks out a laugh and crosses his arms. "Yeah, but the more you're talking and the darker that blush gets, the more I wonder what you're hiding, Hadrian Alkazar."

I spin him in place and shove him toward the door. "Nothing. Go get a couple more boxes, then I'll buy you a beer."

He punches me in the gut, but I sidestep and whack him with my wingtip. I'm so much stronger, he hits the wall with a thud.

Downstairs, Bluebell's got two more boxes in her arms, heading toward us.

"I was kidding about the snooping." I stop her with a hand on her arm. "You've been one of my best friends for two decades, Bluebell. The door's always open to you if you need something, okay?"

"Just not *bestie stuff*," Jasper quips. "'Cause that's a horrifying thought. If I find out y'all are doing fucking movie nights and shit without me, I'm going to throw a literal shit fit."

Bluebell winks at me. "Guess naked yoga's out so we don't hurt Jazzy's feelers."

I laugh as her comm watch rings, and a name hovers over the blue band. She struggles to answer it while carrying the boxes, so I grab them and head for the stairs.

A quarter hour later, she appears in the doorway with Jasper, who's carrying the last box.

"Thank you both." I take it and set it on the countertop, glancing between Bluebell and Jasper. "I'm gonna buy Jasper a beer. Wanna come with us?"

Bluebell grins but shakes her head. "Another time. I've got the dinner shift at Whiskey Business, then I'm closing at Lizard Lick 'cause someone called in sick."

I frown. "You gonna have a chance to get some dinner?"

Jasper elbows me. "You think Bluebell's gonna miss a meal? Have you met my sister? She's basically a garbage disposal."

I look back at her, concerned that she's been working all day and still has two shifts to go. "I can come help, if you want."

She shakes her head as Jasper disappears back into my apartment. "Not sure how much help it'll be when all the single monstresses in town flood the bar to get served by the famous Hadrian Alkazar. Naw, I'm good, but thanks for the offer. Oh hey..." Lifting her hand, she fingers the delicate necklace around her throat.

The one I sent her.

"Thank you for the early birthday gift, it's absolutely perfect."

"No problem," I say even as pleasure ripples through me. She likes it. I knew she would.

"The note cracked me up," she says with a laugh. "It's gonna suck for me one day when you get tired of honoring a promise we made like, literal years ago."

I won't ever get tired of honoring that promise, but I can't tell her that. Especially with Jasper right inside the apartment.

She glances at her watch, seeming to look at the time. "Well, I've gotta get to gettin' but I'll see ya later, neighbor!"

"Sure," I say quietly, wishing she'd allow me to help.

She spins on her heel and heads for the door, hair falling out of her usual space buns. Thin blue tendrils stick to the back of her neck. She's slightly sweaty from all the trips up and down the stairs. My nostrils flare, her usual scent stronger as her heart races from the work.

Thwomp. Thwomp. Thwomp.

That beat. It's slow and steady, as grounded as she is except when her brothers are irritating her. Then it picks up until it's a wild gallop.

I *love* the sound of her heartbeat. I think about it sometimes when I...do things. The rhythm's so beautiful and familiar, like a harmony I can't stop humming.

"Bye, my dudes," she shouts as she flashes us a peace sign from the doorway. When she disappears without a backward glance, I stare after her, wishing she'd throw a look over her shoulder at me. Something, anything that seems like more than just friends.

Jasper flops onto my sofa with a big groan. "Gods, dude, you have so much shit and not a plant to be seen. I'd thought I'd at least grow something nice and big for you, but not a piece of greenery in this place. What the fuck?"

I stare at the doorway where Bluebell left before I turn to him. "Normally, someone's best friend would gift them something like that as a housewarming present, ya know." Planting my hands on my hips, I shoot him a harsh look.

"Not me." Jasper jumps to his feet and heads for the door. "Gifts aren't my love language."

I laugh and shove him. "You have a love language?"

"Beer," he shouts as he heads up the hallway. "You owe me one or ten, Hay! Come on!"

Snickering, I lock up the apartment and follow him down to the alleyway. As my footsteps fall, it occurs to me that it's the same cadence as Bluebell's heartbeat. Some days I just can't seem to get that rhythm off my mind.

Bluebell

"How's the Bodice? Tell me everything." My best friend, Lemon, sips a pumpkin mead as her mate, Furyon, drops onto the barstool next to hers.

I wipe the bar down before placing two menus in front of them, not that they even need a menu at this point. I swear they eat at Whiskey Biz at least three nights a week, always when I'm working. Great tippers, too, even though I've argued about them tipping me like I'm their kid who finally got a job.

"Lem, it's not what I thought," I admit as I go back to wiping the bar down, even though it's spotless and still early in the evening.

She frowns, dark blond brows furrowing into an elegant vee. Her itty bitty fangs peek over the edges of her mead tankard. Setting it down, she cocks her head to the side, perfect blonde waves hanging over her neck and chest to highlight the swirling vampiric house tattoos covering her large breasts. She's so fucking pretty, it's sickening.

"I hate you," I mutter. "You're too pretty to be real."

Furyon smirks, black lips pulling into a satisfied smile as he slides an arm around his beautiful mate.

"It's not fair," I snap, tossing a rag at Lemon.

She catches it easily, dropping it back onto the countertop. "Stop changing the subject, Bluebell Tucker. What's wrong with the Bodice?"

I sigh. "Well, it's been three days since I took over and what's *not* wrong? The back room is actually a mess with no organizational system I can suss out. The building is upset at having been left, I think, but doesn't want any help from me. It's just not what I thought I was getting into."

Furyon eyes me. "So she doesn't want your help? How do you know?"

"We just didn't get off to a great start, and I'm getting weird vibes. I'm sure it'll be fine, though."

"It's probably just an adjustment period," Lemon says smoothly. "Kinda like me and the Keeper's house."

"We still can't figure that one out," Furyon supplies helpfully. "You ain't our Keeper, Lemon, but that mansion loves you."

She shrugs but beams. "Tough not to love someone so sweet and kind, ya know?"

"And humble," I tack on. "Want to come to the Bodice and see if you can make her like me? I don't know what I'm gonna do if she doesn't come around."

"Well, it's been less than a week since you took over, right?" Furyon grabs Lemon's menu, stacks it on his, and sets them both aside. "You're gonna be fine, Bluebell. You've known that business your entire life. It's just gonna take a minute, sweetheart."

"Don't call me sweetheart," I say, making a fake barfing sound. "Save the sweetiepies for your sweetiepie and the Valentines shindig. Or, shit, even the Christmas or Yule celebrations."

"Give us our usuals," Furyon says, sliding the menus toward me.

"Me too," shouts Oz as he appears in the doorway, an auburn pit hell female trailing after him. He crosses the bar and flops onto a stool next to Lemon. The pit hell hops up next to him and leans forward, resting her chin on the edge of the bar.

Oz shuffles his big leathery wings and pets her head. "Bacon cheeseburger for my girl here, please. I named her Ginger, finally!"

I reach over and stroke the half pit bull, half hellhound's silky snoot, looking at Oz. "She finally bond with you?"

He shakes his head, stealing Lemon's mead and downing it in one big gulp. Smacking his black-painted lips, he looks at me. "Naw, but any moment, I'm sure. Which would be cool because then I'd have, like, a personal bodydog, you know, like a bodyguard?"

"Maybe she'd like a gift," Lemon says thoughtfully.

"What do you think the bacon cheeseburger's for?" Oz rolls his eyes.

Lemon matches his expression. "I was talking to Bluebell about the Bodice. I'm saying maybe the Bodice would like some gifts since she's a store."

I turn and punch Lemon and Furyon's orders into the point-of-sale. Once I hit submit, I slide a menu over the bar to Oz. He doesn't tend to branch out in his orders either, but I might as well do the job I'm hired to do. Unless only the dog's eating...

Lemon does karaoke while Furyon and Oz chat over drinks. The pup's burger comes out first, and Oz chops it into small pieces for her. She eats with delicate, quick movements, eyes darting around the bar. She's so cautious, looking constantly to Oz for reassurance. He strokes her with his big purple fingers, his touch delicate.

When she's done, she crawls into his lap, and despite being probably sixty pounds, she tucks her head up into his shoulder-length hair and falls asleep in his arms. He wraps a wing around her, cradling her body, which makes him look like a human with a wing-shaped baby carrier.

Big ole sweeties, all of the Gulch's pit hells. Most of them run wild, although they're all friendly. This one's been following Oz around for a while, though. I suspect a little love story is happening, which is pretty adorable since Oz moved here to escape a love story with a shitty ending.

He deserves this.

"I've got an appointment with a supplier in Santa Alaya tomorrow. They've got some cool gear that's very you-inspired," I say to Lemon. "So I'm hoping the Bodice will be on board for some nifty new things, a little change of pace."

"Tell her I asked for it," Lemon says with a shrug. "She's always happy to accommodate a customer, in my experience. And I'm in there a lot."

"I know you are," I say with a snort. "You're gonna help me keep the lights on in that place."

We share a laugh at that. I can't even imagine what Furyon's credit card looks like now that she's gotten ahold of it.

"Between outfits from the Bodice and potions antiques from the Auction House, you're gonna keep me workin' til I'm dead," Furyon says with a wink at his mate, which answers my question.

She shrugs. "Happy to pay for it myself, if it's an issue, Ranger Zayle."

Hoboy. They've started flirting at the bar, which means one or both of them'll be doing karaoke again soon, and then I'll be thanking the gods I don't have monster senses for the pheromone display.

Oz'll comment on it though.

Lemon smiles at me. "Can you grab me some cool things for the Keeper's mansion? Anything you see that's gothic but a little more modern? I've got a troll builder coming to town later this week to work on some foundation issues, and then I can finish fixing up the back of the house."

Oz leans forward, cradling the pit hell against his chest. "And then what, Lem? It's not like you're gonna move in."

She shakes her head. "I'm not, but we don't have a Town Hall *or* a haven Keeper, and I think the mansion could kinda function like one. We're doing a lot of hiring at the potions house, and I'd like to use the mansion's formal living room as a temporary space. The light's great, and the house is on board. So's Rykan; he'd have to okay it, of course, since he's running the potions house now."

We talk about that for a while, and Whiskey Business acknowledges her approval by shimmying the chunky ceiling beams.

My shift slows to a crawl after Lemon leaves. Thankfully, Oz sticks around to close down the bar, even though he's not working. The pit hell ducks into a bed beneath the bar, falling asleep with her long legs tucked beneath her.

Once she's snoring, Oz leans against the bartop and smirks at me.

I throw the rag over my shoulder. "What? Got something in your eye, Ozifer?"

He shrugs but the smirk remains. "Just noticing that pretty new necklace. Lemme guess...Hadrian?"

I return to my work, tossing the rag down and rubbing at nonexistent spots on the bartop. "I can neither confirm nor deny."

"Still just friends, hmm?" He grabs a second rag and joins me in rubbing water spots that aren't there.

"Oh yeah," I lie. Hadrian hasn't been 'just a friend' in my brain for many years, but it's a secret I've got to keep to myself. "If I went on a date with Hay, Jasper would shit a literal brick."

Oz laughs. "So?"

"Soooo...." I draw the word out long. "That just sounds like more shit to deal with and I am up to my ears in shit."

"Heard," he mutters, and thankfully that's the end of that.

Eventually I abandon him at the bar and head to Lizard Lick Saloon to do the final couple hours until closing. My muscles are dog-tired...It's been such a long week. But there's no rest for the weary, I suppose.

When I step inside, the floor planks wriggle in a path all the way to the bar, the building showing me where to go.

"Sweet girl," I whisper as I rub my fingers just inside the door, leaving a happy spark of magic. The saloon is full to the brim with monsters eating and drinking.

Behind the bar, a cute minotaur male winks at me as he rubs a wet rag over the wooden surface. "Bluebell, I hope you're ready for a long night, girl. The minotaur social club is on a roll this evenin'."

I let out a groan, glancing around him at the large group of minotaurs at the single long table in the back of the bar.

I shoot the bartender a knowing look. "Monthly poker tournament?"

He grins and nods, so I wave him out from behind the bar. "Git. I know you're dying to join them and fleece someone again this month."

He bends down and kisses the top of my head. "Thanks, friend."

* * *

The following morning, I walk briskly through the portal between Pine Gulch and the Grand Portal Station at haven system headquarters. Thankfully, my trip to Mexico's Santa Alaya haven will be quick now that the station connects every hidden monster community.

One of the downsides of the haven system used to be that each monster community was only connected to one other. Originally, it was meant to be a security measure but it made travel a real nightmare. These days, those worries are forgotten.

The haven system is safe. Safe from thrall attacks and monsters who don't want to live within our system for one reason or another.

Jogging across the giant room, I locate Santa Alaya's portal and rush through. I hate to be late, and I got a rough start after Jace showed up at my place at six a.m. with truck trouble. Jasper and Jack were already on a job and couldn't help, so there I was in the middle of Main at the ass crack of dawn, helping him sort out carburetor issues.

Some days, I really regret being the only Tucker besides my father with a penchant for engines.

Now I'm running slightly behind, and I already had a packed schedule today. When I reach the beachy-themed portal station at the other end of the portal tunnel, I resist the urge to call Hadrian. He's in Santa Alaya with the Punishers for the next couple of days for yet another away game. This season's schedule is brutal—he was only home for a few nights this time! I can't imagine doing what he does, traveling around the whole system so much. I'd hate that. I like visiting other havens, but the moment I leave Pine Gulch, I find I can't wait to get back.

Outside the station, Santa Alaya's tropical sun beats down, warming my skin. This haven is packed full of bright plants and flowers that burst out of every crack in the building from the street. It's a paradise of colors. Not for the first time, I wonder how my brothers and mother would feel in a place like this where their green magic probably feels so strong.

Even *my* magic is drawn to the old buildings, wondering who takes care of them because, while they're obviously old, they're strong too. Only a black witch could make that happen. Of course, the shifter queen bounces back and forth between this haven and another, and I'm sure she has monsters with all sorts of magic in her court.

Looking at the map on the back of my daily to-do list, I follow my supplier's directions through sun-drenched streets all the way down to the oceanfront boardwalk. Hooking a right, I continue along for another fifteen minutes, preferring to walk through and feel the sun versus taking one of the popular local taxis.

Eventually, a beautiful pink colonial building comes into view. That's my destination for today, and where I hope I can find some interesting new products to carry at the Bodice, but also a gift, per Lemon's request.

I spend most of the day at the Fábrica Superior with my supplier, Enrique. He's an excellent host, stuffing me full of the most amazing food, all while tantalizing me with glitter and sparkle and gorgeous soft leather.

I buy way more than I should; we'll just call that an investment. But I find some boots and belts I think the Bodice will love, not to mention Lemon. When I casually mention her request of a gift for the Keeper's mansion, Enrique gives me a gothic planter with a cutting of Variegated Hydrangea, something that's only native to Santa Alaya. My brothers can grow the cutting fast, and it'll be stunning in front of the Keeper's mansion.

By the time I reach my hotel, I'm sweating from every pore, still schlepping my backpack with my shit in it, and all I want is a shower. But it's not meant to be because there's a line to check in.

I get to the front and smile at the beautiful dark-skinned pixie female behind the check in desk.

"Hola, señora, how can I help you?"

"Checking in for Bluebell Tucker."

She nods and smiles, nails clacking on her keyboard as she looks up my reservation. Her brow furrows, and she looks back at me. "Tucker is t-u-c-k-e-r?"

I frown. "Yes, that's right."

She clacks more, then calls a manager, and they whisper together for a moment, pointing at the computer screen. After a solid five minutes where I start to feel more than a little snippy, both females look at me apologetically.

The manager speaks first. "Miss Tucker, I'm so sorry, but we don't seem to have a reservation for you in our system. What's worse is that we're fully booked, so we don't even have a room to offer."

My mouth drops open. "For real? I've got my confirmation code and everything."

"I know," the manager says, her tone extra apologetic. "And I'm so sorry because I don't even know how this is possible, but we don't have you in here, and we have no available rooms. Let me call around to our sister property up the street and see if we can slot you in there."

I frown. "How long's that gonna take?"

"Give me five minutes," the manager says confidently.

Twenty-five minutes later, there's no word, and I'm still

sitting in the lobby waiting for someone to tell me what's up. I'm about to go back to the desk for answers when my comm watch rings. Hadrian's name hovers over the band.

I direct the watch to answer him. "Wassup, Alk?"

"You're in Santa Alaya on a buying trip, right?" His deep voice reverberates through the watch face.

Something deep in my belly pools hot and hard. Like always, I shove it down. I can't be lusting after Hadrian, despite how fucking sexy we both grew up to be. Kind of a shame he's basically my brother. And Jasper's best friend.

Except he's not at all *your brother*, the devil on my shoulder whispers. *He's not even human.*

No shit, Sherlock, I mutter to that bitch. *Stop talkin' to me about how hot Hadrian is. He's Hay-Hay, Alk, Big H. Or one of the million other stupid names my brothers call him.*

"Did I lose you?" A soft chuckle.

I clear my throat. "Sorry, no. I'm in my hotel lobby, but they've lost my reservation, and what was supposed to be five minutes to clear the problem has been half an hour of me being increasingly pissy and debating if I need to flip tables or what."

He's quiet for a second. "I'm gonna message you my hotel address. Just come stay with me. There's plenty of room. I won't be home until after the game, but I'll let the manager know you're coming."

I nip at the edge of my finger. "You sure? I'll crash on the sofa or whatever. This is just...I don't know if they can find a spot for me."

"Sending you a message now." Moments later, an address pops up, hovering above my comm watch.

"Are you *absolutely* sure?" I'm giving him one last out, then I'm taking him up on the kind offer because I'm not sleeping in this damn lobby.

"Ask me again, and I'll kick your ass when I see you. Gotta go." He clicks off before I can protest yet another time.

Grabbing my backpack, I slip it on and head out of the lobby.

I'm not going to bother with letting the front desk know I'm leaving. They sure didn't seem to care enough to check on me for the last half hour.

Outside, Santa Alaya is full of laughter and music. I bask in the fading winter sun as I follow my comm watch's directions through colorful, vibrant streets toward Hadrian's hotel. It takes about twenty minutes to walk there, but I'm not in a rush because his game starts in an hour, so he won't be back until who knows when. I'm guessing he'll go party with the team afterward, so I can get in a solid nap while he's doing that. I didn't think I'd have time to go to the game, so I didn't bother trying to get tickets, and I didn't even consider asking him.

His hotel, Hotel las Armas, looms at the end of a gorgeous cobblestone street. Calling it a hotel seems like too much, because it's opulent but small. A black-and-white tiled entryway is open to the street and filled with monsters drinking beautiful concoctions as they mingle in small groups.

A beautiful vampire approaches me with a smile. "Miss Tucker?"

I nod, unsure how she knows it's me.

"Excellent," she chirps. "Señor Alkazar let us know you'd be coming." She hands me a small envelope. "Here's your key and a two-hundred-dollar voucher for the hotel. It can be used in the spa, at the bar, restaurant or for room service. You're in the penthouse suite, which has its own elevator." She guides me around the check-in desk and down a hallway behind it. Plants peek in from open windows down the entire right-side stucco wall. She pauses and gestures toward an elevator at the back. "Simply scan your key down there, and it'll take you directly to Señor Alkazar's suite."

Damn. This is the royal treatment. I always assumed Hadrian got this, but it's sure nice to be on the receiving end of it.

She smiles at me. "Can I answer any questions or send up a refreshment for you?"

I might as well take advantage of this while I can. "Any chance I could get a diet soda of some sort?"

Her smile widens. "I've got pretty much anything you can imagine. Do you have a preference?"

I order a Diet Cherry Pepsi and head for the elevator, wondering how quickly I'll actually receive it. To my fricking deepest surprise, the can of soda sits with a glass of ice on a tiny table just outside the elevator door. There must be a hidden service entrance. Just past the table there's another doorway that looks like I'll key-card into.

After grabbing the soda, I let myself into Hadrian's room. Despite the star treatment so far, I'm still shocked to find a full apartment with a beautifully appointed kitchen and the same black-and-white-checkered tile as the lobby. Big open arches let in the setting sun and give a perfect view of a courtyard filled with monsters having dinner.

A singular bedroom is nestled back behind the kitchen, but I'll be fine on the giant U-shaped sofa between the kitchen and the line of open windows.

Scoffing at how ridiculously gorgeous this place is, I drop my backpack on the sofa and head to the windows, staring down into the courtyard. A few monsters down below glance up at me, whispering and pointing. I guess it's fun to see who occupies the topmost suite. Do folks stare at Hadrian like this when he travels? I bet they do on account of his size and hotness.

All gargoyles are handsome. It's, like, a monster trait they just all possess. But Hadrian's attractiveness is on another level. I don't know if it's because he's bigger and quieter than even the average gargoyle. Maybe it's because he looks like Aragorn from Lord of the Rings, except he's purple. Maybe it's his love of books, which makes him seem kinda nerdy. Maybe it's that he seems even older than his years. *Maybe* it's that he's so impossibly manly and competent. I have no idea what he sees in Jasper, or Jack, for that matter. If I could have picked any of my brothers to be his bestie, I'd have assumed Jace, who's an old soul.

Maybe Hadrian and Jasper are so close precisely *because* they're such polar opposites. I've thought about it plenty of times over the years. I knew when Hadrian picked the Punishers' offer that he'd buy a place and set down roots. I don't think Jasper even has a plan to *ever* move out of my folks' place. He'd be happy to live there forever. It should be awkward, but when he dates—and he dates a lot—he just goes to the girls' place and they're, like, fine with that, I guess?

I sip my soda, thrilled to have gotten my favorite flavor, as I return to the sofa and snuggle in. Opening my computer, I smile at the pic on my laptop screen—me and my brothers, plus Hadrian. The guys must be about thirteen because I'm eight or so. I'm in the middle, and Hadrian's got one arm slung around me and the other around Jasper. Jack and Jace are missing half their teeth, still in that awkward growing up phase. But we look so happy. So cute.

Clicking into my product-tracking software, I work for a half hour before the day gets to me. Before I realize it, I'm falling asleep on the cushiest black velvet couch I've ever encountered.

A scent fills my nostrils, something clean and manly.

Glycerine.

Hadrian. Did I murmur his name aloud?

Reaching my fingers across the sofa, I feel for him.

He's not there...

A poking sensation along my ribs has me jolting upright, blinking my eyes to figure out who or what is tickling me.

I scream at finding shocking purple eyes and sharp white fangs right in front of me.

Hadrian.

He snickers and grins, moving his tail from beneath the hem of my shirt and wrapping it around his thigh like most gargoyles do. I try not to stare at just how much of that thigh is exposed due to the shortness of his Punishers shorts. They can't even be called shorts; they should just be called sho— because they can't have more than a two-inch inseam.

"Get your junk outta my face," I bark, slumping against the sofa as he crosses his arms and beams at me. "When are they gonna get you some shorts that fit?"

He snorts out a laugh and spreads his huge wings wide, flaring them so big, they blot out the light coming in from the windows *and* the light filtering from the chandeliers above him. "Shorts that fit? That ain't in the playbook, Bluebell. I think half the tickets we sell are so that monstresses such as yourself can come stare at our junk while we're running around."

"Facts," I grumble. "I'm partial to the team uniform, if I'm honest."

He drops to his heels and rests his elbows on his knees, cocking his head playfully to the side. "You come to the game to stare at my junk, Bluebell?"

I lean forward until my face is a half inch from his, dropping my gaze to his mouth. Nipping my lip, I hum in the back of my throat. "Would you like me to, Hadrian?"

He rolls his eyes and pushes me to the back of the sofa. "You eat yet? They gave you the gift card, right?"

I pop up and follow him into the kitchen, where he deposits his bag and starts emptying protein shake bottles out of it.

"Didn't eat yet. I fell asleep on that bomb-ass sofa instead."

He raises a single dark brow in an accusatory fashion. "Yeah, with your soda in your hand. It was half dumped over when I arrived."

I gulp. "Err, did you pick it up?"

"I did." He smiles as he tosses the protein bottles in the sink. "Let's get food."

I look around. "Don't you have post-game team shit to do?"

He shakes his head. "I'm not much of a partier. Told them I had plans."

"Argh." I slump onto a barstool. "Don't cancel plans to hang with me. I'm just gonna pass out and be boring and probably work."

He rounds the island and joins me, slapping a menu down on the bartop. "And yet that sounds fucking perfect to me because, again, I'm not a party animal. Let's order room service, watch weird movies, and chill on the sofa. Or I'll take you out if you wanna go out."

I scrunch my nose up, and he laughs, shoving the room service menu closer to me.

"In, it is. Pick a bunch of shit from there. I'm gonna shower, then I'll order, and you can pick a movie.

"Done." I pull the menu close as he rises and heads to the left where the bedroom is situated. I definitely don't watch him go to see if he happens to rip that shirt off on his way to the bathroom.

Ten minutes later, he shows back up in gray sweatpants—my fucking archnemesis, WHY DO GUYS DO THAT?—and a matching gray hoodie that snaps along his shoulders and sides to accommodate his enormous wings. The gray looks good against the dark purple of his skin and all that black hair. It's pulled halfway up into a top knot that shouldn't make my mouth water.

I blame the sweatpants. It's stupid for him to wear them. I'm just a simple woman, and I can only be expected to behave so much.

Scratch that. I'm just a horny woman who hasn't been on a date in about, oh, eighteen months, and I really cannot use the vibrator I brought while I'm in this suite with my brother's best friend. Not when gargoyles have such impeccably strong senses. He'd hear it and smell it, and gods, that would be fucking awkward.

Although, I'm pretty sure I hauled a box of his sex toys when I helped him move. He got *so* awkward about that small one. LOL.

Hadrian flops on the sofa and grabs the room phone. "Give me your food list 'cause we both know you wrote it down."

Laughing, I slide off the bar and hand him the sticky note where I wrote out the food I want to try. "I picked a lot," I admit. "I'll pay."

He snorts. "Imagine if I told Jasper I let you pay for food. He'd rip my head off."

"I dunno, he's not that chivalrous," I mutter. If he was, he wouldn't let me do so much of the shit he should be doing for himself.

Hadrian takes my list and calls down to the attendant, who's apparently on call specifically for his needs. His tone is casual and easy with her, and despite the angel on my shoulder who usually overrules the devil, jealousy rises. The way he talks to her sounds like he knows her. And that leads me to thinking about him out partying with his teammates. And wondering what he'd be doing tonight if he wasn't stuck in with me.

I'm ready to flip tables again thinking about some girl riding his face.

Get it together, Blue, I scold myself.

Hadrian turns to me with an inquisitive look. "You okay? Your scent changed. Did I order wrong?"

I force a laugh. "That's my starving scent. It's the I'm-about-to-be-a-feral-cat-if-you-don't-feed-me smell."

He stares for another moment, then turns to grab the television remote. Handing it to me, he puts his big feet up on the coffee table. I definitely don't admire the three thick claw-tipped toes. He has no arch to speak of. His foot is totally flat. I bet you couldn't knock him over with a bulldozer.

"Pick something you know Jasper wouldn't wanna watch," he says, grabbing a water bottle out of the front pocket of his sweater.

I scroll through the options as I tuck my feet up under me. With the sun setting, it's getting a little chilly, and I hadn't imagined that for Santa Alaya. I should have, because the wind off the mountains in PG makes everything feel twenty degrees colder. Here they've got wind coming off their mountains *and* the sea. Ultimately, I settle on *Galaxy Quest*, a movie I fucking adore that I know Jasper hates.

"Good pick." Hadrian settles his right arm on the back of the sofa. I try not to notice how close his hand is to the back of my head. And I definitely don't think about what it would be like for him to grip my neck and guide me onto his huge lap.

"I'm gonna get a drink," I announce, rising off the sofa and heading into the kitchen, praying there are more sodas or something in here. Turns out his fridge is fully stocked, so I grab another drink and busy myself while I try to tamp down the unfortunate hormones.

Hadrian glances over. "Is this gonna be like a typical Tucker movie night where you can't sit still because you've got a to-do list a mile long?"

I take a swig of the soda, willing the cherry flavoring to chemically alter my brain just for tonight. "Yeah," I admit. "Probably."

He smiles and turns back to the movie.

"Do you ever go out with the team?" I return to the sofa and flop down just past his reach.

He shakes his head, taking another long drink of water. Fuck, the way his throat bobs as he swallows makes me think things. And wonder things. And I've got to rein it in.

I just don't spend time alone with Hadrian. And that's a good thing because being alone with Hadrian makes feelings rise inside me, feelings I've done a great job of hiding over the years. Feelings I've had ever since he got big and brawny and started getting facial hair and a five o'clock shadow.

Finally, he turns to me, scrunching his nose up, which brings out the divot in his chin. "They're younger guys, mostly, like me, but I'm an old soul. They want to drink and party and taste the local delights, if you know what I mean."

I snort. "Are you afraid to say the word 'sex,' Hadrian?"

He gives me a wry look. "No, Bluebell. My teammates love to go out and fuck hard; is that what you want to hear? *Fucking* random women isn't my jam. It's not interesting to me without a connection. And I can't connect with someone hopped up on tequila in a random sex club. It's just...not to mention, it's hard to know who wants to hang out with you for you and who wants the fame and everything that comes with this." He waves around at the beautiful suite.

Returning his focus to me, he smiles. "Remember when you were nine, and we wrote out that pact that we'd get married at thirty if we weren't mated yet?"

My blood freezes in my veins. He's thirty-four.

"Yeah, I remember." I take a deep drink of the coke. *Please please please don't tell me you're thinking it's time for that.*

He shrugs. "Obviously you and I aren't married, but the spirit of that pact still means something to me. We made it because we knew that the basis of any good partnership is friendship and mutual respect. How can you even have that with someone you just met?"

I'm staring, but I can't summon words. I've had plenty of one-night stands. Nothing ever stuck, and nobody was ever right, but that's always been fine for me.

"I've still got the bracelet we sealed our pact with," he says with a little chuckle. "It's at home on my keychain."

My mouth drops open. "Are you for real?"

He scoffs. "You didn't notice when you helped me move in? Do you have yours?"

I gulp. "Errr..."

He shrugs. "I'm sappy. I know. It's symbolic more than anything. I just never met anyone who made me want to throw it away, I guess."

I've gotta do something about this revelation, so I resort to my trademark sarcasm. "Well, you've got two months until I'm thirty, and then you'll be stuck with me for eternity."

He grins as he watches the opening credits of the movie. "You say that like it's a *bad* thing, Bluebell." He winks at me. "I could do worse than you, you know."

I roll my eyes. "You couldn't handle me, Hadrian. I would drive you crazy."

His teasing smile falls, and a muscle works overtime in his jaw, his tail uncurling from his thigh to thwap against the floor. Cocking his head to the side, he stares at me like he's seeing me for the first time.

Heat flares along my cheeks and down my chest, nipples pebbling at that challenging, possessive expression. What do I do with this?!

I'm thankful when a bell dings, and we both get up to grab the food.

Half an hour later, I'm so full, it hurts, and Hadrian's half asleep on the sofa, eyes heavy-lidded as our intrepid Galaxy Quest team struggles to understand that aliens do exist.

I quietly quote my favorite parts as the room gets chillier and chillier. Eventually, Hadrian glances over. “You cold?”

I laugh. “Among the other failures of this trip, I neglected to realize it would be cool at night.”

He shifts upright and yanks his sweater open at both shoulders, revealing miles of taut purple skin and ab muscles so thick they’re like building blocks. They’re, like, fake abs, they’re so good. He could be wearing one of those fake ab *sweaters*. I force my eyes up when he snaps the sweatshirt back together, then turns to me.

Pulling it over my head, he helps me get it fully on and then smiles. “Got it cooled up for ya.”

I wave at his everything. “You won’t be cold?”

“I’m fine, Bluebell,” he says quietly. Then he wraps an arm around my shoulder and hauls me close. “I’m not as warm as a human would be, but c’mere.”

Fuck meeeeee. I’m tucked against his side, my feet under his thigh as he angles sideways so I’m basically resting on his side and chest.

His slightly cool skin smells faintly of soap as he shifts to make room for me, muscles flexing beneath his beautiful dark skin. Resisting the urge to slide my hands over his abs, I carefully rest my cheek on his naked pec. His fingers grip my shoulder even though his eyes don’t move from the television. Is he finding this as awkward as I do? I’m snuggling my brother’s best friend I’ve had the hots for for ages.

But within moments, he’s asleep and snoring softly, manspread all over the couch while I try to take up the minimum amount of space without making this awkward.

He wouldn’t have pulled me close if he felt weird about it. Eventually, I roll with it and try not to pass out on his half-naked body while I’m wearing his clothes. This could be so, so hot if things were different.

Sigh.

Hadrian

When I wake with a raging erection, it takes me a moment to remember that Bluebell's in the bedroom, which is why I'm out here in the living room. We fell asleep on the sofa last night, but I worried about her comfort, so eventually I picked her up. Carrying her to the bedroom and tucking her in was the most sensual thing I've done in a long time, feeling that trim body wrapped in my arms. Taking care of her came so naturally to me, my protective nature loving every second of it. I didn't want it to end.

I'm sure that's why my dick's throbbing and leaking precum all over my sweats.

It's not because I've fantasized about her for years, a secret I'd told myself I'd be taking to my grave.

Soft snores ring from my room. Without really thinking, I rise and tuck my cock down one leg of the sweatpants. Stalking past the kitchen, I open the bedroom door, telling myself I just want to make sure she's okay, that she's not cold.

A lump in the middle of the bed makes the blood rush to my dick, and I resist the urge to fist it and get off right here. I can't do that. I can't *do* that. But she's curled up all tiny, still wearing my sweater. Our combined scents are everywhere in the room.

I jacked off four times *in that bed* before the game. The smell of my pleasure in the same room where she's sleeping has me so hard, I could almost come just looking at her.

She groans and rolls over. Hard nipples pebble beneath the soft fabric of my clothing as she stretches long in the bed. She's waking, and if she wakes up to find me staring at her with a hard-on, things are gonna get weird.

Holding her on the sofa last night was probably a step too far, but I couldn't help myself when she was shaking with cold.

But now it's this morning. Forcing myself away, I return to the kitchen and put a cup of coffee on, thinking about anything I can to get the erection to go down.

Jasper.

Skyball plays.

My dumb parents.

Not to mention the fact that Bluebell and I have been friends for almost three decades. I'd be crazy to risk fucking that up... right?

By the time the coffee's done brewing, I've got things as under control as is possible with *her* wearing my clothing in my bed.

But she's perfect for me, I think as I sigh aloud and step out onto the porch. It's no longer chilly, and the courtyard below is full of monsters eating breakfast that smells delicious from up here. That devil on my shoulder telling me to make a move on my best friend's sister? He's gotta go.

Faint footsteps echo from inside the suite. Closing my eyes, I suck in a steadying breath along with a big gulp of hot coffee. I can do this.

Bluebell appears on the porch next to me, tan legs sticking out from underneath my sweatshirt.

"Are you wearing shorts?" I bark out, sputtering as I choke on a second mouthful of coffee.

She slaps my stomach as she rolls her eyes. "Of fucking course I'm wearing shorts. How awkward would that be if I was, like, naked in your clothing? Better not let Jasper find out. He'll flip his wig."

"He'd rip my wings off," I mutter, thinking about the last time Jasper got it in his head that I looked at his sister wrong. It's been a solid five years since that argument, but I'm careful not to stare too hard at her because of it. He's very...protective. Bill and Elena have always drilled that into him as the oldest.

She lifts her arms over her head and stretches.

My eyes drift to where the move exposes a few inches of her flat stomach. A floral tattoo swirls down her entire left side and thigh. How high up does it go? I don't know.

I'd *like* to know, though.

"Is your tit tattooed?"

Fuck. Did I just say that out loud?

Bluebell roars with laughter but blushes and tucks a long chunk of bright blue hair behind her delicate, round ear.

"Umm, yeah. The tattoo goes up the side and over my shoulder."

"Damn, that must have hurt."

She winks. "You still not a tattoo guy?"

I shake my head. "Can't think of anything I like enough to put it on my body like that. Piercings, though, those interest me a whole lot more."

Her playful smile drops, and she lifts both hands in shock. "Wait, wait. And I'm just hearing about this now? Where the hell do you have piercings?! I saw you shirtless last night."

It's my turn to wink. "They're all places you can't see when I'm shirtless, Bluebell."

She scoffs. "Does Jasper know? Wait, scratch that. If you've got a bunch of asshole piercings, and y'all got them together, I don't need that mental image." She scrunches her nose and shakes her head like she's dispelling that vision that's most surely in her head right now.

I jerk my head toward the kitchen. "Coffee's ready. There's

cream and plenty of sugar so you can ruin yours with all that shit you love."

"Spank you very much," she chirps as she turns to pick her way across the living room.

Jasper ain't here, so I allow myself to watch her as she walks. Long, tan legs are trim with muscle, and the floral tattoo curls down her left thigh. She might be wearing shorts, but they're short enough that I can almost see the swell of her ass beneath my sweatshirt.

And now something else is swelling too, because Bluebell looks really damn fuckable right now.

Masking a groan beneath a cough, I force myself to glance back down into the courtyard, pretending I care about what's going on below until she returns with coffee in hand.

She blows on the steaming cup, and I try not to focus on the purse of her lips. They're blue right now too, part of the spell she uses to dye her hair and freckles. Looking up, she smiles. "So, what's on your docket for today?"

I shrug and lean against the stucco railing of the small porch. "Some guys are sticking around to do a day of practice with the local team. I was planning to head home and take a couple days off before our next home game. It's been a long few weeks of traveling."

She sips the coffee.

I smile. "You wanna go back together? We can—"

A rustle and flash of light from down below grabs my attention. Flaring my right wing protectively around Bluebell, I crush her to my side as I look for a threat. In the courtyard below us, a small group of photographers have their cameras pointed upward, and they're snapping pic after pic.

I usher her back inside, knowing she won't appreciate what they're doing.

"Alk, Alk!" she shouts, pushing against the leathery skin of my wings. "What are you *doing*?!"

I unfurl them and tuck them back behind me, surprise

rushing through me at how strong my protective instinct was in that moment. No heartbeat pounds in my chest, but it might as well for the tension in my muscles.

"Photographers," I grit out. "Taking photos of us. I just assumed you wouldn't want that, sorry. I'm used to it, but I'm sure you're not."

Her mouth drops open, and she looks at the porch, then back at me. Lifting a hand, she places it on my chest. "It didn't bother me, but thank you for thinking it might have. Do you deal with that a lot?"

I nod. "It's near constant, but it's one of the things I love about PG. Nobody there really cares all that much. I've never seen a photographer around with the exception of the *Gulch Gossip* gals. They're pretty harmless, though."

She looks back toward the porch. "I was going to ask if you wanted to grab breakfast, but maybe we'd better not if that makes you uncomfortable."

I laugh. "It doesn't bother me, but imagine if the Tuckers see us splashed all over some newspaper somewhere having breakfast."

She rolls her eyes. "Good point. I don't have the energy to deal with a Tucker inquisition right now. I got enough nonsense going on."

Her comment about the Tucker inquisition is spot on. They're a nosy bunch. That doesn't bother me. But the comment about nonsense pings my instinct.

"What's going on; what do you mean?" I slide my hands into my pockets to resist touching her.

She sighs, taking another sip of coffee before she answers. "The Bodice is messy. She's mad at being sold, and even though I've known her my whole life, she's not interested in our new partnership. It's going to be a rough transition, I fear."

"But we live upstairs," I manage, thinking about how she seems perfectly peaceful in the apartment across the hall from mine.

"And that seems fine," she says with an exasperated look and a shrug. "But she won't let me fix or organize anything, and she makes all sorts of awful noises. I'm sure it'll work out in the end, but we're not off to a strong start."

I take a sip of my coffee, letting its temperature burn all the way down my throat. "If anyone can fix it, Bluebell, it's you."

I mean it as a vote of confidence, but some of the light seems to die in her eyes when I say it. It occurs to me that maybe that's because Bluebell fixes so fucking much, for not just herself, but the entire Tucker clan.

And maybe...just maybe...she doesn't like it that way.

Bluebell

Lemon's gasp of surprise has me turning to where she stands just outside one of the Bodice's two small dressing rooms. She steps onto a small platform and twirls in front of the half circle of mirrors, eyeing the black cowboy boots on her tiny feet. I've been home a few days and managed to unpack most of what I bought in Santa Alaya.

"That turquoise buckle is a game changer, Bluebell," she says, voice full of awe. "It's subtle but still so damn gorgeous."

Above us, the Bodice shimmies her ceiling beams—the first happy noise I've heard her make.

"You gotta get 'em," Oz states before crunching into a crisp red apple. He munches loudly as Lemon and I share a smile. At his feet, Ginger shuffles and puts her head on top of his foot.

Oz looks over, swallowing the bite. "You get the Bodice a gift while you were in Santa Alaya?"

The building goes silent again, and discomfort prickles up my spine. Black magic sings through my fingers, anxious to be of use. It's almost painful to hold it back and not *help*.

"Yeah." I wave at Lemon's shoes. "These and a bunch of other options arrived early this morning, and there's a stunning metal display cactus in the back. I'm planning to use it in the front window to hang belts on."

Oz looks up at the building. "And...you love it or what, sister?"

The Bodice remains silent, and he and I share a warning look.

"Just channel me." Lemon spins in place, admiring the boots. "Rest easy knowing your exuberance wears everyone down eventually."

The Bodice lets out a warning shimmy, and the walls tremble. A few of the western prints fall off and slide to the ground.

"Not sure she agrees," I say with a frown. "But one thing we *can* agree on is that those boots suit you, Lem."

"Give me the same ones in purple," Oz says, rising and flaring his wings only to retuck them. He cocks his head to the side, his long horns flexing and straightening. "Tell me you got gargoyle purple to match my eyes." Reaching up, he nudges his brand new slutty little glasses up the bridge of his nose.

"Those are darling," Lemon says with a little clap. "I know you don't need them but you look so *studious*, Oz my sweet."

He takes a little bow.

The Bodice emits a series of squeaks and rumbles, which we all take as an affirmation of her agreement about the glasses. Heading into the store room where this morning's shipment is still waiting to be fully unpacked, I grab Oz a pair of purple boots with a giant inlaid turquoise buckle. They're hella impractical but absolutely stunning.

When I emerge with both boot boxes beneath my arms, I'm surprised to find Hadrian standing there with his hands in his front pockets. Lemon and Oz are both silent, staring at him.

"Alk, hey," I say, nearly breathless at seeing him again this afternoon. We just said goodbye yesterday, but I half didn't want to leave. There was something so nice about hanging with him away from PG and my family and all the trappings us Tuckers come with.

He smiles at Oz and Lemon. "I'm in no rush, Bluebell, but I

was hoping you could fit me for some new clothing when you have a sec?"

Heat rushes to my cheeks, and I'm thankful to be so tan right now because hopefully I don't look like I'm blushing.

"We'll just pay and get outta here," Lemon says, barely masking a huge smile. Next to her, Oz is smiling politely at Hadrian, his hands clasped at his waist where he still holds his apple.

"Erm...nice game in Santa Alaya. I heard you scored, like, a buncha goals."

Oh my gods. I'm gonna slap Oz. He doesn't know the first thing about skyball despite having gone to a half dozen games with me.

"Thanks, Oz," Hadrian says. "Appreciate that. It was a fun game."

"You know my name?!" Oz shrieks, looking between us all in apparent shock. "I had no idea!"

Hadrian laughs, and it's so deep and sexy, I bite my lip and cross my legs at the ankle as I ring Lemon up.

"Yeah," he says to Oz. "You've probably served me two dozen times since I moved home. Sorry if I haven't actually introduced myself. I forget to, and I've got my nose buried in books more often than not."

"Well, that's adorable," Oz says. "Gotta love a bookish man, don't we?"

"Wait," Hadrian says, cocking his head to the side. "Are the glasses new, though?"

"Yeah!" Oz chirps, shuffling his big leathery wings. "I mean I don't actually *need* them, they're just cute, you know?"

Of course we fucking do, I'm about to hiss. *Stop talking!*

We all fall silent, and I resist the urge to kick Oz or slap him or just generally tell him to stop being weird.

I ring him and Lemon up faster than I've ever rung up anyone, begging them with my eyeballs to leave without saying anything else random. Lemon grabs Oz by the elbow and directs him toward the door, thanking both me and the Bodice. The building quakes and squeaks happily as they leave.

Hadrian winks at me. "Long time no see."

I wave him toward the back as I grab my measuring tape. Rebekah, the vampire I bought the Bodice from, gave me a primer on measuring for custom clothing just before she left. Hadrian's going to be my first customer, though, so hopefully I get it right. I'm unexpectedly nervous, but it's hard to tell if that's because I'll have to touch him or what.

"Stand in front of the mirror, please." I head to the storeroom and grab a small step stool because there's no way I can reach his neck and shoulders on my own. When I emerge, he's standing on the small platform eyeing himself in the mirror with a frown.

I open up the step stool next to him and climb up it, resting my forearm on his shoulder as I meet his gaze in the mirror.

Play it cool, Bluebell. Friends. Friends. Friends.

"Why are you glaring at yourself, Alk?"

He cocks his head to the side, which brings his gorgeous long horns close to my face. "Irritated that none of my shit fits anymore and wondering if I'm gonna have to do this again in a few months. Coach wants me to bulk, though, so here we are. All of that to say, maybe I can get some clothing with a little stretch to it like Furyon has?"

I eye Hadrian's broad shoulders. He's right that he's pushing his current clothing to its absolute limits. The fabric over his chest is pulled tight, the buttons barely holding back his pecs.

"Furyon's fabric's hella expensive because it has to stretch to accommodate his large form, like three times his normal size. I don't think we need to do that for you, but we can if you think you'll grow that much."

He glances over at me. "You're the expert. What do you think?"

This is actually a great chance for me to include the Bodice, so I look upward.

"Hey, Bodice, what do you think? If he's going to pack on ten or twenty pounds, will a stretchy jean fabric work, or do we need something like—"

She rumbles happily, and I take that as agreement.

"Stretchy pants it is," I say with a laugh. "Tell me what all you need, and I'll take all of your measurements."

"Sweatpants, hoodies, jeans, pearl-snap shirts and a couple tees too. V-neck ideally. Nothing I have at home fits at all."

"'Kay, stand real still for me, alright? I'm going to grab a notebook and take down all of your measurements. For an order like this, it'll take about a week. Is that alright?"

He nods. "Yeah, for sure."

Hopping down from the step stool, I grab a notebook and pencil, then return and set them on the floor next to his huge feet.

Back on top of the stool, I start with his neck, and move my way down to his shoulder and back. He's quiet while I work, perfectly still and silent. When I move to his front and direct him to lift his arms, I try not to stare at the way his muscles flex beneath the too-tight shirt.

"Hold there," I say quietly, taking measurement after measurement, which I add to the notebook. When I'm done up high, I move in front of him and wrap the tape around his chest. Working quickly so it doesn't get awkward, I measure around the top of his chest and right beneath his pecs.

It's then I notice Lemon and Oz standing at the front window, staring in at us. I blow out an exasperated breath, shaking my head. Hadrian doesn't turn to look, but he chuckles.

"What was that for?"

"We've got onlookers," I mutter.

He sighs. "I'd like to say you get used to it, but most of the time, I want to hide at your house."

I snicker. "Remember when you first got recruited to the Academy team, and Dad ran that minotaur reporter off with a shotgun?"

Hadrian's eyes sparkle. "Yeah. And remember when I moved here and everybody was staring at me in Whiskey Business, and

Jasper told off the entire bar? It's what I love about your family. One of the many reasons I prefer yours over mine."

I take another measurement at the end of his rib cage, trying not to notice how hard his abs are beneath the shirt's fabric. "Where are your folks right now, anyways?"

"Somewhere in Brazil still," he mutters, his tone frustrated. "You know how they forget that time passes faster here inside the havens. They think they've been gone for two months, and it's years for us. Their research into gargoyles in ancient cultures always sorta came first, but I'm not bitter or anything."

It's impossible not to see it bothers him, but it's a conversation we've had many times. And it's one of the reasons he started spending summers with us at eight years old. His folks and mine are old friends, and they love to disappear into their work for years at a time. It often takes them deep into dangerous jungles and they never liked to bring him. It's *my* opinion they just didn't want to have to deal with a kid tagging along and asking a million questions. Buncha a-holes.

"I'm sorry they're not around much." I slide the tape down and pull it carefully taut over his belly button.

He says nothing, but he's tense.

Oz and Lemon are still in the damn window. I can see them from the corner of my eye, but I ignore them as I turn from Hadrian to jot down his mid-waist measurement. He's quiet, but it's fine because we're friends, and it's *never* awkward between us.

Until I get to his inseam.

"Spread your legs," I command in a deep voice, wiggling my eyebrows at him.

He snickers and steps his feet out to hip-width. "I'm at your command, milady."

Dropping to one knee, I look up with a serious expression. "For real though, don't move, or I'll accidentally touch your junk, and it'll get awkward *real* fast."

His nostrils flare, horns flexing nearly straight as he looks over me to the mirror. I work quickly, bringing the tape to the top of his current inseam. It's hard *not* to notice his package when it's right fucking there in front of my face. Not that I haven't looked a time or twelve, but is it....is it growing?

Oh shit.

Moving quickly, I measure all the way to his heel and then the other leg inside and out. I go to his back and measure over his fantastic bubble butt to his heel.

"All done?" His tone is clipped, tight.

"Yep!" I force brightness into my voice until horror hits me. "Oh damnit, I didn't write any of those down, I was so focused on going fast."

He barks out a laugh and crosses his arms. "Bluebell Delia Tucker, did you do that on purpose?"

I lift a finger. "First of all, don't ever say my middle name aloud again. If Oz or Lemon learn it, they'll just call me that, and it's game over, man, game over." I shoot him a warning glare. "And secondly, no, it was an unfortunate accident."

"Just get it done," he says, still chuckling as he shuffles his wings, rubbing the sharp tips together.

I work as fast as I can, but this time when I drop to my heels in front of him, there's an unmistakable bulge, thick and hard down the front of his thigh. And it's growing. Gods, it would happen to any male, I'm sure, having a woman on their knees in front of them. But I can't make it weird, so I say absolutely nothing, studiously avoiding the horrifyingly enormous erection right at eye level.

The problem is it's mouth-wateringly beautiful, too. If I really, really stared, I bet I could see every vein because these pants don't fucking fit him.

"Done for real," I manage, smiling up at him.

He steps off the platform with a soft smile. "Cool. Just let me know when to pay or when they get here. And also, you working late? We have a couple days off before the next home game. Jasper's supposed to come for a movie tonight, but you should join us."

"I'd love to, but I'm on at Whiskey Business. Closing," I tack on. "I'll try not to stomp down the hallway when I get home."

"No worries." He grabs a chunk of my hair and tugs on it, something he's done since we were kids. "See ya later, Tucker."

"Bye." I watch as he strides across the floor and opens the door, sailing out with all that gargoyle grace and elegance.

No sooner has he disappeared across the street than Lemon and Oz swan back in looking pleased as punch. Oz carries two cones of chocolate ice cream from BrewHaHa Beans, and he hands me one as he takes a big lick of the other.

"Spill, bitch."

"Spill what?" I ask innocently as I take the offered cone and lap gratefully at it.

Lemon smiles, but that smile is full of all her vampire deviance. "Bluebelllllll, don't act like you don't know what we're talking about. There's a vibe between you and Hadrian. I saw it at the rodeo a couple weeks ago, and I'm seeing it again now."

I nip my finger hard as I look between them. Lemon's smiling softly, but Oz's mouth is dropped open, eyes wide as he waits for me to talk.

Reaching out with a wing, he slaps the back of my head. "Spill, bitch. Do I have to say it *three* times?!"

At his feet, Ginger the pit hell looks up at me with those sweet golden-brown eyes.

The whole story about Santa Alaya spills out of me then. How they lost my reservation, so I stayed with him, slept in his bed and wore his sweatshirt.

"It's not a *thing*," I finish, biting the top off the ice cream cone. I groan at how it freezes my front teeth. "I just mean we've been friends for literal decades, and that's more important than anything else. Plus, can you imagine what Jasper would do?"

"Who cares?" Oz asks with a dramatic hand flourish. "You could be banging Hadrian Alkazar tonight, Pine Gulch hottie and all-around hunk."

"Someone's been reading the *Gulch Gossip*," I mutter,

thinking about how they covered Alk's non-dating dating life in a recent column. Or ten.

"I don't know," Lemon says with a shrug. "This place has a way of making people fall in love, doesn't it?"

"Facts," Oz says, pointing at her. "We kept you, and we thought you were a killer!"

We all laugh at that. Lemon couldn't hurt a fly, I swear.

But I think about her comment all the way until closing time.

I'm not falling in love, right? But I might be in a little teensy bit of lust. Love is catching, my mama always says.

I have someone perfect in front of me, but I absolutely cannot have him—not without ripping apart at least one friendship. At this point, I'll take a solid partnership with my store or a personal assistant to do some of my to do list.

Except that's a lie I'm telling myself to avoid the uncomfortable truth—I most definitely *want* Hadrian Alkazar.

Hadrian

"Can you deliver this to my ranch?"

The minotaur male behind the checkout counter at Feed & Hardware nods. "Same as the prior shipments? Set it on the right side of the main house?"

Jasper yawns next to me.

"Yeah, that's perfect," I confirm. "Any time this week is good."

The big minotaur grins. "Knock 'em dead tonight, Hadrian. We hate it when the Sao Paulo Silents come to town."

Unsurprising. I've had a run-in or two with their shitty coach, Gil Stoneswallow. He's brash and arrogant, and he coaches dirty, which means his players *play* dirty, and I hate that shit.

"I'll do my best," I assure him.

Jasper yawns a little louder, kneeing me in the thigh. "Dude, when are you gonna give up and just hire someone to do the work for you? That ranch is a mess, you don't have time, and you have a shitload of money."

I smile as I thank the minotaur clerk and turn to my best friend. "Like I've told you at least a half-dozen times, I *want* to do the work myself. I might be slow, but I'm thorough, and it makes me happy. Plus, it's a good excuse not to go party with my team-mates after games."

Jasper blows air out of his lips. "I'll literally never understand this about you. You could be partying all over the haven system, having the time of your life, and you'd rather be up to your horns in wood shavings, pine dust, and books than enjoying the fruits of your labors."

"We like different fruits," I deadpan.

"You can say that again," he snarks back. He waves at my crotch. "I still don't understand why you even got that fucking piercing if nobody's getting the benefit of it."

A grin overtakes me as I consider how it feels good for me. I'm sure one day someone else *will* appreciate it.

I grab the door to the store, opening it as he sails through. "Hey, have you seen Bluebell around today?" I haven't seen her for three days since she fitted me for new clothing. Three a.m. rolled around that night, and Jasper fell asleep on my sofa, but I never heard her come home. She's up at dawn every morning and back late as far as I can tell. I don't know if she even *sleeps*.

Jasper shrugs. "Long as she gets the invoicing and scheduling done on time, that's what I care about. Who knows what that girl even does with all her time?"

It's on the tip of my tongue to say that she's fucking working nonstop, and I'm pretty sure she's twelve seconds from burnout. Why the hells did she buy a business to add on top of everything else? She's a twitchy, busy person. She never could sit still. But the Bluebell I'm seeing now who lives across the hall is busier than any monster should be.

Jasper walks me to my truck.

"I'm gonna run a few more errands," I say offhand.

"Dude, you promised me burgers," he groans. "I didn't eat breakfast."

"You'll be fine." I shove him with a wing. "Take yourself for burgers. I'll see you after the game."

"Not if you're going out to that ranch to do whatever the fuck you're doing out there." He spins so he's walking backwards as he winks at me. "Knock 'em dead, buddy. Oh." He pauses and reaches into his pocket. “I got you something on our recent buying spree.”

My brows lift. “You did? I thought gifts weren’t your love language?”

He grins and hands me a small envelope. “They’re not, so literally don’t expect this ever again. But if I haven’t said it, I’m really glad you moved home. I’d have been miserable without you. I love my brothers, but you’re my favorite, *not* that I should have one.”

Grinning, I pull him close with my left wing. He stumbles toward me, eyeing the envelope with a little smile. Not the usual smirk but just a regular old smile. It’s almost tender.

“Oh my gods,” I whisper. “Are we having a bromance? Is this a love letter?”

He scoffs and elbows my wing. “As if. You took my sweet moment and ruined it. I’m leaving for the burgers you promised me, asshole.”

Spinning on his heel, he shoves my wing aside and walks up the street, lifting a middle finger as he goes.

“Awww, come on back, sweetie pie,” I shout after him. “Love you, bro!”

He lifts the middle finger higher even though the sound of his laughter echoes back to me.

Now I’m intrigued, though. Opening the envelope, I pull out what looks to be a printed receipt. Scanning the contents, I gasp. It’s a first edition of *Beasts of Bateau*, a suspense mystery written by my favorite author, Mirabelle Megaux. She died over a century ago, and first editions are impossible to come by.

A note at the bottom of the order receipt lets me know the actual book will be coming soon.

Holy shit. It’s a level of thoughtfulness I would literally never have expected from my best friend. He’s always there for me, always by my side. He’ll back me up in a fight and come anytime I need him. But thoughtful gifts? Not in the Jasper Tucker wheelhouse.

This is *wholly unexpected.*

I stare up the street as he disappears into Lizard Lick Saloon. He's partial to their burgers, but I'm more a fan of Whiskey Business myself. Maybe that has something to do with a certain blue-haired bartender, though. Not sure.

Movement in the Buxom Bodice's front window catches my eye. A flash of blue hair confirms what I thought I saw as Bluebell comes into view, placing a giant metal cactus in the center of the platform behind the window. She spins it this way and that, eyeing it with an armful of belts looped around her left wrist.

Without really thinking, I stride across Main Street toward the Bodice. Sweet building that she is, she swings the door open for me. When I enter, Bluebell turns with a smile. No sooner has she done it than the Bodice jerks the entire platform Bluebell's standing on. She goes flying off it, landing on the ground, but as soon as she drops the belts, all the floor tiles ripple, and the belts go flying like bullets around the room. A few land toward the back, one lands on my horn, and a couple end up on the ceiling beams.

Bluebell's mouth drops open as she looks around.

Above us, the ceiling beams clatter.

The building is laughing. That much is clear.

Bluebell is decidedly *not* joining in that laughter as she crawls to her feet and plants a hand on her hip.

I pull a black leather belt off my horn and hand it to her. "You okay?"

She blows out a raspberry as she looks up at the laughing ceiling. "I don't know how to get this building to chill." She waves at the cactus in the window. "I brought that gorgeous gift home from Santa Alaya, but she won't let me stage it. I thought gifts would be helpful, but nothing I'm doing is working."

"It's been about two weeks, right?" I pick up a couple belts off the floor and hand them to her.

"Yeah," she says, frowning. Double lines between her dark blue brows tell me she's stressed.

I glance up at the ceiling. "Hey, can you take it easy with my friend Bluebell? She's the best person in this whole haven, and she really wants to be your friend."

Silence.

"I'm serious. Would you behave this way toward a customer?"

More silence.

I point at the ceiling beams. "You want me to grab those?"

Bluebell shakes her head. "Nah. I gotta get my tall ladder anyhow because there's a hole up there, and I need to patch it, even though she hasn't wanted me to."

Dismay and discomfort fill me in equal measure. It's obvious the building and she aren't on great terms yet. Falling from the front window platform is one thing, but what if the building messes with her when she's on top of a ladder? It's got to be fifteen feet to the beams.

"Let me help you," I offer, looking back at Bluebell.

She frowns. "You think I might fall?"

I shake my head. "I think if you *did* fall from that height, it would really suck, and even though you could heal yourself, it would be painful and scary."

She cocks her head to the side. "Shouldn't you be getting ready for a game, Alk?"

I shrug. "I'm always ready, Bluebell. I can help you for a couple minutes."

She looks between me and the ceiling again. The Bodice is still silent.

"Alright."

Something inside me feels immense pleasure that she agreed to my help. I don't like the idea of her up on that ladder. Not at all.

"I'm gonna put you on my shoulder," I say, stepping close.

A clipped nod is her answer, but she's visibly tense, rubbing the fingertips of her right hand together, the furrow still between her brows.

Dipping down, I slide my left arm around the backs of her

legs and lift her up to my shoulder. She's bitty enough to fit nestled right there, her right hip up against my head.

I glance up at her. "When I take off, it'll be a slight up and down movement."

"Just don't drop me," she demands.

Her tone has the quietly dominant side of my nature rising hot and heavy. It's a side that doesn't come out that much since I don't casually date. But being in close proximity to her since I moved back has it rearing its head more and more. This is going to become a problem. My *pull* to her is becoming a problem.

And I don't know how much I care.

When I flap my wings and push lightly off the ground, she wobbles and yips on my shoulder. I clutch her knee tightly, but she grabs my left horn and grips it hard.

I choke back a groan at feeling her tiny, warm fingers on the sensitive length of my horn. But she must be more worried about falling, because she hangs on for dear life as I flap slowly and carefully up toward the beam. I focus on the destination, careful not to let her fall as I near the beam. Once there, I grab a beam with each wing tip and alight on the one "wearing" the belts.

"This close enough?"

Her face is right up near a visible crack in the ceiling. While it doesn't rain often in Pine Gulch, the ceiling crack could let in critters and moisture, none of which are good for the building or her wares.

She leans forward. "Hang on to me so I don't fall, 'kay?"

Reaching up, I grip her waist as she shifts forward and upright, lifting her hands to the ceiling. The move exposes several inches of her belly beneath my fingers. Her skin is soft and warm, and this close, she smells of something tangy and rich like citrus and chocolate. I breathe her quietly in as she presses both palms to the ceiling.

The Bodice shudders but remains quiet.

I've had the privilege of watching Bluebell's brothers and mother use their green magic many times over the years—growing plants, healing injured or infected plants, pushing strength into the ground.

But black magic? I've rarely witnessed Bluebell use hers.

Dark sparks flit from her fingertips and disappear into the air. She's quiet on my shoulder, although the furrow between her brows is back. As I watch, the ceiling knits slowly together until all the wood connects like new. Bluebell remains quiet, black mist swirling around her fingertips as the beams shift and straighten slightly.

When she removes her hands, it's impossible to tell where there was damage. The Bodice is silent as Bluebell folds her hands in her lap, eyeing her handiwork.

"Looks good," I murmur as I stare at the spot she fixed. "Your magic is remarkable, Blueb—"

The beam I'm on spins like it's in a log rolling competition, and I lurch forward. Bluebell flies off my shoulder and into space. I grapple for her as terror fills me. She spins in slow motion as she falls toward the ground. Clawing through the air, I reach for her as I dip a wing beneath her body. Her mouth is open, eyes wide as she stretches for me.

She hits my right wing with a thud, head falling back as her hair splays all over the bones. I flap with my left wing as I yank her close until she hits my chest. She's breathing rapid-fire, heart thudding like a machine gun as pink tinges her cheeks. We're breathing the same air, my mouth close to hers and her body tucked tightly against mine.

Pert, small breasts are pressed to my upper chest. My eyes drift to her open mouth and that pink, soft-looking tongue. Those navy-blue lips are tinted a shade darker by her favorite berry-flavored lip gloss.

"Holy shit," she breathes, wrapping her arms around my neck and pulling me even closer until my face is pressed to her neck and shoulder. "Thank you." It's a whisper as she starts trembling, thin arms around me and face against mine.

I slide both arms around her body and hold her close, moving my tail up to wrap around her waist. I'm holding her steady with every possible appendage, willing her to know that I will never let her fall.

"I've got you," I whisper into her neck. "That was frightening, Bluebell."

"No shit," she murmurs back. "I didn't think she'd really hurt me."

I lift my head, staring deep into those turquoise eyes, so bright they're nearly iridescent. "You're not allowed up on that ladder without me, okay? It's not safe."

Her eyes drop to my mouth, her blush growing. Her scent deepens, and I soak it in, flaring my nostrils as I drop my mouth closer to hers. I want to kiss her. In that moment, nothing is clearer to me than that desire. Every inch of my body is focused on her, on calming her, on protecting her, on infusing my scent into her pores so she never smells like Bluebell again.

I want her to smell like *us.*

I'm shocked the Bodice tossed Bluebell right into my arms, but when I really think about it...what if she wasn't trying to knock Bluebell down? What if she was just trying to push us together? I don't know why the building would do that or even care, but my senses ping.

There's more to this story. I just need to figure out what it is.

Bluebell

Hadrian's mouth is so close to mine, I could lean up and kiss him. And gods fuck me, I want to. Not as a thank you for saving my life just now. But because those purple lips are slightly parted, a darker purple tongue barely visible. I can't stop staring at him, and he's doing the same. For the first time ever, there's clear and obvious desire in how he's looking at me.

Is Lemon right about us?

But he doesn't make a move, and the moment stretches long. I can't be the first. It'll be so damn awkward if I try to kiss him and he doesn't want that.

Wriggling against him, I brush my long blue bangs away from my face. "Umm, I think I'm okay, if you want to put me down."

Black lashes flutter against his high, masculine cheekbones. "Of course, sorry, I...I got lost there for a second thinking about you falling all the way down." He frowns, black brows bunching together to form a concerned-looking vee. "You know I wouldn't let that happen, right?"

I laugh as he flaps carefully toward the ground, alighting on the creaky wooden floorboards. He lowers me, sliding me down his body until my feet hit wood.

"Yeah, of course," I say with a shrug. "But maybe I won't get on any more ladders without you around. I wouldn't have pegged the Bodice for a killer."

I'm joking, but around us, the entire building quakes and shakes, emitting a series of angry-sounding squeals and clatters.

Hadrian's eyes go wide. "Guess she doesn't agree with you."

At this point, I'm not sure I care. I'm beyond frustrated, and now she's put me in a super awkward position where I don't know what to say next. I tried calling Rebekah again for advice, but she must be traveling with her new grandbaby. That's why she left town, anyhow, but it means getting ahold of her is hit or miss.

He rubs his chin, looking around at the building. "Do you suppose Pine Gulch's penchant for running would-be Keepers out of town is rubbing off on her? Maybe she got the idea she can do the same thing? So, it's not you, really, just the fact that it's someone new?"

"I don't know but I've got to prep for the game," I say with a frown, desperate to move on to a topic where I know how to talk to him. Reaching up, I grab a space bun in each hand and close my eyes, focusing on "healing" my hair into another color.

Hadrian laughs when I remove my hands and glance at my long bangs—gold and black, as expected.

"It's wild watching you do that," he says with a smirk. "Can you do mine? Could you make my wings black and gold?"

"Shit," I bark out, mouth dropping open. "I...don't know? Maybe? I've never tried anything past my hair and freckles."

He steps closer, grabbing my hand and shoving it on the leathery inside of his wing. "Try it; I wanna see." Purple eyes glitter with hope.

Now I'm touching him again. Resisting the urge to trail my fingers up the strong, dark bones of his inner wing, I flatten my palm against the cool, leathery skin. I close my eyes and focus the same way I do with my hair, imagining the bones in gold and the wings in a purple so dark, they're almost black. Hot magic combines with the chill of his skin, pulling goosebumps onto mine.

"Fuck me," he breathes, "that's incredible, Bluebell. You did it."

I open one eye, and he's right, his wing bones glow a faint burnished gold, and the leathery skin connecting them is an eggplant purple so dark, it's almost black.

Waving my left hand in a circle, I take a bow. "You're welcome. But maybe don't tell everyone I'm open for business because I don't need yet another venture to take up my time."

His smile falls. "You're busier than I would have imagined is possible for a person to be. You ever think about slowing down?"

No. Because if I slow down, I'll probably crash out. It's best for me to keep moving so I don't think about how I never have time for myself at all. I'm okay like that. I really am. As long as I don't stop.

Hadrian flares his wings wide, and they blot out all the light from the front window. "Looks good," he murmurs. After a few moments admiring the changed colors, he glances back at me. "How long will it stay like this?"

I shrug. "Hard to say because I've never done anything quite on this level, but my hair usually fades after a day or two."

My comm watch rings, and Sheriff Rygold's name hovers above it. When I direct it to answer, our sheriff-masquerading-as-keeper is as brusque as ever.

"Bluebell? Someone called a human from the outside world. She's arriving in a little bit. Gonna introduce her to what we really are at the game. Can you be there as a friendly human face in case the presence of monsters comes as a shock?"

I glance up at Hadrian, whose dark brows have risen high.

"Yeah, of course," I say quickly. "Who called her?"

"One of the skyball players," Bishop says roughly. "Been traveling to the outside world and met her there. Fell in love and asked me to summon her a while back, although she's just now finding her way to us. I ain't great at the Keeper magic, so it's taken her longer than it should. Might oughta head back to Hearth Headquarters to get re-spelled. Shit, I'd rather us just find a damn Keeper. I'm gettin' too old for this shit."

It's well known that our sheriff spends more time in his stone gargoyle form than not since it's easier to heal like that. Old war wounds plague him, he says, although I've always thought it was an excuse not to think about his troubles. Some days I think, if I could turn myself to stone, I might do it to escape the world a little bit.

"Bye," the sheriff says brusquely, clicking off before I can even ask him anything about the new person.

Hadrian tucks his giant wings tightly at his back, grinning at me. "That's exciting, huh?"

"Did you know?"

He shakes his head. "I didn't, but if I had to guess, I'd guess it's Shroud, one of the older guys on our team. He's been quiet lately, lost in thought."

I look around the store, hating that I'll have to close. But nobody will be around during a skyball game anyhow. The whole haven comes to a standstill when skyball's going.

Hadrian smiles at me, offering his arm. "Shall we, Miss Tucker?"

I slip my hand through the crook of his arm and head for the front door. He flips the Open sign to Closed, then grabs the door for me.

"Bye, Bodice," I call out to the store. She doesn't answer, but I have to keep trying despite my mounting frustration.

Outside we find Main Street full of monsters waiting for Mabel the train. A few folks turn to look at us when Hadrian appears in the street.

"I should be going," he says quietly. "I'll fly, but I'll see you at the game, right?"

"Always," I assure him, grateful that our vibe is back to normal.

"Okay, well, see you later." He flares his wings wide.

Whispers rise up around us at the black-and-gold coloring, but I do my best to ignore it.

Until I see Merit and Bryony, PG's resident pixie snoops and owners of the *Gulch Gossip,* snapping a pic of his wings. I'm probably in that pic. Ugh.

Hadrian gives me a final look then pushes gracefully off the ground and up into the sky. I force myself not to watch him flap away as I look around. I recognize most of the locals waiting for the train, but it's always exciting when out of towners visit for skyball.

A train whistle announces Mabel's arrival. Two minutes after the shrill sound, the train herself chugs slowly into view up Main Street, her red-and-black engine shiny with a fresh coat of paint after a recent run-in with a truck parked on her tracks. You couldn't tell, though; she looks great.

And I did that, using my black magic to heal the engine so she could be repainted.

Mable choo-choos happily when she sees me standing there. Like always, I wait for the visitors to board her first, and then I board near the end. It'll mean I have to stand most of the way to the skyball arena, but that's okay. I love monster-watching the others as they experience Pine Gulch through the perspective of the train.

Forty minutes later, we disembark into a huge crowd tailgating outside our beautiful skyball arena. Everyone's still in monster form, so the new human must not be here yet. The idea of another human in town pulls my lips into a smile. My brothers and I grew up in Pine Gulch, but my mother called my father here the same way one of the players called this woman.

It's a lovely bit of magic that helps us expand when a monster feels strongly about a connection in the outside world. I wonder how he met her? How he knew of her? Since he's a gargoyle, he must have met her in the human world to know she was his mate. Now she gets to learn about his world.

Following the crowd into the arena, I flash my season pass and head for our seats with a Pine Gulch welcome book under one arm. My brothers and parents are already there, decked out in the Pine Gulch Punishers black and gold. The team isn't on the field yet, but Sheriff Rygold stands in the middle of the field with a microphone in one purple hand.

He's looking better than usual, stronger despite the broken horn and the giant scar that bisects the left side of his face.

As the stadium fills, he clears his throat. "Welcome, one and all, to today's Punishers game! We thank you for visiting our beautiful Pine Gulch, and today is particularly special because we called a human here from the outside world, and she'll be arriving any minute. For those monsters who don't know, I serve as this haven's Keeper, so I'll be glamouring the entire stadium. Like in any haven, I'll pull the glamour down once our calling monster has had a chance to make contact. Thanks again for being here."

He lifts a cowboy hat and slots it down over his horns as he clicks the microphone off and stalks off the field with his tail lashing behind him like an angry cat.

"That's the most pleasant I've ever heard him be," my mother mutters, glancing at me. "How you doing today, sweetheart? I hoped I'd see you at breakfast."

I smile and pat her knee. "All good, Mama. Just busy, like always."

"Don't work yourself into a lather, dear," she says sweetly, putting her arm around me. "You like to stay busy, I know that, but come to breakfast soon. We miss having you at home." She leans in close, bring her mouth to my ear. "I'm outnumbered and it sucks."

Holding back a laugh, I lean into her as the sheriff comes back on the microphone to let us know he's going to place the glamour.

He stands on the sidelines up from us, and it's as fascinating as ever to watch him mutter a spell to make everything appear human. A glittering line of magic sinks down over the stadium, transforming all the monsters into human form. The skyball pitch shifts and moves until it looks more like a football field. It's fascinating to look around and see monsters I've known my whole life in glamoured human form.

There's Varek Shorthorn, the minotaur land developer, looking like Shrek's human form with a huge square jaw, piercing chocolate eyes and a fantastic head of brown wavy hair.

Off to my left, Lemon looks like Lemon except her vampiric tats are gone and her eyes are a beautiful bright blue. Next to her, Furyon's a dark-skinned human with white hair and pale blue eyes. Strikingly handsome.

A giant man with pitch-black hair tinged white at his temples stands on the sidelines, looking through one of the hallway entrances expectantly. He's got to be nearly seven feet tall and hugely muscular, his thighs barely contained by tight jeans and a white collared shirt open enough to reveal salt-and-pepper chest hair.

"Damn, Shroud looks *good* as a human," my mom mutters.

Dad slaps her thigh with a little tsk. "Don't be gettin' any ideas, woman."

She barks out a laugh.

Everyone acts normal around us as the giant screens announce the team will be coming onto the field shortly. Shroud brings his hands together, rubbing them like he can't wait to do whatever's next. I've never been more thankful for field-level seats so I can see what's going on with the couple.

"There you are!" a small voice echoes up the entry corridor, and Shroud breaks into a huge grin, opening his big arms wide. It takes a few seconds for a human woman to come into view. She's shortish, maybe five-foot-six; she jogs to him and then hops into his arms. Long chocolate hair cascades down her back in shiny waves. She's plump with a great ass hugged tight in cutesy jeans.

Shroud pulls her into his arms, closing his eyes as he buries his face in her neck. He says something quietly, but I can't hear it from this far away.

Someone announces the team, and they come onto the field. I

can't pull my eyes from Shroud and the woman as he sets her down and takes both her hands. They have a brief exchange, and then she steps back, looking around as if uneasy.

Annnnnd that's my cue. Pushing past Jasper, Jack, and Jace, I walk onto the sidelines and make my way toward the newcomer. When I halt next to her carrying the book, she looks over at me, her expression unsure.

"Hey, I'm Bluebell," I chirp, holding a hand out for her.

She eyes it, looking between Shroud and me. "What's going on here?"

"Wellllll," I wave at Shroud, "I'm guessing my friend here just let you know this town is actually a hidden monster town, and he's not actually human, even though you met him looking like the hottie he is in this form."

She puts a hand to her forehead, feeling like she's expecting a fever. "I'm going crazy, that's it. This is *not* happening."

"Oh, it's happening," I say again, keeping my tone light. "We can prove it, and Shroud can go first, assuming he's okay with that."

"It's still me, Vela," Shroud says quietly. "I'm the same man who met you in that bar. The same man who's been sending you gifts. The same man who asked you to come meet me today for the game. This is my team, and I'm a player. I'm not human; I'm a gargoyle."

She takes a step closer to me. "No. Monsters aren't real. This is...a dream. A weird dream. Am I drugged?" She's starting to look like she might freak out.

The sheriff joins us, his shiny star badge clearly visible on the front of his tan uniform.

"Hey there, Vela, my name is Sheriff Bishop Rygold, and we're mighty pleased to welcome you to Pine Gulch on behalf of my friend Shroud, here. What these folks are telling you is true. The arena and its inhabitants are glamoured to appear human, but most of us are monsters. Shroud 'n' me? We're gargoyles. But I asked my friend Bluebell there to join us because she's human like you, although a black magic witch. She grew up here."

"And I can answer any questions," I offer. "But why don't we show you the truth of what we are? It's *so* fun, I promise. Makes the human world seem so blah in comparison. My folks met like this, actually. Totally adorable and disgustingly in love to this day." I flash a brighter smile and lift the welcome book. "We've literally got a welcome book for newbies!"

Vela barks out a disbelieving laugh, but waves at Shroud. "Okay, I guess. Show me the truth."

Shroud smiles as the sheriff closes his eyes and whispers the glamouring spell. Everything happens in reverse, a glittering golden line moving out from the center of the arena toward us.

Vela squeaks and leaps over it when it passes beneath her. Then she jolts and shrieks again when she sees Shroud.

He wears the same clothing, but now he's in full gargoyle form with beautiful dusky-purple skin and long arched horns. His wings are tucked tightly at his back, and he's got his tail wrapped around a thigh, probably so he doesn't wrap it around *her* and scare her to pieces.

"You're safe," I remind her when she backs into me with a hand over her heart. "You're totally safe, Vela. We're all friendly, and you can leave any time."

Shroud lets out an unhappy noise at that comment, but it's something I always say because it's every human's first question.

Am I a prisoner?

"Shroud?" She takes a step closer to him. "I mean...you look like my Shroud but...am I dreaming?"

He unsnakes his tail then and wraps it around her wrist, using it to pull her closer. "No, my sweet. You're not dreaming. It's still me, and I am so, *so* glad you're here. Normally, I'd play in the game, but I asked for this game off so we could watch it together. Will you sit with me?"

She eyes the tail around her wrist, then looks up at him. "Can I touch your face?"

Shroud dips low and watches her closely as she lifts a hand. She brushes her fingers down his nose and over his high cheekbones, then moves them to his square jaw.

"It's you." Her voice is awed, reverent as she moves her fingers to his horns. "And these?"

He shudders when she draws her fingertips along the length of his left horn.

"Sensitive," he says gruffly.

She laughs. "Oh my God. I don't know anything *about* you now!"

"You know all the important parts," he corrects, "except for this. Shall we take our seats, my sweet? I can't wait to introduce you to skyball."

Her mouth drops open. "I thought you coached *football*!"

He shrugs. "Closest story I could go with, Vela."

When he offers her his hand, she hesitates a moment then takes it, threading her fingers through his. I hand Shroud the welcome book for later—going through the scavenger hunt at the front will be the perfect way to introduce Vela to Pine Gulch.

As they make their way to two empty seats on the sidelines, the entire arena breaks out into cheers. The kiss cam moves to them, showing a shocked-looking Vela and beaming Shroud as they sit in the empty seats.

I follow them over, promising to be there after the game to tour downtown if she wants a human friend to accompany her. Unsurprisingly, she looks pretty okay with Shroud by her side, staring at him like she's totally shell-shocked.

It's always a little like that when we call humans from the outside world. I'm sure it's a weird experience for them to easily enter our town just because they feel drawn to it, and then for us to unglamour everything to reveal the ward that protects us from the outside world, and—oh, by the way—we're all monsters. Most of the humans who live in the haven system are some sort of witch, too. The odd human has no magical ability at all, like my dad, but that's less common.

Leaving Vela and Shroud to it, I return to my seat. Uncharacteristic moroseness fills me as I sit between Jasper and my mother. The game starts, and the players come onto the field, but I can't stop my eyes from drifting to Vela and Shroud. They're engrossed in conversation, and he's obviously enamored. He's missing the entire game, his head propped on his fingertips and one hand wrapped around her knee. She talks emphatically, and the only time he even looks at the field is when she seems to ask a question about it.

Eventually, I pull my eyes from them and focus on the players. My mother leans over. "Did you do Hay's wings? Looks awesome, sweetheart!"

I smile. "Yeah, he asked me to try. No idea how long it'll keep, but it looks pretty badass, huh?"

Jack snorts. "Gaudy as hell. I'm gonna make fun of him after the game."

I shake my head, fairly certain that the twins' and Hadrian's friendship is built on a foundation of their snarky nonsense and Hadrian's utter unflappability. It surprises me anew that it's not Jace and Alk who are so close. They're more alike. But perhaps that's precisely why they're not drawn together.

On the other side of my father, Jasper sits with his head in a book about green magic. Of my three brothers, he has to work the hardest, although he's usually not inclined. It's the same because his magic is so damn *strong* when he chooses to apply himself. In some ways it surprised me he wanted to study for the level-three mastery test. I don't think Jack'll ever bother with it.

Glancing at Vela and Shroud again, my heart leaps into my throat at seeing his huge fingers trailing up her jaw. He stares at her in absolute wonder, eyes hooded and the slightest smirk on his face.

And I know that look, because it's the way Hadrian looked at me earlier.

Hadrian

"Everything alright, Alk?"

I look up to find my coach, Rip Shorthorn, sinking onto the couch next to me with a seasonal mead in his hand.

Smiling, I nod and wave at the rest of the team who are playing touch football in his enormous backyard while the coach's grown sons grill steak and vegetables for a post-game family-style meal. We don't always do this after home games, but when we do, it's one of the only times I hang with the team afterward.

"How you feeling about things, son? You've been here for a few months now..."

His deep voice is comforting, reassuring. I like him as a coach more than I thought I would. I'd been so hopeful Manorin would take the Punishers job and I'd get to play under him still. That was the main reason I stayed at the Protector Academy as long as I did. But Rip reminds me of Manorin in many ways—quiet, observant, doesn't suffer fools and sees through monsters to what they really are. In a short time, I've come to rely on him more than I imagined I would. I'm glad I kept an open mind.

He takes a deep sip of his mead, throat bobbing as he enjoys the brew, crossing one muscular leg over the other.

"I've noticed you don't party with the younger guys. Not that there's anything wrong with that, but I wanted to make sure it wasn't a fit thing or you not feelin' welcome."

I shake my head, leaning onto my forearms. "Nothing like that, Coach. The team has been incredibly welcoming. I'm just a homebody." Waving at the grill and his sons, I smile. "This is more my speed than anything else. Shit, if I had it my way, the team would spend their free time helpin' me fix up my ranch. I like to get my hands on things and work, I guess. Never was much of a partier. Do you think it's a problem?"

He smiles, the move pulling his thin lips wide and exposing bright shiny fangs. "No, son, I don't. I never used to be able to understand that perspective myself, though, until my calves came along. I loved to go out with my team and party. But now? I don't even like traveling for games. Perfect night for me is spending time with family, eating a good home-cooked meal and staring at my beautiful mate over a dinner table filled with our calves and grandcalves."

"That sounds perfect," I breathe, my mind going immediately to Bluebell and our near kiss earlier. I was so close. I could have—*should* have done it. I'm regretting it now. But once we cross that line, there's no coming back from it. The knowledge that I tried it will always be between us, and it'll be awkward if she doesn't reciprocate.

But part of me is pretty sure she will based on the way her scent changes near me, especially since I moved home.

My comm watch pings before I can say anything else, and the coach takes his leave. Jasper's name hovers over the band.

When I answer, he's laughing, and Jack's yelling something in the background. "Great game, Hay!" Jasper yells. "You out with the team or what?"

I take a swig of my mead. "At the Shorthorns' ranch having dinner."

"Come out with us!" he shouts into the watch. Sounds of a scuffle follow the loud demand. That'll be Jack starting shit like he always does.

"I should stay here for a little while longer," I hedge, looking at my teammates as they wave me onto the field to join the tag game.

"Fine," Jasper says with a groan. "But we're getting Bluebell outta her head tonight 'cause she's been working too hard at the Bodice and she's being rude as hells. I gotta butter her up because I've got about fifteen things I need her to do next week. Come join us, it'll be fun. Might even go swimmin' in the gulch after, if you're down."

Bluebell at the bar? Bluebell possibly swimming in the gulch?

We don't swim *clothed* in the gulch.

"I'll be there," I manage, taking another deep swallow of my drink as everything inside me tenses and tightens in anticipation of seeing her.

Knowing I can't dip immediately out of this shindig, I head onto the field to join my teammates. I manage an entire half hour of play before I can't take any more. Irish goodbye-ing my way out of a party ain't my way, but I do say goodbye to the coach before I head out.

Flapping up into the sky, I relish the cool breeze on my face as I bullet toward downtown. I pass a few other gargoyles on the way, waving as we glide along the currents. When downtown comes into view, several of the buildings wriggle their roof tiles at me. Below, Main Street is full of revelers, lights strung from one side to the other like we do for every home game.

Or maybe it's because of the new human Shroud called to town. They joined us for a few minutes of dinner, but it was clear they wanted nothing more than to be alone. Vela seems lovely, but all I could think about was how it's the second time in a few weeks I've seen a human and gargoyle couple who looked blissfully happy.

The dance hall comes into view at the far end of Main Street. A line out the door tells me it'll be slammed inside, but if I know Jasper, he was probably already there when he called me. I consider going home and changing into something better than my post-game jeans and black tee, but I'm so ready to see Bluebell, I don't consider it for very long.

Dropping into the street, I'm careful to tuck my wings without knocking into anyone despite the gathered crowd. I get more than a few stares and whispers, but thankfully the minotaur bouncer at the door lets me bypass the crowd and head inside. Groans follow me, but it's one of the perks of being a PG local—we don't wait in the line.

Inside, the dance hall is packed from floor to ceiling with monsters of all species. A long two-story bar takes up most of the left and middle of the narrow building. The mechanical bull and a stage are somewhere off to the right, although I can't see them. Outcroppings of seats scattered around the ceiling are best-suited for winged monsters like myself, so I hop into the air and drift up to the nearest available one.

Perching myself on a thin ledge, I look around the room, twitching my ears this way and that to pick out the various voices. Knowing Jasper wouldn't be caught dead on the mechanical bull, I focus on the bar area first. Jack's a bourbon guy, Jasper's into tequila, and I don't even know what Bluebell's into these days because every time I see her, she's working.

That's when I spot her down below. She's on the godsdamned bull, one hand thrown back in the air and laughing raucously as she nods to the pixie in charge of running it. He flips a switch, and the bull starts rocking back and forth slowly. Hoots and catcalls rise from the audience as she rolls her hips easily in time with the machine, a smirk on her face.

It's too easy for her. She grew up around here. She's probably never ridden a real bull, but we've ridden horses since we were kids.

She shouts, and the pixie turns a dial. The bull moves a little faster, spinning this way and that, but all she does is press her knees tighter in. Her blue lips pull into a satisfied smirk when the bull spins and she goes nowhere. A couple of males shout from the crowd, and something hot and possessive inside has me snarling.

Bluebell's hips move when the pixie turns the dial again. She shifts her upper body back and forth in time with its bucking, but all I can stare at is how her body rolls and rocks. I'm always hot after the physicality of a game. Even so, I have to mop sweat from my brow as I stare at her. Maybe it's seeing human and gargoyle pairs all over lately, but I can't pull my eyes from Bluebell's trim waist or that gorgeous head of black-and-gold hair. The space buns are gone, and her locks are long, waving down her back to tickle the top of her pants.

I had my hands all over that body earlier when she fell. For a moment, terror filled me, and all I knew was I couldn't let anything happen to her.

I should have kissed her. Godsdamnit.

I'm not normally a male to waffle like this. Being decisive is a character trait I pride myself on. But this thing with Bluebell? It's got me tied up in damn knots.

"Hay!"

A voice drifts up from below, pulling my attention away from Bluebell riding the bull. Glancing down, I find Jasper and Jack down below with three drinks. Jack's talking to a pretty female gargoyle, and Jasper's staring up at me expectantly.

Dropping off the ledge, I flap my wings once to land in the crowd without slapping anyone. Jasper hands me a drink with a huge smile.

"Nice game, dude. Listen, I've been thinking. We should be helping you more with your place. Wanna work on that tomorrow? Jace is down to help, too, if he can raid your library once it's done."

I grin at that. Jace and I are kindred spirits when it comes to books. Clinking my glass with Jasper's, I nod. "Sold, buddy. I'm ripping out carpet tomorrow, so it'll be a smelly good time."

He groans. "Fuck, I shoulda asked next week once the carpet was out."

Rolling my shoulders, I take a drink of the bourbon. "Could be worse, you coulda offered when I was dealing with the septic tank."

He scrunches his nose, pale eyes flashing with disgust. "Let's don't talk about that at all. If I never have to think about you taking a shit, it won't be soon enough. I gotta study all morning for my level-three test, though. Then we can charge more and travel for work. This prep is kicking my ass, but I'm tryna set a good example for Jace. I don't think Jack'll ever do it if I do."

"Unsurprising. Jack's happy to just go along with whatever you two do."

Jack Clinton Tucker isn't the most motivated being I've met.

Smiling, I tuck my wings tightly together because the crowd is nearly pulsing with energy. I wrap my tail around my thigh, hanging the spade inside my knee so it doesn't get tugged. When I'm not careful in public, it's not uncommon for others to bump into me or try to touch my wings or tail—sensitive spots for any gargoyle male.

Spots I only want one person to touch.

"You alright, Hay?"

I glance down at Jasper, who's staring at me with eyes narrowed.

"You've got that look, dude," he says. "That determined look. What did you just figure out?"

Coughing to mask my surprise, I shake my head. "Nothing, man. Nothing at all. Just thinking about the game." It's a lie, but if he can tell, he doesn't press me on it.

Bluebell bursts through the crowd, eyes wide and heart racing. It shocks me that I can hear it so clearly over the crowd, but I'm focused. Getting obsessive. It's nearly impossible not to stare at her as she joins us but I make myself scan the crowd in case her brother's watching.

"I made it all the way to level seven!" she shouts, high-fiving both of her brothers at once.

Jasper yanks on her hair. "Thought you'd make it to nine for sure. You off your game, sis?"

She rolls her eyes. "You know, it's a scientifically proven fact that women with two or more brothers are prone to dying early. Probably because you're such a pain in my ass."

He only grins bigger. "Oh, you love me."

"I do," she grumbles, grinning at them both, although Jack's already turned to flirt with the female gargoyle again.

Jasper claps my shoulder. "Wanna grab another drink? I need to grab Bloob one too."

If I'm honest, all I want to do is get outta this crazy crowd and find a quiet spot to enjoy a drink with my Tuckers.

"C'mon, Alk!" Bluebell gushes, grabbing my arm and beaming up at me.

In that moment, I know if this woman wants me to hang out at the bar all night, that's where I'll be. Because I'm lost in those glittering blue eyes and the tiny wrinkles at the corners when she looks way up at me.

"Lead the way, Tucker," I say with a laugh, flaring my wings just enough to help part the crowd in front of her.

She drops my arm and spins, pushing through the crowd toward the bar. Jasper and Jack trail behind me. It's always easier for me to get us through a crowd. Wings and my general size are useful in that way.

At the bar, Bluebell orders us a round of drinks. Not that it'll do me much good. It takes a metric boatload of alcohol to get me remotely drunk. I'm curious to see Bluebell three sheets to the wind, though, floundering around like a ship with all its sails amuck. Gods, I might be the only monster nerd who knows the meaning of that expression about being drunk.

Jasper cheers when the big troll bartender shoves four shots across the bar toward us. Taking them in hand, we clink our glasses together in universal cheers. Bluebell throws her shot back, staring at me while she does. She's a little unsteady, slumping to one side as she downs the shot. Reaching out, she grabs my forearm with one hand, hanging onto me as she wipes her free hand over her mouth and grins. When she sets the shot glass back on the bar she smiles up at us.

Her hand is still on me and I dread the moment she moves it. She touched me so easily and I don't want to lose that.

Is it hours later that we finally agree it's time to leave? I've lost track of time because we've been at the bar drinking and laughing, and it's everything I can do to pay attention to Jasper and Jack and *not* the beautiful woman living it up and laughing more easily than I've seen in many years.

She needed this. That much is clear. And that's why I stay out so long. Eventually, though, her energy flags, and she sits at the bar with her chin in her hand, smiling at her brothers.

Jasper clinks yet another shot glass to mine. "Dude, take my sister home, would ya? She looks like she's about to pass out on the bar, and that would be embarrassing for the Tucker reputation." He rolls his eyes. "I'm gonna have to cut out early to study for a few hours, but I'm cutting her off now. Can I pass caretaking duties to you?"

Chuckling, I wrap an arm around Bluebell's back and under her right arm. She shifts easily off the stool, although when she stands, she sways against me.

"You two are assholes!" She points at her brothers. "I did the Tucker reputation super proud, stayed on until level seven. I'd like to see you stay on past that."

Jasper winks between us. "Don't you worry about how well I ride, little sister. That ain't ever been a problem for me."

Bluebell makes a gagging sound and taps my arm. "That's our cue to go, Alk. C'mon. Take me home, big boy."

The command isn't inherently sexual, but the way she says it tightens my sack anyhow.

"She's a mess," Jasper mutters.

"No, she's not," I bark before I can stop myself.

Jasper's dark brows rise, and he looks between Bluebell and

me. “Okay, big guy, if you say so.” He claps me on the shoulder. “You want help getting her home?”

“I think I can handle it.” I force a smile so he knows we’re good. Pulling Bluebell carefully with me, I leave the other Tuckers behind as we head toward the exit.

She’s quiet all the way back to the Bodice, humming softly with her arm around my waist. The scent of tequila radiates from her, but it mixes with her natural essence until I’m rock-hard thinking about licking that tequila from every inch of her body.

Gods. I’m down bad. I don’t know if I even fully admitted it to myself until this very moment. But if I had my way right now, I’d be *having* my way with her up against the wall. Then again in our stairwell. At least once in our hallway. And then over and over and over again in my nest. And when she passed out, I’d let her sleep, and I’d rub all over her, massaging that sexy body and loving on her until she woke again. I wouldn’t get sleep for days. Not with Bluebell Tucker in my bed.

I’m slowly going insane with need. Every moment I spend with her breaks down the walls I’ve put up over the years. It was easier when I was in school and didn’t see her so frequently. But now? A switch in my brain has fully flipped, and I’m barely holding back from following my deepest, most basic primal instincts.

This zero-to-sixty obsession is so typically gargoyle, but if I’m honest with myself I’ve been holding it at bay for such a long time, I just can't anymore. It’s impossible with her living right across the hall.

We make it all the way to her door before she looks up at me with a silly, open smile. “You’re cute, Alk, ya know that? Too cute for your own good.”

“You’re drunk,” I say with a laugh, thumping her nose with my left hand.

“Not so drunk,” she corrects. “It was a fun night, though. I enjoyed myself.” She slips her hands over her head and stretches tall from left to right. "Good to get out of my head sometimes, ya know? I'm just so busy all the time."

That's a conversation I'd love to have with her sometime when she isn't drunk.

She slips her keys out of her back pocket and swings them around her finger, but they go flying and hit me, sliding down my body and hitting the ground with a clink.

"Shit," she mutters, dropping to the ground. As she does, her to do list falls out of her pocket and lands on the keys. She moves so slowly to grab them that I get a quick look and holy shit—is this all for a single day?!

Cottage healing at units 234 and 712.

Follow up with dad about purchase paperwork.

Check with supplier about the Mead Cute order for the Bodice.

Reorganize the storeroom.

Invoices through Wednesday.

Call Rhubarb Ranch about final decision re: spring planting

And that's just what I see at a quick glance.

Her hair falls to either side of her head, exposing the sunburst tattoo on the back of her neck. I reach for her before remembering I shouldn't just touch her like that. Not yet.

When she rises, her face is flushed, and her scent explodes between us, thickening until I'm choking on pheromones and need.

"Bluebell." My throat is rough with need. I bracket my hand on the wall above her head, dipping low as she backs against the solid surface.

"Hadrian?" She stares up at me, heart racing and mouth slightly open.

Drifting closer, I bring my mouth to her ear, loving how she mewls softly and shudders. I nuzzle the edge of her ear, deciding that a tease might be exactly what she needs right now.

A soft groan escapes me as I drag my mouth along the curved shell of her ear. "You smell good like this, Bluebell. Relaxed."

She turns her head just enough to hover her mouth close to mine. "Is this supposed to help me relax more, Hadrian?"

Dropping my voice low, I let out a satisfied chuckle. "No, my pretty little neighbor. Not at all." Straightening tall, I grin at her as I shove my hands into my back pockets and tuck my wings behind me. I want to take that first kiss, but I don't want it when she's drunk. I don't want there to be any confusion when I kiss her for the first time.

"Good night, Miss Tucker."

She lifts her chin, shooting me a snooty, imperious look.

I love it. That sass. Beneath it all, there's a tender side of Bluebell. A side that's in desperate need of someone in her corner. That's me, even though she probably doesn't know it yet. She needs someone for those quiet moments between the rush and mess. The two a.m. cuddle sesh. The post dinner clean up. And everything in between. She does it all alone and I really, really hate that for her.

She shoves her keys in her door lock and opens it. After disappearing inside, she pokes her head back out and sticks her tongue out at me. "Tease." That said, she goes back inside and slams the door.

Chuckling, I turn and head into my apartment. Inside, I change out of clothes that smell like a bar and into gray sweatpants. I forego the shirt. There's no one here to be offended by my state of half nudity.

Faint singing filters through my door from Bluebell's apartment. Normally, I don't listen for her, but tonight I'm amped and hot, and her scent is buried in my nostrils so deeply. My cock hardens against my thigh, stretching against the fabric of my pants as I twitch an ear to listen.

She's singing and humming, although I can't make out any particular song. Stalking across the hall, I press my ear to her front door. It's not like anyone is going to come up here. We're the only two apartments on the Bodice's second story.

The sound of clothes hitting the floor has me holding back a groan. I reach down and grip my dick through the sweatpants, stroking down the length just once. Heat flares from the base of my shaft, my skin tingling as my sack tightens. Precum drips from me like a faucet at the mere idea of Bluebell naked on the other side of this door.

Springs squeak as she drops into bed, still humming. Moments later, the sound of something vibrating reverberates from inside. I do groan then, as the vibrations rise and fall. Her moans are soft and inconsistent at first, her bed springs squeaking faintly. Fuuuuuck.

She must not realize quite how good my senses are. I'm pressed to the doorway, hand on my cock, and I start stroking faster up and down my rigid length, pulling gently at the piercings that line the underside. Squeezing my tip, I gather the moisture there and use it to jerk myself roughly. Soft groans fill my throat, growls following as the sound of her vibrator amps my lust.

I press my forehead to her door, shoving my hand inside my pants for skin on skin. Gripping my cock, I choke out a groan as heat spears through me, my abs tensing and tightening as Bluebell cries out inside.

Something clicks, and her vibrator whirs faster, her bed squeaking rapidly. Wood cracks and splinters. Gods, is she gripping her headboard? It's what I imagine she's doing as I jack myself hard and fast.

"Say my name, baby," I beg softly through the door. If she utters my name, I'm ripping this door off the hinges to get to her.

"Oh gods," she moans. The vibrator makes sounds like a jet engine taking off.

I'm dying, moaning against the hard surface of her door as she masturbates inside.

"Say my name," I plead again. "Bluebell."

She makes a choked sound, then a muffled scream like she has her hand clapped over her mouth. The scent of her coming undoes me, and orgasm hits me like a freight train. Baring my fangs, I ride out waves of pleasure, jerking my hips against her door as I fantasize about being buried inside her.

"Say it," I beg softly once more. "Fuuuuuck."

I'm whining with need by the time her orgasm fades. Mine drags long, and I'm still coming like a fucking faucet as she rolls out of bed and turns the water on. When she steps into the shower and starts humming again, I flip against the door, panting so hard, I'm seeing stars. I stalk across the hall, sweatpants soaked through and dripping cum all over the hallway floor.

She didn't say my name.

Fuck me.

Bluebell

"Bluebell, I'm here!"

Tiana's voice drifts from the Bodice's front door to where I am in the storeroom.

"Back here," I shout, knowing she'll easily find her way to me.

Moments later, the beautiful purple-haired troll appears in the storeroom door, amethyst brows rising high. She plants both big hands on her hips and looks around.

"My oh my, what is going on here? This place is a bit more of a mess than I would have expected."

I stand and pull her in for a quick hug. "That's exactly why I need you, friend. The Bodice and I aren't exactly seeing eye to eye, and I thought she'd appreciate a friendly face."

She cocks her head sideways, big tusks sticking up from her lower jaw. "Exactly how *not* getting along are you?"

Overhead, every ceiling beam creaks and wriggles. Shoe boxes fly off the shelves, hitting me. Although, at this point, it's happened enough that I lift my hands just in time to avoid getting a box corner to the eyeball.

"Okayyyy then," Tiana says. "Buxom, girl, you should be ashamed of treating Bluebell like this. She was a customer for decades, honey."

Thank you, I mouth when the Bodice lets out a sorrowful series of groans.

"I thought you'd be happy to see an old friend," I say loudly to the building. "She's going to take over some of my shifts."

Tiana drops to a knee beside me, gathering up an armful of boxes. "Listen, honey, I've got this, and I'll be here until closing. If this is like any other day of yours, I imagine you've got a to-do list a mile long. Why don't you get on outta here and I'll see if I can figure out what's going on?"

I squeeze her shoulder as I flash her another grateful smile. For the first time when I leave, the Bodice opens the door for me and doesn't slam it behind my back.

Outside, I stop in the street and lift my arms like I just won a gold medal. Hopping up and down, I squeak out my excitement.

"Making progress with the store?"

Hadrian's deep voice shocks me, and I freeze, turning slowly to find him standing to my left. I run a hand through my hair, laughing. "Yeah, I think so. Just a little bit, but yeah? I mean... we'll see."

He looks at the front door, lifting a hand from his pocket to wave. "Hey, sweet girl, you being nice to our neighbor?"

Silence.

"Just a bit of progress," I admit.

"Keep at it," he says softly. "I know you'll get there. I think you could win over anyone you want, Bluebell. Anyone. And I mean that."

Fuuuuuck me.

His eyes drift to the leopard-print leotard I'm wearing as a shirt today. It's rare I let my whole arms hang out, but I was doing porch yoga this morning, and I ran out of time to change.

He smiles. "Can you take off today?"

I yank my to-do list out of my pocket and wave it at him. "I don't know, Hadrian. Whatchu got in mind? Because this is all the stuff I've got to get done today. Where's Jasper?"

"I don't know," he says simply. "I wanted to hang with you."

"Are we doing this?"

I don't realize I actually asked that aloud until he smiles at me. "We've been best friends for two decades, Miss Tucker. What could be more normal than hanging out?"

Not hanging out?! Not almost kissing?!

I shrug. "Right, yeah, of course you're right."

He hands the to-do list back to me. "Why don't I come help you with some of the stuff on that list? Then we can grab some lunch together. As friends." The saucy look on his face suggests "friends" might not be exactly what he has in mind. Last night showed me a side of Hadrian I wasn't expecting, but in the light of day, I sorta thought I dreamed it up.

I'm second-guessing that right now.

"Okay," I chirp. "Now that Lemon's moved into Furyon's place, I've got to get hers fixed up for a new tenant. You want to come help me clean?"

He laughs. "Can't imagine anything I'd rather do. Why don't the Jays help you with this stuff?"

I bark out a laugh at his nickname for my three brothers. "Jasper cleaning?" I shrug as I wave for us to head toward the rental cottages around Main Street's corner.

"He would," Hadrian says. "If you asked."

I suck in a breath. "But would he do a good job? That's the thing. And that first time a new renter walks in the door sets their expectation of how our rental relationship will be. Not to mention, he's actually pretty freaked out about his third-level test. He's been *studying,* if you can believe it."

He sighs. "You sound just like your mother when you say that."

"I suppose I got it from her," I admit. She taught me most of what I know about running our business, then promptly stepped away so she and dad could spend more time renovating Tucker Ranch. That process has been going on for a very long time.

When we arrive at cottage number four-thirty-two, she waggles pale blue shutters at us.

"Hey, sweet girl," I call out. Smiling up at Hadrian, I fish around for the keys in my pocket. "We shouldn't need to be here too terribly long. I just need to clean up and make sure she's feeling alright. The new family moves in next week."

He's silent as I open the door for him. Pressing my palm to the doorframe, I close my eyes and allow the black magic course through me. Sparks tickle my fingertips as I receive the house's sentiment. She's happy, healthy, doesn't need healing of any sort. She shouldn't, because I check on all of our buildings regularly, and with twenty-two properties around Pine Gulch, it's a lot.

Smiling, I remove my hand and head inside, halting when I see the way Hadrian's looking at me.

"Your magic is astonishing," he says.

"You said that last time you saw me use it," I tease.

"And I'm astonished anew." He grabs the cleaning supplies. "I'll tackle the bathroom?"

I cock my head to the side. "I...I know you offered to come do this, but for some reason, I really didn't see you cleaning bathrooms."

He gives me a fake shocked look. "Right? Hadrian Alkazar, star skyball player, scrubbing toilets and pulling blonde vampire hair out of the shower drain? I've done worse. You should have seen me fixing the septic out at the ranch."

I tsk. "You should have called me for that!"

He shrugs and heads for the bathroom, glancing at me over his shoulder. "I like the hard work, Bluebell. I like getting my hands dirty. Maybe I should tell you a little more about how I got them dirty last night?"

I freeze as he disappears toward the bathroom, shuffling his wing tips together as he goes. He's got his tail wrapped around his thigh, his huge beefy thigh.

Did he really just say that?

It's blissfully quiet as he cleans the bathroom and I start in the bedroom. For an hour, we work in silence. When he eventually emerges smelling of bleach and lavender cleaning solution, I smile.

It's fake, though. I don't know where we stand after his tease just now and what he said against the door last night. Because I couldn't possibly forget the way his mouth felt against the curve of my ear.

He sets the cleaning supplies down on the small rectangular dining table. The moment stretches long as beautiful purple eyes focus on me.

"We need to talk, Bluebell," he says in a voice so quiet, so commanding, I feel it all the way in my bones.

"About what?" I whisper.

"You know what." He removes his hands from his pockets, unfurling his tail from around his thigh to lash it behind his back like a cat.

Or a predator.

My heart leaps into my throat. "Okay, Hadrian."

His lips pull into a half smile. "I know what you did last night, Bluebell, after you went into your apartment."

I gasp, embarrassment hitting me hard and hot. "I...I—"

He shakes his head. "I'm not saying that to embarrass you. I'm saying I know, and because of that, I did the same thing in the hallway against your door."

A full gasp leaves me then.

"I can't stay away from you," he says. "And if I'm honest, the main reason I came back here is *you*, Bluebell." His gaze softens. "I know it's a lot to admit this fast. I told myself I'd try kissing you first, but it turns out, my self control's shot when you're around..."

Black stars dance behind my eyelids as I struggle to figure out what to say. We've been avoiding this attraction since he came home and we shared that *almost* kiss. But there's been nothing obvious since then.

Or has there?!

"Hadrian," I begin, but just as I say his name, his comm watch rings.

He groans and lifts his wrist. His coach's name hovers above it. He shakes his head. "I'll call him back later. Like I was saying—"

The watch rings again, insistently.

"You should get that," I offer. "For real, I'm good."

"Fuck," he hisses, running a hand through his black waves and looking between me and the watch. "I really should take this, I'm so sorry."

I lift both hands as I back toward the door. "We'll finish this conversation, I promise. I'm just going to head into town, but call me later, okay?" Part of me is desperate to run from the conversation because I don't know if I'm ready for it.

His tail lashes faster, and he sucks at his fangs, staring at me like he's not sure if he agrees with my suggestion. "Call you later, I promise."

Nodding, I spin toward the door and do my best not to break into a run. I speed-walk until I get half a block away from the cottage, then I lift my wrist and comm Lemon. She picks up on the first ring.

"Bluebell, hey girl. You've been busy this w—"

"I need you," I hiss. "And Oz. Meet me at the boats right now!"

"Okayyyy," she says. "Right this second?"

"Yes," I bark. "I promise you have nothing better to do than what I need right now. I have never called and asked you for anything, but—"

"I'm coming now," she says. "Don't worry, friend. I've got your back. You want to call Oz, or should I?"

"I'll do it."

She clicks off, and I call Oz next. "Meet me and Lemon at the boats right now, Oz. I need your help. It's a friendmergency."

He sputters, but I close out the call and break into a jog. Hooking a left into the alleyway between Whiskey Business and the Welcome Inn, I head into the hidden tunnels below Main Street. Then I find my way to the handful of boats and the hidden river that runs beneath all of Pine Gulch's downtown.

Neither Lemon nor Oz are there yet, so I busy myself hopping into a boat and settling onto a seat. I can't sit still, though, so I tap my foot incessantly until I hear footsteps. Oz arrives first, swanning into the room with a swish of his hips, wings held high behind him.

"Girl, this better be good." Ginger trails behind him, her nose practically touching his tail as she slinks into the light.

"Oh, it is," I mutter as he hops into the boat. He has to kiss the dog to get her to join us, and she tucks herself between his thighs with her head on his knee.

He rolls his eyes but scratches her neck anyhow. "This girl is obsessed."

I eye the pretty thing. "But she hasn't bonded to you yet?"

He runs big purple fingers down her neck. "Nah, not yet. This is a normal amount of hovering, I'm told. Once she starts giving you the stink eye for hugging me or something, that'll mean she's bonded."

Lemon smiles and reaches down to pet Ginger's head. "That's right. She'd follow you around like she does but potentially attack anyone she thought posed a threat to you."

Lemon flounces into the boat and sits between Oz's knees next to the dog, who shoves her butt in Lemon's lap but doesn't move her chin from Oz's knee. Oz's thighs are spread wide around both of them but he doesn't seem to mind in the slightest, if the grin on his face says anything.

"Okay," Lemon says with a cutesy little purr, waggling elegant brows at me. "Tell us *everything*, girl. I've never heard you sound like you sounded when you called."

Grabbing the boat's oars, I slip them into the supports and start rowing up the jewel-toned river away from the pier. The tunnel is lit by elegantly flickering sconces, but it's the last thing I notice as I suck in a breath and consider what to do.

They're quiet until I've rowed a few minutes in silence, considering how to break this news and what I even want.

"Hadrian's flirting with me," I finally bark out. "Like...I

wasn't sure, but now I'm super sure, and he's definitely flirting with me."

Lemon beams and looks up over her shoulder at Oz. "You owe me."

Oz scoffs and tugs on her long blonde hair. "I just said it would take longer."

She shrugs. "And I said it would be faster. This is faster. Shit has already happened, obviously."

I look between them in disbelief. "You two have been discussing this?"

Lemon beams at me, looking every inch the vampiric predator she is. "Yeah, girl. I knew when you two took me to that skyball game, and you made me leave room for him. The way you chanted his name? The way he tugged on your space buns? And then when we were at the rooster races, and he handed you your rooster, his fingers touched yours. I knew for sure then."

"Well, I didn't know!" I shout. My voice echoes off the stones above us. "Am I oblivious?"

"Tell us absolutely everything," Oz demands, still stroking the pit hell's head lovingly. "We'll set you straight, since you can't be trusted with your own love life, apparently."

The whole story comes out then. The banter and back and forth over the last few weeks. How Hadrian's my neighbor now. What happened last night and his commentary before Coach Shorthorn called.

My friends listen in silence, but once I'm done, Lemon leans forward and places a hand on my knee. "What does your heart say, Bluebell? Do you want something with him?"

"Yes," I admit, "But—"

"There you go," she says with a grin. "That's actually all you need to know."

I shake my head, rowing to expel the nervous energy. My heart's still running a damn sprint in my chest. "We've been friends for decades, not to mention how much Jasper's going to freak out."

"Why would he, though?" Oz asks. "For real. Why would he care? And why do you care if he cares?"

I'm not even sure I can fully answer that question other than knowing that, over the years, he's mentioned Hadrian steering clear of me dozens of times.

"It's just what big brothers do?" I finish lamely, not entirely sure other than knowing that, in my heart, I'm certain Jasper won't take it well.

"I think you should let it happen," Oz says. "I, for one, would love to know more about how Hadrian Alkazar is in bed."

"Eww." I scrunch my nose. "None of your business, Oz."

He waves at me and Lemon. "This is all our business, now that you've involved us, bitch."

"I don't want to ruin my friendship with him, or Jasper's," I tack on. "What if it doesn't work out?"

"Tap that ass," Oz says again. "Nobody has to know. Keep it a secret for a minute or two, but what if he's your mate?"

What if he's your mate...

Lemon smirks at me. "Has he brought you snacks yet? It's a whole gargoyle thing, I'm told."

I shake my head. "I mean, yes, but not like a formal presentation or whatever?"

She offers me a reassuring smile. "Honey, if you belong together there's nothing you can do to stave this off, especially now that he appears to be pursuing you. Might as well just give in to him, ya know?"

Oz nods and strokes the top of Ginger's head. "And then of course tell us every bitty detail because I am literally salivating over this love story."

It takes them the better part of ten more minutes to convince me to let Hadrian kiss me next time the opportunity arises. And just like that, it's decided.

I'm going to kiss my best friend.

Hadrian

Not finishing my conversation with Bluebell rankled. Being forced to an emergency team practice session for the upcoming away game rankled more because it meant I didn't get a chance to share any of what I planned to. I called her after practice, and she answered, but she was working a dinner shift at Whiskey Business and then closing at Lizard Lick again.

She got home late, very late, trudging to her door.

My sweet Bluebell...

I wanted nothing more than to pull her into my nest and hold her 'til she fell asleep on my chest. But that conversation crouched like a tiger between us? We absolutely have to finish it.

I didn't sleep after I listened to her go into her apartment and flop onto the bed. Within minutes, soft snores rang out from her place to mine. I spent most of the night lying there considering how to move things forward with her. What's really held me back all these years is both her friendship *and* Jasper's. Hers because I didn't want to fuck it up, and his because he's protective of her, and I think part of him resents me being friends with anyone but him.

Now that I'm home, though, I don't think losing her friendship is what would actually happen. Jasper's another story, but he's a grown-ass man, and he can deal. By the time the sun began to rise, I'd made my decision.

It's time I'm forthright with her. There can't be any wishy-washiness. Jasper's gonna be a problem. She's right that he'll freak out—the last time he thought I was staring at her, we got into it, and he was mad for a while.

But at the end of the day, I'm banking on his love for her and long friendship with me to mean more than his upset at my romance with his baby sister.

The following morning, I rise early and head to Mince Fine Art and Flowers at the far north end of Main Street. When I appear in the doorway, Tissant, the pixie owner, smiles at me, her white wings fluttering at her back.

"Ah, Hadrian Alkazar, I wondered when I'd see you here."

I grin. "Am I that transparent, or have you just been reading the *Gulch Gossip*?"

Her smile matches mine. "I'm observant."

I shrug. "I need a floral arrangement that'll be like Pine Gulch come to life, but with a splash of blue, dark blue if you have it."

She snickers. "I don't even need to guess who that might be for."

I join her at the checkout counter, eyeing the far-left wall that's covered floor to ceiling in beautiful blooms. Every other surface is covered in art of various sorts—paintings, rugs, tapestries, quilts. This shop's probably overwhelming to some, but I love how creative it is.

Tissant writes down a few notes on a pad then glances up at me, lips pursed. "Will you be waiting for it, or shall I deliver it to you or somewhere else later?"

"I'll wait," I confirm.

She gestures at the door. "Why don't you hop down to Brew-HaHa and grab us both a latte, and I'll have it done by the time you get back?"

I love the bossiness—it makes me feel like I belong—so I promise I will and head out the door back along Main. This early, it's quiet, although a handful of monsters mill about in front of the Welcome Inn and outside of BrewHaHa. The sunflowers painted on the front of the building lend it a cozy warmth. One of the things I love most about Pine Gulch is the unique way we add beauty to town. Colorful murals, constant parties, the pumpkin maze behind the buildings.

A quarter hour later, I return to Mince with two lattes in hand. When I show back up, Tissant stands there with a stunning bouquet. Flowers drip down the sides and up over the top. It's mostly rusts and golden shades reminiscent of the Montana landscape, but splashes of bright blue dot the arrangement.

"It's perfect," I breathe, setting both lattes down so I can fish for my wallet.

"Let me know how she likes it," Tissant whispers.

I sign for the bouquet then retrieve it gently out of the holder it's in, winking at the proprietress. "Just don't tell Merit and Bryony who I bought this for, and I'll owe you extra."

She rolls pale blue eyes. "Those nosy biddies don't come in here. There's *history* there, if you can imagine."

I tuck my wallet back into my pocket. Her gossip isn't something I need to get into, although I bet she'd tell me if I asked. Instead, I thank her again and head for the door. It takes me just a minute to get halfway down Main Street to the Buxom Bodice. The building clatters her front siding at me in a welcoming way when I grab the gold door handle and pull it open.

Inside, I don't immediately see Bluebell, even though a bell dinged to let her know someone was here. I'm assuming she's working this morning, but I could be wrong. That won't be go—

"Hadrian! I didn't expect to see you here." She emerges from the storeroom in the back, a blush spreading across her pretty high cheekbones. Sliding both hands into her back pockets, she eyes the flowers. "Those are pretty."

I pick my way across the store until I'm close enough to hand them to her. "They're for you, Bluebell."

Bright eyes flick up to me, her blush growing a darker red and traveling down her neck and across her chest.

"This might seem like too much too soon, but I mean to pursue you," I say. "We've been dancing around this for a week, and I don't like the idea that it's not clear to you what I'm trying to do. So this is me telling you I'm interested in *more*. That I've *always* been interested in more and always worried I'd fuck up our friendship if I made a move. I don't think that's what would actually happen though, do you?"

Her mouth drops open, but she quickly zips it shut as she takes the flowers. "Let me just put these in some water," she murmurs, turning from me and heading back into the storeroom.

She's skittish, and I understand it. She probably feels like a lot is riding on the line if we try to date, and it doesn't work out.

"Bluebell," I call out as I follow her into the storeroom.

She grabs a vase from a table in the back and unwraps the flowers, sticking them in the tall glass vessel. That done, she rejoins me and looks up, cradling the flowers against her chest.

"I want that too." Her tone is so quiet, I probably wouldn't hear her if I didn't have such excellent hearing. She lifts her chin and smiles. "I've wanted it for a while, and I tried to tell myself I didn't because of...things. But I have and I do."

Joy fills me, and a huge smile overtakes my face. I slide my hands into my pockets, knowing it flexes my chest muscles, and she'll look.

"What about Jasper, though?" She frowns up at me. "He's made his opinion clear about a million times."

"He's gonna freak; you're right about that." I think about that book he got me, and I know my being home is a big deal to him. "My friendship with your brother doesn't have to change because of you and me."

"It will, though," she says. "It'll definitely change."

"Not all change is bad," I counter.

Goosebumps trail across her forearm, and she starts quivering.

Gods, this is going to be so fun. I'm not flirtatious with

anyone. But with Bluebell? Teasing and playfulness are as easy as breathing.

"We can take it a day at a time," I say. That's not natural for me at all. It wouldn't be natural for any gargoyle. But for her I can try.

"Okay, Hadrian." She smiles up at me. "Hey, your clothing arrived this morning," she says. "Wanna try everything on? That could be fun..."

I chuckle. Oh yes, I think this will be a *lot* of fun.

"You know where the changing room is," she says with a wink.

Grinning, I turn and walk to it, just thankful it's built with bigger monsters in mind so I don't have to crunch my wings up to fit. Bluebell joins me with a stack of clothing.

"Here's the nicer clothing first, then we can work our way to the casual stuff. I'm super pleased with the quality. I hope you are too."

Around us, the Bodice creaks and squeaks.

"I think she's also pleased," Bluebell whispers.

Another series of squeaks affirms the building's feelings.

I take the clothing and set it on a ledge. Bluebell pulls the curtain closed. I'll allow that for now because I'm going to tease the hells out of her in a moment. But when I change into the next outfit? I'm leaving that curtain wide open.

When I've got the jeans and collared shirt on, I hike the curtain back. Bluebell's standing outside, leaning against the opposite wall with one foot propped up on it. Her arms are crossed, highlighting her small, pert breasts. Reaching down, I begin rolling up one sleeve to reveal my forearm. Like I expected, her eyes trail the movement, and her breathing picks up pace, heartbeat matching it.

"How does it feel?" She walks to me and starts nitpicking at the fabric, pulling it over my muscles this way and that.

"This set's perfect." I turn to the mirror, watching as she joins me, looking around my big body. "I want you to take it off so I can try on the next shirt."

Navy lashes flutter against her cheekbones as she looks way up at me.

"Do it now, Bluebell." I focus on those eyes and the way she's staring, the way her scent explodes and strengthens when I play with her. I'm working on pure instinct but willing to bet that's just fine for her. In fact, I'd bet every dollar in my bank account that anything I try will be a fit for her.

She reaches up and undoes the top button, trailing her finger down my pecs to the next one. Her skin is warm, her touch light enough to send shivers down my abs as they crunch and flex in response to her. Never looking away, she pulls each button slowly open, then undoes the tiny zippers along my shoulder blades, separating the front piece from the back. It falls off around my wings, and she grabs the shirt, laying it over her forearm as she quirks a brow upward.

"What would you like to try on next, Mister Alkazar?"

I slide my thumbs into the belt loops of the jeans, pulling them low enough to reveal the vee of my abs. It doesn't take a genius to see she loves that by the way she nips her lower lip. Her heart's galloping along, and I'm having fun.

"Do you think these fit me, Bluebell? Wanna come measure again? I think I've gotten a little bigger since we did this..." I run a thumb along the waistband, tugging it low enough to reveal the faintest hint of pubic hair.

"Fuck," she whispers. "You're killing me, Alk."

"Good," I say. "Because I'm having a shitload of fun teasing you."

"How long are you going to torture me for," she quips, slapping my bare stomach. "Don't you have a game this afternoon?"

I flare my wings wide, loving how her eyes follow the movement, admiration obvious in the way her gaze softens.

She turns from me and grabs another shirt. "Here, try this one on next."

For half an hour, I slip in and out of clothing. She nitpicks the fit on several of the pieces, but most of them are perfect. We agree to send a few pieces back. I should be able to get them in a few days. When it's time to leave for the game, I can barely drag myself out of the store. Thank fuck it's a home game, and she'll be there. When I linger too long, she shoves me toward the front door.

"Don't be late! I don't need to end up in the *Gulch Gossip* as the reason you can't ever be on time to a game! I'll hold everything here and you can pick it up after, or whenever."

Trailing my fingers along her jawline, I brush my thumb over her lower lip. "I'm not gonna kiss you right now because I don't want to rush when we have our first kiss, Bluebell. But after the game tonight? We're stealing away. and I'm *taking* that kiss."

She lifts her chin and nuzzles into my touch. "Alright, Hadrian."

"Not only that," I watch her snuggle against me, "but I want to remind you that your friendship is one of the most important things to me in the whole world. I'll always protect that, Bluebell, alright?"

"Deal," she whispers. "Whatever we do, we've always got that first, right?"

"Always," I whisper as I stare into those beautiful blue eyes. "And that's never changing."

* * *

Hours later, Coach Shorthorn screams out a warning as a big minotaur player from the other team barrels into me, one of my wing bones crunching under the female's enormous weight. I'm distracted, and I can't let that happen. But the only thing on my mind is Bluebell Tucker and the fact I decided teasing was the thing to do. Except I'm edging myself into oblivion as much as I'm edging her, and I don't think I can take much more.

The Punishers barely eke out a win, but when I head to the

Tucker bench, Bluebell's not there. Mr. and Mrs. Tucker embrace me, and I get high-fives from all the Jays.

"Where's Bluebell?" I look around, still surprised she's not in her usual seat.

Jasper shrugs. "It ain't like her to miss a game. I tried calling her but didn't get an answer. She's probably just up to her eyeballs in boxes at the Bodice. She's been over there most of today, far as I know." His focus drops once more to the level-three mastery textbook propped on his thighs.

I nod, knowing I can't ask much more about it right now, but I'm worried. I don't think she's ever missed a home game the entire time I've known her. She doesn't answer when I put my comm watch on and call her.

After the game, the team wants to hit up Lizard Lick Saloon for post-game brews. I agree to go because Jasper and Jack want to, but it's my intention to slip out the moment they get drunk enough not to notice. It doesn't take long, and it's good for me to get in a little bit of time with the team.

Half an hour into it, I slip out the side door and jog across Main Street to the Bodice. The front door's locked, but I stroke my fingers down the glass pane.

"Sweet girl. Is she in there? I need to get in and make sure she's okay."

The building creaks, but the lock unclicks. Clicking the handle, I push my way inside, shut the door, and lock it behind me. A faint heartbeat is my indication that Bluebell's still here.

Then I hear the sniffling.

Sprinting to the back of the building, I run into the storeroom and slide to a halt when I find her in the middle of the floor surrounded by mountains of shoe boxes. Most of them are open, shoes spilled out all over the floor. Some of the other stored items that looked to be in order earlier are now askew and in random piles.

And in the middle of it all, Bluebell's on the floor sobbing. Her eyes are red-rimmed, tears streaming down her cheeks.

Dropping to my knees, I slide boxes out of the way until I can pull her between my thighs. I tuck soaked hair behind her ears as I scan her for any injuries.

"Baby, what happened? Talk to me."

She waves around at the building, brows furrowed. "I thought we were making so much progress, but then I tried reorganizing something, and she threw the hissy fit of the century and tossed this shit everywhere. I have had it up to *here* with this godsdamn building!" Grabbing a box, she tosses it at the wall and screams, "Screw you!"

Looking back at me, Bluebell yanks a soggy piece of paper out of her pocket and hands it to me. "And look at this damn to-do list, Alk. I had so much to get done before the game, and I didn't manage *any* of it. The Mead Cute Festival is coming up, and I was supposed to finalize a couple things because I'm on the fucking organizing committee, and oh my fricking gods, I didn't even make it to the game!"

Lurching forward, she throws her arms around my neck and buries her face just beneath my ear, sobs racking her frame. Her body's tense and tight in my arms as I slip them around her, holding her close with my nose against her neck.

"I'm here," I whisper, placing a tender kiss just beneath her ear.

She shudders, squeezing me tighter. Her sobs don't slow when I hold her close, dragging my mouth down her neck to her shoulder. I place tender, soft kisses on her exposed skin.

"Let it out, Blue, then we'll tackle this together if you want. I'm here," I whisper against her soft, warm skin. "I'm here..."

The better part of ten minutes passes before her crying slows. She's shaking in my arms and covered in goosebumps, although her racing heart eventually slows. Her pain is tangible, its taste sour in my mouth as I continue kissing my way up and down her neck and shoulder.

I just mean to reassure her, but as the crying stops, she begins angling her head to the side to give me more space. Staring at her exposed, creamy neck, I wonder if it's entirely purposeful. When her arms tighten around me, I decide this is exactly the opening we both need, and maybe what she's telling me is that she wants the connection.

Dropping my jaws slightly open, I close my mouth around the spot where her neck and shoulder meet, pricking her slightly with my teeth. Bluebell jolts in my arms, letting out a soft moan that unleashes me. Biting again, I press harder as one of her hands snakes up into my hair, fingers trailing the base of my left horn. The tantalizing tickle does something to me, something primal and filthy.

Threading a hand around her long blue locks, I guide her head backward and move up her neck, alternating between hungry bites and ravenous licks. Bluebell writhes in my arms, thrusting her hips against my stomach as she grabs on to both of my horns and lets her head fall back into my hand.

Snarling, I bite harder and harder until I reach that tender spot just below her chin. If I bit her there, her life would be in my hands. I want it. I need it. Surging forward, I clamp my teeth around her throat and shake slowly from side to side. It's possession and lust and desire all wrapped in a tidy, tight package. Bluebell yips but sinks harder against me, the tiniest amount of blood welling to the surface of the wounds.

Releasing the bite, I nip up the underside of her jaw, up over her chin until I reach those delicious blue lips. I hover for a moment, dragging my fingertips over the soft, plump things. My entire world recenters, then, on that mouth and that soft-looking pink tongue peeking out.

Closing my eyes, I close the final inches between us and slant my mouth over hers. For a moment, time stands still. Then she moves first, dragging her nails down my horns as she bites my upper lip.

That's it. I'm finished. There'll never be someone else who tastes this good, this right. Growling, I swoop my right wing around her, crushing her to me as I devour her, cocking my head to one side and the other as we lose control together. My hands rove entirely of their own accord up beneath her shirt, my fingers arching to touch her pert nipples.

I tug softly at them as she pushes off the surface of my wing, trying to wrest control of the kiss.

"No," I command. "I don't think so, Blue."

Shifting forward, I lay her on her back atop my wing, splaying her gorgeous hair over my skin. It tickles, and even that makes me hard. Dipping low, I take her mouth again, thrusting my hips against hers as I muse over how much fucking bigger I am. Our kiss gets wild, hot, out of control until I'm biting and kissing and sucking on every inch of her I can reach. I've got my lips and mouth on her chin, her neck, that delicate shoulder and down the inside of her arm.

Bluebell's scent envelops me, mixing with mine until I can't tell us apart. There's just our lust, our need, and the knowing that she is mine, mine, mine.

I couldn't tell you how long I kiss her before she parts from me, chest heaving.

"That was a hell of a kiss, Alk," she whispers, slipping a hand up my shirt to rest it over my silent heart.

A heart that'll beat when I claim her. I'm sure of that now. Because there's no other woman in this entire world who could fit me like Bluebell Tucker. I'll never want anyone else. Kissing her cemented what I was already relatively certain of, something I've been feeling for a very long time.

"I'm yours," I whisper into the scant space between us. "You know that, don't you?"

A smile overtakes her, blue freckles along her cheeks highlighting her beautiful burnished skin. "All mine? Sounds nice. Nothing's ever been all mine before."

"Until this place," I correct, waving at the Bodice around us. "And because I'm yours, that means I'm hers too. And as a unit, we're going to figure out how we can live and work together in partnership. Right?" I glance around.

A soft clattering comes from somewhere behind Bluebell.

"We can do this, honey," I say to the building before looking back at my woman. "I'm not going anywhere, Bluebell. I'm in your corner, alright?"

She strokes her fingers down my jawline. "Are we *really* doing this, Alk?"

I nip at her fingertips, sucking them into my mouth, then grabbing her wrist and biting the inside of it. "I think you mean, 'Are we really doing this, baby?' Or mate. Or whatever term of endearment you want to give me. But I don't want the nickname you've used our whole lives. I want something new, something special, something you call me at three a.m. while I'm fucking you in front of our fireplace. Pick a new name, Bluebell."

Her mouth drops open, and the blush returns as she shifts in my arms. "I...I can't think of one right now, but I'll figure something out."

I shift back onto both hands. "See that you do."

Silence stretches long before her comm watch rings. Jasper's name flashes over it. When she answers, he shouts in relief. "Girl, we thought you might've died. Where are you, and do you have Hadrian? He disappeared!"

"Got him," she says evenly. "I've got a meeting with Lemon and Oz about the Mead Cute Festival, but do you want to come retrieve your wayward bestie?"

I grin and pinch her nipple again. She jerks away with a barely withheld laugh. Oh yes, I think I love this new dynamic where I just put my hands on her when I want to—assuming she's down, of course.

Jasper asks something else, but I don't pay attention because my eyes fall to the to-do list she dropped when she yelled at the Bodice. I grab the list, and my mouth drops open at how fucking much is on it, just like before. When she hangs up with her brother, I wave the sheet of paper at her.

"We're gonna talk about this, Bluebell. This is more than one human is literally capable of achieving in a day."

She shakes her head and grabs for it, but I lift it high over my head. "No," I say again. "I'm helping you. Tell me what on there I can do, and I'll take care of it with you."

She wriggles in my lap. "Well, you could help me with the decorations tomorrow, if you want. Lemon, Furyon and Oz are planning to as well, but I'd be open to that if you want."

"I'll get the Jays too," I offer.

She snorts. "Jasper sucks at decorating."

"He'll learn," I promise. "This is non-negotiable. You cannot take on all of this stuff by yourself. We'll learn to do it your way, so you don't feel like you have to redo it for it to be right, but I absolutely insist on helping you."

Her answering smile is soft. Silence goes long again, and it could be awkward, but it's not. Not until she hops off my lap and runs both hands through her mussed hair.

"Get some clothes back on Mister Alkazar," she commands. "You're still my dirty little secret."

Fuck me. That sounds good for now. But in the long run, I won't be able to stay like that. Because I want the entire world to know Bluebell Tucker is mine. One day? One day I'll shout that news from the damn rooftops.

Bluebell

Hadrian is quiet as I gather up his new clothing and bag it. Now that the game's done it'll be easier for him to haul the bags home. Plus, I can help. He stands there smirking while I ring it up, debating about whether it's weird or not to charge my...whatever he is...for a service. When I open my mouth to debate that with him, he shakes his head.

"Don't even think about *not* charging me, Miss Tucker. You provided a service I needed, and I want to see you be successful."

The Bodice shimmies around us, but this sound is happy as she clatters the wall displays. Buckles jangle together on their hooks, and the shoe boxes shimmy loudly. The playful sounds bring a smile to my face.

"You did a great job," I compliment the building, hoping that what Hadrian said earlier will sink through to her. I really thought we might be done for when she ruined my organizing efforts. I've got to figure out how she wants to be worked with because what I'm doing isn't panning out.

She seems to like Hadrian, though, so maybe we can finagle that to my benefit. It's worth a try, if he's willing to help.

He pays cash and leaves a stupid tip that I try to refuse. When

I put up too much of a fuss, the building lets out a series of warning creaks. She doesn't like me saying no to a customer.

Hadrian chuckles and leans onto both beefy forearms, winking at me. "Seems like the Bodice and I are on the same page, Bluebell. Take the money and don't fight me about it. Your success and your partnership with her are important to me because *you're* important to me, alright?"

I stuff the money in the cash register, determined to return it to him later. Maybe I'll shove it under his apartment door or stick it in a bag when he's not looking.

He might be reading my mind, though, because he grabs the large bags and slots it under his arm, then slides his hands into his pockets. Behind his back, his sharp wing tips hover, reminding me how very predatory he could be if he wanted to.

A shiver skirts down my spine, pulling goosebumps to my skin.

Hadrian's nostrils flare, his pupils darkening as a furrow appears between his brows. He's utterly still, utterly focused, staring at me like he might rip the counter from its supports and shove it aside to get to me.

"Hadrian," I whisper. "What are you doing?"

His tail begins to lash side to side as he takes a step forward, then two, until his body hits the counter. "Bluebell," he growls out. "You want me. I smell it."

Oh gods. Anybody could come in at any time, and Jasper already called looking for him.

"We can't do this right here, right now," I whisper-hiss. "My brother will—"

"You want something only I can give you," he continues. "Don't you?"

I run both hands through my hair, glancing at the front window. I can't see any of my brothers yet, but it's just a matter of time. And something about the idea of being caught has me throbbing with a surprising anticipation.

"I'm gonna put you on this countertop and take care of that

soaked pussy, Bluebell." He leans over and grips my throat carefully, pulling me to touch the opposite side of the counter as he rubs his giant thumb pad over my lower lip. His eyes drift to my mouth, and he smirks. "I want that mouth open while you scream, pretty girl. My name. My nickname. Any of those works for me. Hop on up here." He pats the countertop.

"No." I cross my arms. "We've got to go, Hadrian."

His dark brows lift. "You're denying me? Me? After you've wanted this for so long?"

This kind of play is right up my alley. I always fantasized about Hadrian being secretly dominant. But the fact that he is and getting more dominant by the minute is *exactly* what I'm into. This male is *trouble.*

The shop bell dings, and I gasp, wheeling around to the front door. Hadrian never looks away from me, his gaze as tangible as his fingers on my mouth just a moment ago.

"Well, well, well," says Merit from the doorway, her sister, Bryony, hovering behind her with a smile. They cross to us, Merit waving a piece of paper. "Fancy seeing you two here, although it seems like you two are being seen plenty of places together."

I scowl at the nosy pixies. They're Pine Gulch OGs, but damn they love to get into everyone's business so they can publish it in the weekly Gulch Gossip paper.

They cross the store and I'm thankful when the ceiling beams creak out a noise I take as warning.

Merit slaps the paper down on the counter between Hadrian and me. When I look at it, my blood runs cold—it's a photo of him and me standing on the balcony in Santa Alaya. His wing is around me, and I'm staring up at him, smiling. We look...shit. We look like we're in love or, at the very least, romantic.

"It's not what it looks like," I shout. "And don't go flashing that thing around town either. For once, can you mind your own business please?"

Bryony shrugs. "Aww, Bluebell, we were just poking fun. Are

you two not dating?" She pulls a notepad and pen from her crochet purse.

I stare up at Hadrian, willing him to rescue me from this conversation.

"Ladies," he says evenly. "I've been the subject of your column a few times in the last couple weeks. I'd greatly appreciate a reprieve, even if it's just for a short time. Why don't you try talking to Shroud and Vela since Vela's new to town? I'm sure she'd love to be on the *Gossip's* front page."

Merit looks between us while Bryony nods happily.

"I'm not dropping this," Merit says, lifting her chin. "But obviously we don't want to be rude, so I'll leave it alone for a minute, but if we can break the story first, we want to."

This isn't breaking news! I want to shout. And Pine Gulch doesn't need a damn gossip newspaper. We don't even have a *regular* newspaper. But I guess that's all the two old biddies have to do with their time.

Merit points between us. "No idea why you're hiding this, but we can respect it. When you decide to go public, I'd like an interview about how it all got started. Inquiring minds want to know!"

I snort, but Hadrian just grabs the photo and shoves it in his pocket.

"Interview granted. I'll reach out when I'm ready to talk. Sound good?"

Bryony claps and flutters her wings. "Of course, Hadrian, that would be absolutely lovely! More than reasonable. Thank you!" She grabs her sister by the shoulders and spins her toward the door. "We're going now. Enjoy your evening!"

No sooner have they opened the door than my brothers pile through it, mead glasses in hand. Jasper's level-three prep book is tucked under one arm. He groans at seeing us at the checkout counter.

"Alk, dude, you promised me dinner, and I'm wasting away. All of this studying is eating up my brain cells. Betty's is doing a burger competition, so let's go down there. Free samples!" He waggles his brows at us both. "Bloob where'd you get to anyways? Did you just come here to *work*?"

Hadrian looks at me and ignores my brother. "Come with? You've got to eat too."

"Free samples," Jasper reminds me with a ferocious grin. "You know you love free samples, girl."

I smile at the crew. "Let me just lock up."

We walk together down to Betty's Burger Bar. Tents set up on the sidewalk are full of monsters grilling burgers. Even with my human sense of smell, I can pick out a handful of scents—onions, smoked gouda, pickled jalapeños. I wonder what it's like for Hadrian?

Jasper yanks the door open and holds it for us. Inside, Betty's is packed from wall to wall, but Betty herself drags us to a table in the back with Hadrian's name on it.

"Good thing you called ahead of time, Alk," Betty says with a smile.

"Thank fuuuuck," Jasper moans. "I couldn't have waited in that line."

Hadrian claps my brother on the shoulder. "I know, dude. I thought ahead."

And just like that, I'm *definitely* falling for the big gargoyle. Scratch that. I've fallen, completely fallen. Hadrian's always been like this—always planned ahead, seen every angle, noticed every-fucking-thing. But the way he cares for everyone in his life is maybe the thing I love most about him. Despite having such a huge family, it seems like I'm the one who ends up doing most of the Tucker caretaking and I don't love that.

It's hard for me to force myself not to stare at him as we slide onto the bench seats and pick up our menus.

Dinner's a loud affair with the building herself tossing drunkards out the front door if they get too rowdy about the competition. I down two entire burgers before my hunger is sated...it's impossible to choose with so many good options. The macaroni-filled burger was a surprise winner, but, hot damn, it was fucking good.

Eventually, my to-do list starts burning a hole in my pocket, so I take it out to have a quick look. Hadrian stares at me while the Jays joke about the shit that's always reliably in my pockets. The guys decide to stay for a beer when I beg leave of them to finish my stuff. I'm sure Hadrian would come with me if it wouldn't seem suspicious.

On my way out the door, a young female gargoyle stops me. She's maybe nine or ten years old. Bright amethyst eyes flash as she shoots me a friendly smile. "Excuse me, hi! Is that gargoyle over there Hadrian Alkazar, the skyball player?"

I grin. I suppose I should get used to this. He's still a celebrity even though he's just my Hadrian.

Mine.

"Yeah," I say with a big smile. "That's him."

"Great!" she chirps expressively, eyes wrinkling in the corners. That smile is so stinking cute. "I'm gonna go say hi!"

"Alright." I turn with a chuckle, watching her pick her way across the restaurant toward Hadrian and my brothers. She taps him on the arm, and he looks up, face breaking into a genuine smile. He's so good with the fans.

And he says he's mine. Am I really that lucky?

Hadrian

I smile at the young gargoyle female standing by my side.

"Oh, I'm so excited to finally meet you!" She lets out a high-pitched squeal and jumps up and down. "Dad told me how to find you, but I thought it would be harder." She holds out a hand to shake mine. "I'm Petra, your sister."

Across from me, Jasper chokes on his food and starts pounding on his chest.

I blink as I look from him back to the gargoyle, who's staring at me expectantly.

Cocking my head to the side, I eye her suspiciously. "Hey, young one, I don't have a sister. You must have me confused with someone else."

She reaches into her pocket, sticking her tongue out of one side of her mouth as she does. "Oh, don't worry, I was a surprise to him too! Technically I'm your half-sister because your dad dated my mom a long time ago in the human world. Well like, ten years ago there, but that's what inside the haven system, like almost three hundred haven years?"

I blink rapidly as I try to follow her train of thought. She's three hundred years old? Pinching the bridge of my nose, I struggle to deal with this information.

She hands me a crinkled envelope with my name written on the front. My mouth goes dry. It's my father's handwriting. The way he connects the "d" and "r" in my first name is so distinctive.

The girl hands me a necklace next. It's a mini stone arakna spider, similar to the necklace my father gave my mother as a mating present. The arakna only exists in a sprawling haven in Brazil where they've been doing their research for the better part of two haven decades. And now this young gargoyle is holding one with a letter in my father's handwriting.

Hands shaking, I take the envelope and withdraw a single sheet of paper. My mouth drops open at seeing his handwriting here too.

Hadrian -

This is Petra, your sister. So sorry we haven't had a chance to tell you about her. She was quite a surprise to us as well! You know that whole time difference thing means we lose track when we're working. Petra found us after searching for a long time in the human world. Her mother, an old flame of mine, passed, so Petra stayed with us for a time, but she was so excited to have a brother. We could barely hold her back from visiting you once she learned where you were. Hopefully you're okay having her around for a little bit. We're headed deep into the jungle for a few weeks where it's not safe for her, but we'll be back soon!

As always, we love you,

Dad

"What the fuck?" I bark.

To my right, the girl, Petra, blanches.

Jasper snatches the letter out of my hand. He and Jack put their heads together as they read it. I stare at the young gargoyle who's now lashing her tail side to side, brows furrowed as she bites the edge of her finger.

"How old are you?" I ask.

She crosses her arms at her wrists, threading her fingers together. "Umm, I'm nine. Well, in human years."

I shift uncomfortably, glancing at Jasper and Jack. Jack finishes reading the letter first and holds out a fist toward Petra. "Welcome to the family, lil dudette! I'm your Uncle Jack."

She looks askance at him. "Uncle? You're...human."

"Witch," he corrects. "But yeah. Hadrian's lived with us every summer for almost three haven decades. So I'm your Uncle Jack." He elbows Jasper. "This is your Uncle Jasper. You've got an Uncle Jace too and we've got a sister around here somewhere. So, yeah, welcome."

Petra tentatively fist-bumps his outstretched hand.

I throw both of mine in the air. "Wait a second. Am I dreaming right now? This can't be happening, can it?!"

A sister? A fucking godsdamned sister? My parents gone for *years*? What in the ever-loving shit is happening?

"Umm, I'm hungry," she says softly, eyeing the half-eaten burger on my plate. "Can I have your burger while you finish freaking out? I haven't eaten all day."

Jack and Jasper burst out laughing, and Jasper pats the seat next to him.

"C'mere, honey. Sit by Uncle Jasper, and we'll order you your own thing."

She takes a seat, looking nervously at me until Jasper hands her a menu. I'm still staring at the three of them in utter disbelief when Jack lifts his drink to mine, clinking it. "Congrats on the surprise sister, dude."

A million thoughts fly through my mind at once. How do I know she's really my sister? How do I know the letter's not a fake? Could this be some weird stalker fan thing?

"We need to see the sheriff," I mutter.

Petra's mouth drops open, and she frowns like she might cry. "Why?!"

I run both hands through my hair. "Just to verify some details, okay? It's not that I don't believe you, but it's better to be sure, right?"

She purses her lips. "And when you figure out I'm really your sister, you'll take care of me, right? Because Dad said you would, and it was a lot of travel from Brazil. It's taken me, like, two whole days to get here."

Jasper gasps. "They let you come by yourself?"

The girl shrugs, still eyeing my burger.

One of the Jays says something else, but time and space blur into television fuzz in my brain. I can't find words. I just kissed the woman of my dreams for the first time. I just promised to be in her corner. I *just* told her I was hers. And now I've got a surprise kid sister literally dropped onto my doorstep for fucking years.

Leaning forward, I press my forehead to the table and pray for peace of mind. This can't be happening.

"Just give him some processing time, sweetheart," Jasper says confidently. "You shocked your big brother. You probably knew about him, right?"

"Oh, yeah," she says with a laugh. "I knew he didn't know about me, but I guess it didn't really sink in until right now. I thought they'd have said something when I was on the way."

I lift my head. She sounds a little heartbroken. "Grab some food, Petra. We'll figure all of this out, okay?"

She nods just as the minotaur waitress reappears at our table.

Half an hour later, I'm still in shock as Petra licks burger juice from her fingers. Jack and Jasper have her in stitches, but I'm still staring at her trying to decide if we look alike. When she turns a crooked smile on me and I notice the same dimple in her chin that I got from my father, it all hits me like a ton of bricks.

I've got a one-bedroom apartment across the hall from my fucking mate, who I just started pursuing. One nest. No extra room. I don't even know where Pine Gulch's elementary school is or what grade Petra would be in. I don't have the first clue what to do with her while I'm in games or at practice. Who babysits in Pine Gulch? I don't fucking know. And I cannot add another thing to Bluebell's to-do list.

When dinner is done, I call the sheriff to verify he's at the office up the street. Petra follows me there in silence, her footfalls impossibly light as she hops in and out of the railroad tracks.

"How come you don't believe me?" she asks when I grab the door handle.

I sigh, dropping to my heels and clasping my hands together. "You caught me by surprise, little one, and I'd like to verify all of this. Imagine if a random kid came up to you on the street and said they were your sister."

She frowns, shooting me an exasperated look. "I'd obviously be excited, and then I'd ask them to go play." She crosses her arms and taps her foot. "Dad said you'd be, what was the word? Kerfluffled. Is that what this reaction is?" She waves at me.

I purse my lips. My father is the only monster in the entire world I've ever heard use that word.

Fuuuuck me.

Rising, I grab the door and open it. "Let's go, Petra."

Inside his office, Sheriff Rygold sits behind his desk with both big feet up on it as he reads the newest issue of the *Gulch Gossip*, the one with me on the skyball pitch on the front.

Petra runs up and grabs it right out of his hands, scanning the words. "Oh my gods, Hadrian, this is so cool! You're in the newspaper!"

Rygold rises and eyes her, then me. "What can I do you for, Alkazar? Bit late to be here, ain't it?"

I point at the little one. "Petra here seems to think we're siblings, and I was hoping you could help me verify."

Rygold barks out a ragged laugh. "For real? Surprise relation? Don't see that every day."

Petra sighs and throws the paper back onto his desk. "Hadrian doesn't believe me. He's kerfluffled about it, but he'll come to terms with it. Dad said he would. Also, what happened to your face?" She points at the sheriff's half-horn and ripped lip.

I resist the urge to start shouting at...someone. It won't do any good. I'm not close with my parents, but I never thought they'd casually drop a sibling on my doorstep. I'm comm'ing them the moment I get home.

"Can you help?" I'm practically begging.

Rygold nods and looks at Petra. "Hand me a piece of your hair please."

Petra reaches up and yanks out a strand, then lays it in his outstretched hand.

He looks at me, and I do the same.

Rygold stalks toward the back of his office and shuffles around in a cabinet, withdrawing a beaker and a vial of purple liquid. Returning to us, he sets the beaker on the desk and drops both hairs into it.

"Now, if you're related, when I put this purple liquid in, it'll turn black. If you're distantly related, it'll go pale blue. And if you're unrelated, it'll stay the same color."

My mouth is as dry as the gulch's wheat fields as Rygold dumps purple liquid over the hair. Almost immediately, black swirls through the shade. In moments, the entirety of the beaker is filled with obsidian liquid.

Rygold chuckles. "Ain't never seen it turn quite that fast." He looks between us, his smile crooked because of the huge scar running down the left side of his face. "Guess y'all are family." He reaches into his desk and withdraws a blue-banded comm watch. Handing it to her, he wiggles his brows. "Young lady, you know how this works? You can make calls within Pine Gulch but not outside of it. Need a comm *disk* to call other havens."

Petra hops up and down as she fastens the watch around her thin wrist. "Yes! I have a brother! That is the best thing in the entire world. I'm so excited, Hadrian. I want you to show me everything about the haven system. Dad's been teaching me about how time moves faster inside havens, and how thralls are drawn to the protective wards...which is so dang creepy. I've never seen one of those in real life but—"

I tune her out as I stare at the sheriff. He stares right back.

What in the actual shit am I gonna do now?

Bluebell

I'm just finishing my evening meeting with the Mead Cute organizing committee when my comm watch pings, Hadrian's name hovering above the band. Merit and Bryony look at my watch with obvious interest, then Lemon and Oz shoot me matching satisfied looks as I rise from the table. Heading for the door to get some privacy, I breathe a sigh of relief that the porch is empty. Thank gods most monsters are still terrified of the Keeper's house and won't come inside the property. It's just Lemon who insists we meet here, and the house loves her, so she allows the rest of us in.

Something's happening there, I'm just not entirely sure what, and I can't wait to find out.

"Hey." I can barely hold back a huge smile when I answer him.

"Hey, Blue," Hadrian says softly. "You done yet?"

"Yeah." I slide a hand into my back pocket. "Just finished."

"Listen, baby, I'm out at the ranch working on some things. Can you come hang? It's late, and I want to see you. I've got some news."

Heat radiates through me, and I hop in place, the smile fully overtaking me. "Yeah," I agree, heading for my truck. "I'll come to you now."

"I like the way that sounds," he says, his voice low and gravelly. "I need you, little witch. It's been a day."

Oh boy, I bet I can help with that...

"Loving the new nickname," I admit as I haul my truck door open and slip inside.

Hadrian laughs. "I might try out a few more to see what you like best, though."

I've never driven so fast or been so thankful that Sheriff Rygold doesn't hang around in speed traps. By the time I get to Hadrian's long rocky driveway, I'm practically slinging gravel as I barrel toward the house. Reminding myself to have at least a little bit of chill, I slow down. This is Hadrian; I don't have to make this weird.

I'm still not ready when I pull into the driveway and he walks around the side of the house shirtless, jeans slung low on his hips and a bottle of beer in one hand. His wings are half flared at his back, tail lashing from side to side. He looks so... *expectant.*

When I put the truck in park, he stalks toward me with a secretive smile.

Except I don't want him to be a dirty secret. I already know that. It's not fair to him or me. We're grown-ass people. I'm almost *thirty,* for gods' sake. I'm going to tell him. We'll talk to Jasper. It'll be fine. Right?

He promised he'd protect our friendship, and I believe he will.

Or maybe we'll just make sure this doesn't end in disaster before we tell anyone. His friendship with Jasper isn't the only thing at risk—he's been my best friend for almost my entire life. I'd be devastated to lose that.

He gets close enough to press me to the truck hood, flaring his wings wide as he dips down and slides his hands under my ass. Pulling me onto the hood, he slots his huge body between my thighs and leans his forehead against mine. Staring into my eyes, he runs his hands up my arms and down my back, touching everywhere.

"Thank you for coming all the way out here," he says quietly, pressing my upper body closer to his. "I gotta tell you something that's gonna complicate matters, Blue."

I freeze despite how fucking fabulous his big three-fingered hands feel on me.

Brows bunched, I stare up at him. "Something worse than my brothers?"

He nods. "Something I just found out about today." He takes a step back and yanks his hair out of the high bun in a frustrated move that highlights his thick arm muscles. "It might be better to show you."

I'm frozen on the truck hood, though, because why is it that every time we get close, something seems to pop up? My brothers. The Bodice. The fucking *Gulch Gossip* ladies. Now something else?

"Okay," I say, hopping off the truck. "Talk to me, Alk."

He grins, but it doesn't reach his eyes. "Still waiting on a better nickname, Blue."

I'd come up with a witty retort, but I'm too worried about whatever he asked me out here to say. He grabs my hand and pulls me toward the door. Following in silence, I consider all the possibilities, but nothing makes sense. Twenty years of friendship haven't left any stones unturned. I'd swear I know *everything* about this male, so whatever he has to say must be *bad* bad.

All of that changes when we enter the beautiful old ranch house. He's redone so much of the inside, although it's not quite livable yet—hence why he's currently my neighbor. But across the living room in the room's singular leather chair lies a young gargoyle female.

Wearing one of Hadrian's sweatshirts. Skinny legs hang out from beneath it, cloaked in dirty jeans. Her tail thwaps loosely against the edge of the chair as she snores softly.

I blink rapidly, trying to process what I'm seeing. Wait...she looks familiar. I realize it's the young girl who asked me about him earlier.

"Wait..." As I glance up at Hadrian, his smile is totally gone.

"That's Petra, she found me earlier today just after you left Betty's. She's...Shit. She's my sister, Bluebell. Well, half-sister."

My mouth drops open, and I look rapidly between them. Her face is lax in sleep, but the resemblance is uncanny. She's got the same cute dimple in her chin but heart-shaped face with a wide, angular jaw. Feminine, but similar. And earlier I remember thinking her eyes were such a pretty, familiar color. Brighter purple than the average gargoyle.

Just like Hadrian's.

"Is this for real?" My voice is barely a whisper, and Hadrian nods, crossing his big arms as he stares at the sleeping female.

"I took her to Sheriff Rygold, and he verified she's my sister. My father sent a letter with her too, pretty much saying, 'Hey, this is Petra; we just found out about her, but she wanted to meet you.'" He runs a hand through his hair. "So they told her how to come find me, and here she is."

A disgruntled gasp leaves me. Hadrian's parents have never been attentive. I've known him for twenty years and met them twice. They were always more than happy to send him to us for entire summers at a time, claiming he preferred to be with us anyhow. Most of the time, *we* got him ready to go back to school. I'm both shocked and somehow unsurprised at this. But an entire extra sibling?

"Where has she been living?"

He pulls me toward the back door. "Human world with her mother, an ex of my father's. Let's talk outside."

Quietly, I allow him to guide me out the back door and across a rough stone patio to his firepit. A fire rages within it, spitting golden orange sparks into the sky. In the human world, you could never do a fire like this outside for fear of burning up the whole state. But here in the monster world, we've got a potion for keeping that from happening.

Hadrian takes a seat in an oversized chair, pulling me onto his lap with a sigh that sounds like it carries the weight of the entire damn haven system.

"Apparently, her mother died, and she spent a lot of years looking for my father. She found him and stayed with them for a time, but she wanted to meet me. She was...excited to have a brother. It's kinda detailed here. She told me the rest at dinner." He reaches into his shirt pocket and withdraws a crumpled piece of paper then hands it to me.

I unfold it and scan the contents. My eyes spring wide. "They want you to keep her for *years*? Are they fucking serious?!"

"Surprise," he says in a glum tone. "I need a drink. Would you like one too? I've got some of that plum whiskey from the coach's private stores."

"Make mine a double," I mutter as I reread the letter, freshly shocked by the absolute godsdamn gall of Hadrian's parents to send her without even calling. Even if she wanted to come, they should have come too.

A surprise sister and *oh, by the way, please watch her for some unspecified amount of time*? What in the actual fuck?! I know they've always been locked into their research, so forgetful of the fact that time moves faster inside the haven system than outside. A week for them in the human world is a whole month here so they've lost years with Hadrian. I think it's why he's so much the opposite of that now.

"She's got nowhere to go," he says, tucking a stray lock of hair over my shoulder. "Showed up with just a bag of clothes but wanted one of my sweatshirts at bedtime. I don't know how to take care of a nine-year-old. I couldn't hide her from you, Blue, but I want you to know that her sudden appearance changes nothing about my intention toward you."

I stuff the letter back in his shirt pocket, considering my response. "Don't you think it's weird how stuff keeps coming up, though? Between us, I mean?"

He scoffs. "Just because something is challenging doesn't

mean it's not worth pursuing, Bluebell. But I will make you a promise right now. I won't run from this, and I will always talk to you, because the foundation of *this* house, *our* house, is built on decades of friendship. Don't run from me, little witch, and I will honor that bravery by doing the same."

Those words make me care for him more than anything he's said since our attraction became apparent. But they don't soothe the worry inside me.

"How you doing with this, Bluebell?" He slides a hand up my back and into my hair while he pours a glass full of whiskey from a bottle next to his chair. "I know it's a lot to lay on you, and I put you in my lap so I can read your scent. Talk to me, please."

"It's a lot," I admit. "She's so young, it's like you became a *dad* this afternoon."

"I tried comming my folks," he says with a sigh. "No answer, of course. I suspect it's true that they're so deep into the forest that they won't come out for years."

"How are *you* with all of this?" I stroke my knuckles along his angular jawline. "I know it always bothered you how they left you here for such long stretches, and now they're doing it again."

"They're...unusual," he says with a shake of his head. "I guess I thought, eventually, I'd put all of that behind me. That somehow once I was grown, the power dynamic between us would change simply because I didn't need parenting. I barely spoke to them while I was at the academy. But now? Her? She's so...tiny. Just a youngling. She needs guidance, a mother, a father."

"I'm here for you," I whisper. "Even as a friend I'd help you, you know that."

He shakes his head. "I won't ask you to do that, Bluebell." He sucks at his teeth. "I've seen your to-do list." Reaching around my waist, he pats my back pocket, and we share a wry chuckle at the sound of crinkling paper.

I shrug and thread my arms around his neck. "I'm in shock. I'm worried for you and for her. But I'm here for you no matter what. This isn't the last convo we'll have about Petra, I'm sure."

"No." He bites his lower lip, staring at me. "Can we set that topic aside, though? I needed to tell you immediately, but I'll admit to having an ulterior motive in getting you out here alone."

The drag of his knuckles along my collarbone to my shoulder sends shivers skating down my spine.

I lean forward, resting my forearms on his chest and staring up into those gorgeous purple eyes. "Oh yeah?"

"Yeah." He smiles, but it's soft and tender at the edges, tinged by what I can only assume is the weight of today's revelation.

For a long minute, we say nothing. Hadrian rubs my back. I'm sure we're both lost in thought and I can't think of anything else to say on the topic right now. I'm gonna need some time to process that.

He shifts beneath me, moving his hips while the chair creaks under his immense weight. "Blue, have I ever told you about my sex toy collection?"

My brows rise at the very welcome change of subject, and I shake my head. "Might those be the toys I carried into your apartment that had you blushing dark purple?"

"The very ones," he says with a grin, handing me the glass of whiskey. "All of my toys are shaped like human pussies, Bluebell, because I thought of you every time I fucked them. And I fucked them near constantly."

My mouth goes dry.

His smile becomes a full-on smirk. "You wanna see me do that sometime? Maybe tell me about what you like? If I had a guess, I'd assume there's at least one or two gargoyle-shaped cocks in your arsenal. Am I right?"

A hot blush fully overtakes me.

"That's what I thought," he says while he pours a second glass of whiskey. He takes a sip and lets his head fall back against the chair, throat bobbing as he swallows.

My fingers itch to run down over that muscular column, maybe cover it with bites and kisses. But I'm also shocked as shit about discovering Petra, and even though he asked to move on from that convo and decided to talk about *sex toys*, my mind keeps drifting back to it.

Hadrian swoops a big wing around my back, cloaking us in darkness as he tightens both big arms around me. I can't see him like this, although I bet he can see me just fine with his excellent senses.

My big predator.

"I can tell your mind is still spinning, Bluebell," he says with a low snarl. "Allow me to distract you..."

When I'm quiet, waiting for him to make a move, he shifts forward and brushes his cool lips over mine. "Give me permission, little witch."

"To do what, exactly?" I can't help the snark. Sassing him is almost easier than breathing, and I've got soooo much practice.

His answering chuckle, low and throaty, has my pussy clenching on nothing, desperate for the first taste of him. "Whatever I want, Bluebell," he croons. "I want to get you off, to see it for the first time. I want to taste it. So say yes before I start."

"Yes," I manage, the word nearly choking me. I want him so badly, and I have for so long. Is this really happening right here? Right now?

"Undo my jeans, Bluebell." Cool breath coasts over my mouth. "I want to watch you see me for the first time. Nobody's ever seen these piercings outside of the male who did them for me."

Reaching down, I pull the button of his jeans open and slide the zipper down. He moves his wing enough to let faint light in, shifting his hips so I can pull his pants farther down. He's wearing dark briefs, but the outline of an alarmingly huge erection strains the front of the fabric.

"More, Bluebell," he commands as he lifts his glass to take a sip. His throat bobs as I stare at him, reaching for the waistband of his briefs. I'm about to see my *friend* naked, and he's talking to me like he's about to teach me what it means to fuck hard.

Another shiver racks me, and I shudder. Hadrian laughs, lifting his wings and resting them over the back of his chair.

"Gods, this is going to be fun," he rumbles.

Pulling the briefs down, I watch as the tip of his dick appears. To be more precise, his dick appears first and a line of piercings second. Because the underside of his dick is chock full of metal.

"What the fuck, Hadrian?" I blurt out, flashing a concerned look.

He's smirking, his horns flexing straight, a sign he's aroused. "There's more where that came from, little witch, so keep going."

"More?" I gulp as he shifts his hips enough to help me pull his briefs the rest of the way down. My mouth drops open at seeing multiple parallel bars through the underside of his soda can-sized dick.

I slap a hand over my mouth, shaking my head. There's no way this will work. No fucking way. Between the metal and the size, and I'm just a human. We're gonna need a potion to even remotely help our private parts fit together.

"It'll fit," he says confidently, setting his whiskey glass down. "Stand and take your pants off, Bluebell."

"It won't fit," I confirm, although I do rise and shuck my pants and underwear off. But I point to my pussy as I raise both brows to show him how deadly serious I am. "I've spent plenty of time buried inside my own pussy, and I'm telling you, that monster isn't gonna fit."

He chuckles and slides off the chair, dropping to his knees at my feet. Pressing his lips to a spot below my belly button, he stares up at me with hooded eyes. "It'll fit if you're wet enough."

Before I can say a word, he curls over, dipping low until he can nuzzle his way between my thighs. When his lips brush over my clit, my knees buckle. But Hadrian's already there for me just like he's always been, hands running up my ass and back as he holds me up. Shaking his head side to side, he laps at my clit as shock and awe shatter through me.

His tongue is soft but cool, even though everywhere he

touches me feels like fire licking my skin. Gripping his horns, I hold on for dear life as he starts to groan, his voice ragged, his movements rough. Cheek stubble scratches at my inner thighs, and even *that* threatens to throw me into the abyss of pleasure because it's so fucking good. So masculine.

And when I look down to see my best friend on his knees, eating my pussy like I'm his last meal? My legs are limp noodles at the sight of it.

Orgasm hits before I can even finish that thought. It comes out of the blue, rocking me like a car wreck as my body shakes and shudders, channel clamping around his tongue. Those magical lips never stop moving, and every time I clutch and claw at his horns, he lets out a desperate low growl that prolongs the bliss. Suddenly, I'm anxious for us not to be heard, not to be caught, so I clamp a hand over my mouth when screams threaten to burst from me.

Ecstasy goes from great rolling waves to tight pleasure so hot, it borders on painful. He must sense it, though, because he pulls back and stares up at me, flattening his tongue and stroking softly. It's almost a soothing move, if his fingers weren't tightening at my hips.

My gasping, stuttered breaths begin to slow as I struggle to find words. It takes me a few minutes to accomplish that.

"Did we just do that?"

He grins up at me as he licks slowly again. Moving his mouth to my thigh, he bites softly up to my lower belly. "Might want to add me to your to-do list just so you can check me off, baby."

"Speaking my love language," I mutter. I immediately regret using the word "love" even though I didn't use it in the traditional sense, and I freeze.

Hadrian rocks back into the chair and pulls me onto his lap once more, threading a hand through my hair. "We're gonna take this slowly, Bluebell, but I promise it'll fit because you were made to fit me, and I think we both know that."

Gods, he might as well be *confessing* love for the power of that statement. But I can't find a single iota of my being that's willing to deny him.

My mind fills with mental visions of him fucking other women during all the years we've been apart. Unbidden, a soft growl tumbles from me. Hadrian's eyes spring wide, black brows lifting.

"That sounded a little jealous, Bluebell. You want to tell me what's going on?" Reaching between us, he slips his dripping cock between my thighs so I'm riding the top of its length. Fingers digging into my hips, he drags me from his crown to the root, then rolls his hips so he rubs against my clit.

Heat shatters through me, my eyes rolling back into my head. "Thinking about you learning how to do this with some other bitch makes me mad," I admit, reaching out and grabbing one of his horns. I yank it, pulling his face close to mine. "It makes me feel a little bit stabby, if I'm honest."

Hadrian nips at my mouth and pushes me back down the length of his cock, then forward again, soaking his dick with my honey.

"There weren't many women in all those years, Bluebell. The whole time I was chasing something that might feel like you, though. And every time I did this, I can admit to thinking about you, wishing it was you, fantasizing about you the whole time."

He shrugs as his cock pulses between my thighs. "Probably not fair to those few partners, but I always wanted to come home to this."

Channeling jealous rage into heat, I use my grip on his horns as leverage to thrust along that huge cock, letting it kiss between my pussy lips and nudge my clit from side to side. Just as quickly as before, bliss builds until my belly's on fire with need, legs quivering.

Hadrian never stops watching where we're connected, not until he reaches down and guides his cock more upright. It pushes against my pussy, nudging me partway open. Even like this, I'm split wide around him.

"It'll be perfect, little witch," he croons softly. "Let me do it. You relax."

"Relax, yeah," I mutter.

But he uses his left wing tip to push me back onto his outstretched right wing, like a cushion behind and beneath me, angling me so he can thrust upward.

"Grab ahold of my wing tip, baby," he commands, jerking his head toward the wing holding me aloft.

Reaching up, I grip the base of the sharp tip like a handle. He groans and shunts his hips, and the head of his cock breaches my channel. The metal bars drag along my inner walls in a way that sends heat curling through me. But he's big, so fucking big.

He slips back out, and immediately I cry for more. I could do more than an inch, I swear I can.

The next push of his hips sends several inches inside, and I gasp at how stretched, how full my pussy is. It's too much, and I claw at his wing, gasping for air as his cock kicks inside me.

"Fuck, Bluebell you're gonna be the death of me if you keep clenching like that." His lips curl as he slides back out. "Relax, baby."

"*You* relax!" I bark out. "You're not the one taking a giant monster dick in your human-sized pussy!"

"Count the inches for me," he rumbles as his tail spade sneaks between my ass cheeks, poking at my back hole.

"Oh gods," I gasp out, "that's too much; give me a second!"

"One, Hadrian," he commands. "Let me hear it, little one."

"One," I manage as he rocks softly into me, just barely.

"Two," he murmurs.

"Two," I repeat. "Fuuuuck." Those delicious piercings inch magically further as my thighs start to quake.

"Gonna give you three through seven a little faster," he says with a low, sexy chuckle. With a quick snap of his hips, he thrusts deep inside me, filling me so full, all I can do is dig my fingers into his skin and beg for mercy.

"You got a few more inches, baby." He reaches down and

guides me on and off his cock while I fall forward on his chest, doing my damnedest not to come too fast.

After pulling out, he thrusts back in and leans into my ear. "Eight, Bluebell, let me hear it." Moving his hands to the hem of my shirt, he pulls it carefully over my head. My bra is next to go.

"Eight," I sob as he teases with gentle, methodical thrusts.

"Nine," he croons. "Almost there, sweetheart."

My thighs shake so hard, I can barely hold myself up, so Hadrian reaches down and grips my ass in both huge hands. Pulling me on and off, he works his cock deeper until I've fully lost count of the piercings and inches. All I know is he touches something inside me that needs more heat, more roughness, more depth.

"That's it, Blue." His fingers dig into my hips as he pulls out and slides his cock over my clit. "Gods, you're so fucking wet, little mate."

I clench, and he sighs. "So wet and pretty, and I'm dripping all over you. Can you feel it?"

Risking a glance down, I gasp at seeing how he's depositing sticky strings of precum all over my clit and pussy lips. Gods, could anything be hotter than this? He growls again and shifts between my thighs, snapping his hips a little harder, sending his length inside me again.

"Almost there," he pants. "You're doing so good. How does it feel to ride your best friend, to know we both wanted this for so damn long?"

"Oh fuck," I manage, shifting my hips and spreading myself wide around him.

He hisses out a deep groan and halts. "Wait, baby. If you do too much of that, I'm gonna lose it and go too hard."

"Do it," I groan, wriggling to get more. Everything's on fire, everything's tight and achy like if I don't get all of that dick, I might actually expire.

He plunges faster this time, plunging nearly to the root, cock throbbing inside me as all those piercing do the work of several sex toys.

I press off the inner surface of his wing, using the claw like a handle as I sit down harder on top of him. We let out matching groans as heat flares through me, his piercings nudging me that much closer to exploding.

Hadrian leans forward and pulls my left nipple between his teeth. The shocking pain of his fangs mixed with the hard, cool suction has me mewling and falling forward over his head. I move my hands to his horns and rest on my knees, spread around his waist. The new angle means I get to be in charge of how fast and hard we do this.

And I like being in charge.

Snarling, I sink all the way onto him, a triumphant cry leaving me when he gasps and halts, both hands digging into my thighs.

"Gods, oh fuckkkkkk," he snaps. "Give me a moment."

"Say please," I bark, barely able to give the command but loving that this is my Hadrian, and I can say whatever I want.

He looks up between my forearms, eyes flashing as his tail snakes down to nudge at my back pucker. "Two can play that dangerous game, Miss Tucker," he says in a low, devastating tone. "I could make you say please right now."

"You first," I manage as I slide off him and then sink back down.

His second hiss is more desperate than the first as he reaches his right arm behind him and grips the back of his chair. "Fuck, do it again, little witch. You're close; I can smell your need."

"I'm not," I lie as I rise up and then impale myself for a third time. Now that I've adjusted, he feels better than ever.

"Lies," he barks, flaring his nostrils as he surges forward and closes his mouth around a spot along my shoulder. When he bites, the pain throws me over the edge, and orgasm smashes me from the inside out. My pussy clenches around him, bliss radiating in waves that batter me so hard, time and space disappear. There's nothing but the kick of his cock as he unloads inside me, the messy slap of his hips against mine and all that cum and honey dripping out of me to form a pool at the base of that magical coke-can dick.

His teeth press harder as he groans into my skin, and that sound prolongs the ecstasy until I can't see or hear anything. Nothing exists outside of how we're connected.

I don't know how much later I begin to notice the chill of the night or the faint electrical hum of crickets out in the field. Hadrian breathes rapid-fire against my neck, his muscles trembling and tense until I slump against him with a desperate groan.

He wraps both wings and arms around me and sinks back into the chair, still buried deep inside me. Aftershocks roll through him, and he moans softly, little thrusts stroking my G-spot and threatening to start this all over.

I can't talk. Can't think. Can't manage anything other than breathing against his neck as I wrap my arms around him. He smells like he's always smelled—glycerin soap and something deeper and decadent like rich chocolate.

He sighs happily and rubs his head against mine. "The real you is better than any dream I ever dreamt, Bluebell. Better than any fantasy. You're a gift, little witch."

Mate. I want him to be mine. I want it with an intensity I've never let fully fill me before. But I'm full of that intensity now.

And just like that, it's "stick a fork in me, and I'm done." Hook, line, and sinker. Game over. Or whatever other metaphor there might be. Because Hadrian Alkazar started this thing between us, and I don't think I could go back to a life without him.

Hadrian

When I wake in the morning back in my apartment, soft snores echo from my nest. Which is about the moment I remember I have a little sister. Dismay rushes through me, quickly followed by depthless frustration. I don't know what to do with a kid. After everything with Bluebell last night I gathered Petra up and drove us all back into town. Both girls slept on the way and my need to protect had me practically feral the whole way home.

I'm in no way set up for this—not here in my apartment and not yet at the ranch. It's barely livable out there, and with my game schedule, I figured it'd take me the better part of winter to get it fully ready. And that was fine. I'd wrapped my mind around that.

The realization that I was on the precipice of having everything I wanted, and now there are considerably more roadblocks has me frustrated beyond belief. Glancing over from my spot on the sofa, I stare at Petra. She's asleep in the nest, body curled around a pillow, flopping her tail softly in her sleep. She looks even younger than her nine years.

What am I going to do with her?

Rising, I run my hands through my hair then stalk to the door. I cross the hall and knock on Bluebell's door.

The soft pad of feet announces her arrival, and when she opens the door, she looks like she slept about as well as I did. Lifting a hand, I drag it along her angular jawline, smiling when she nuzzles into my palm.

"Good morning, little witch," I whisper. "Was last night a dream?"

Her beautiful blush makes an appearance. "Which part? The part by the fire or the part where you have a little sister?"

My smile grows bigger. "All of it, honestly."

Bluebell's eyes drift to the open door behind me. "She still asleep?"

I nod, sliding my hand down her arm to slip my fingers through hers. "Yeah. I was just lying there thinking about how I have no idea what to feed a kid or do with a kid, and—"

"Let me help," she says softly.

I shake my head. "I don't want to pile another thing on your plate, Bluebell. If you'll remember, just yesterday, I promised to take a few things *off* there."

She smiles. "Yeah, and I'm gonna let you, too. Why don't y'all help us with decorating downtown later? There are a few things I like to do manually before the sheriff glamours Main Street to look more festive. And it could be a good way to introduce Petra around, assuming you want to?"

"Will do." I wrap my tail around her waist, cocking an ear to make sure Petra's not up and observing. "I have a late practice, and she can come with me, but we can help until about six, if that works?"

She nods. Just then, my comm watch rings. When I lift my wrist, Jasper's name hovers over the band.

"Hey, bro," he says when I answer. "You figure out what to feed a kid yet? I'm coming over with groceries."

Bluebell's dark brows lift. She looks impressed.

"I was just talking to your sister about that," I say with a smile. "C'mon over."

"Already there," he quips before clicking off.

Bluebell steps backward, and I unfurl my tail from around her waist as I slip toward my doorway. Moments later, the downstairs door opens. Jasper's a loud, exuberant presence as he shoves through the doorway and bounds up the stairs. When he joins us with a huge smile, I take two bags of groceries from him.

"Morning, sis," he says with a big smile, reaching over to noogie the top of Bluebell's head.

She rolls her eyes and swats him away.

He waves at her pajamas. "You might wanna put more clothes on, girl, 'cause none of us want a view of those itty-bitty titties first thing in the morning."

Bluebell barks out a laugh, then disappears into her apartment, padding toward her bedroom in the back.

Jasper jerks his head toward my door. "Shall we?"

I lead him back into my apartment, and we set the groceries down on the small wooden island in the kitchen. Jasper glances over at my nest, then back at me.

"Dude, this is crazy, right? How are you feeling this morning?" Wide green eyes focus on me as he pulls groceries out of their bags.

I shake my head as I do the same. "Shocked. It's gonna take some time for this to sink in, you know?"

Petra yawns and rises from the bed, stretching her wings out wide. When she sees Jasper standing with me, she beams. "Hi, Uncle Jasper! How come you're here so early?"

He waves at her. "Hey, kiddo. I was worried your brother would have no idea what to feed a little girl, so I brought pancake mix, syrup, a bunch of fruit, and then these little sponge cake cup things your brother loves."

Petra bounds across the room and slips onto one of the barstools, smiling at the groceries. "This is awesome! Can I help put it away?"

"Sure," I say with a smile. The apartment door opens, and Bluebell comes in wearing tight jeans, brown leather work boots and a hot pink V-neck tee. It highlights every inch of her muscular figure. Her hair's up in the typical space buns, long tendrils framing her face.

She stops next to Jasper, bumping him with her hip as she smiles at Petra. "Morning, kiddo. How'd you sleep?"

Petra beams. "So good. Hadrian's nest is the best; it's so soft. Have you ever tried it?"

Bluebell barks out a cough, and Jasper laughs. "They ain't that kinda neighbors, sweetheart."

Oh my gods. I was very sure she didn't overhear any of what Bluebell and I did last night, but now I'm having doubts.

Bluebell recovers faster than I do. "I make the best pancakes. Should we make some while the guys put the rest of the groceries away?"

Petra flaps up off the barstool, clapping her hands together. "Yessss! I'd love that! Let's do it?" Purple eyes flick to mine, and her smile falls. "I mean...if that's okay? I shouldn't assume we can use your kitchen."

The protective side of my nature rears up, hot and hard. Despite the surprise of Petra's appearance, I don't like her feeling uneasy around me. I remember feeling that way for a while the first summer my folks dropped me off at the Tuckers'. They quickly made me feel at home, but it was awkward until I adjusted.

"My apartment is your apartment," I say with a smile. "Knock yourself out, kiddo."

Petra's smile lights up the room. She and Bluebell move to the other side of the island and start hunting around for bowls and everything they need to make pancakes. I grab a bowl and mixing spoon and push it down the island toward them with a thankful smile aimed at Bluebell.

Half an hour later, Petra scarfs her third plate of pancakes. Bluebell, Jasper, and I stare at her in a combination of awe and shock as she munches the last pancake, eyes rolling back in appreciation.

"My gods, this was so good. I've never had this before, but it's really tasty. Well, we had something kinda similar, but I haven't had it with this syrup stuff. Gahhhh, so *delicious*!"

I zip my lips closed. I've got no idea what Petra's actually been exposed to and what she hasn't. Do they have pancakes in Brazil?

Bluebell gives me a look then jerks a thumb toward my door. "I've got a to-do list a mile long, so I'm gonna head next door and grab my stuff. Be back in a minute, alright?"

Jasper just waves her off without looking up from his practice book.

I glance between him and Petra, but Petra's staring at me with a wary look.

"Be right back," I say as I push Bluebell carefully toward the door.

She's silent as we head across to her apartment. I follow her inside and drag her all the way to her retro green kitchen, the farthest spot from the front door.

Last night we connected in a way that has me surer than ever she's mine. But humans don't mate like that. Despite our years of friendship, I'm sure she's having reservations this morning. I can *feel* them like worms crawling beneath my skin, because my sense of her, the way I read her? It's getting stronger by the minute.

"Talk to me, Blue," I whisper. "I see regret in your eyes."

She shakes her head, planting both palms on my chest. "Not regret. I could never regret last night." Blowing out a breath, she laughs. "It was...life-changing. But what if this is a whole right person wrong time thing, Hadrian? I mean, Petra, my brother... maybe we should just take this slowly."

"Gargoyles don't work like that, baby; you know that," I say gently, hoping it doesn't sound too much like I'm downplaying her opinion. "Is that what you *want*? Or is that just what you think makes sense because you're so damn pragmatic?"

She bites the edge of her thumb. "Erm, the second one."

I smile and grab her hands, shoving them up under my shirt to rest over my heart. "That's what I thought, Bluebell. We can't hide and dance around this forever. But we can keep this quiet for a little while until other things calm down, if you want. It might even be fun to pretend I'm your dirty little secret, but I don't think either of us will be satisfied with that for very long."

She purses her lips while she considers my words. After a moment, she looks up. "You're right. I want to hold your hand in public. I want to yell at Merit and Bryony that I don't give a fuck if they share a picture of us. I don't want to hide you."

"Good," I whisper. "Put me at the top of your to-do list every day. We'll find time. We'll keep it a secret. For now."

Dark blue brows lift. "Sounds to me like you might need help with your house, on account of me being a black witch and all. Maybe help with your cutie pie little sister. I'm going to be around a *lot,* Mister Alkazar."

I bend down to brush my lips against hers. "Good, Miss Tucker, because there's nowhere else in this entire universe I'd want you to be."

Bluebell

Petra smiles up at me as we descend the stairs toward the side of the building. "So, you need help with decorating or something today? Can I help? I helped Dad and his wife with their research for a while. I'm an excellent listener; Dad said so."

Something breaks inside me at her words. She's never been in a haven, never had pancakes, never met her brother until yesterday. I mean, they basically dumped Hadrian with us when he was about the same age, leaving him for the summer and conveniently only showing up every few haven years.

We just loved him so much that we kept him.

"I'd love to have your help with the decorating. Normally we glamour most of downtown because it's an easy way to decorate but there's a couple hours' worth of work we prefer to do manually. I'm meeting my friends Lemon and Oz to knock that out. Pine Gulch hosts a lot of festivals, and monsters from all over the haven world come to visit us."

She hops up and down, wings flapping at her back. "What kind of festivals? What are you celebrating?"

I tuck both hands into my back pockets. "Let's see. There's the Fall Ball in autumn. Mead Cute is coming up and that's kinda fall themed too. Yule Love It happens in the winter and then of course there's a new year bash and a Sweetheart Ball right after. And that's just the next couple of months!"

She looks up at me. "Do you do human Halloween? I always loved watching humans on that holiday even though I obviously didn't participate."

"We do," I say with a laugh. "Even though it confuses most monsters because, well, we're *already* monsters."

Her smile goes soft as I hold the door open so we can exit into the alleyway between our building and the next one. "So which festival is this one?"

"Mead Cute," I say with a smile, waving her toward Main. "It's a good time for the younger monsters too. Maybe you can meet some kiddos your age."

"I'd like that," she says, wrapping her tail around her waist.

Jasper and Hadrian trail behind us until we get to Main. At the corner of the building, Lemon and Oz stand with matching coffees in hand.

"Morning, bestie," Lemon chirps, handing me one of the coffees. She glances at Petra. "Who's this cutie?"

Petra smiles between Oz and Lemon. "Hi! I'm Petra. I'm Hadrian's sister. I just got here."

Lemon's mouth drops open as she looks between all of us over to Hadrian and back. "Sister? I...was not aware."

"Nobody was," Petra says. "I surprised everyone, so, surprise!"

Lemon and Oz go silent, but Oz speaks first. Reaching out, he claps Petra on the shoulder with his tail.

"Girl, you are gonna *love* the Gulch! There are tons of gargoyles here. Not to mention your brother is, like, our star skyball player. And we're gonna be decorating town all morning, *plus* Bluebell plied us with lunch, so it's honestly gonna be the very best day." The pit hell lurks around his feet, sticking her face between his thighs as she looks up at Petra. "This is Ginger," Oz explains.

Petra smiles at him and lifts her tail spade up level with his chest.

I chuckle when he slaps it with his. It's such a childlike thing to do. Next thing I know, she's going to slip that spade under someone's shirt to feel their heartbeat...another thing gargoyle children seem to adore.

That heartbeat obsession makes me think of Hadrian and... last night. I desperately need to catch up with my besties.

"Well," Lemon says, "y'all ready to do this? We all know Bluebell's got an entire to-do list in her back pocket."

I smirk as I glance down at Lemon's feet. Today she's wearing her iridescent turquoise boots...hardly the most practical of things. But then again, Lemon never did care about practicality.

"Let's do it." Hadrian pushes me gently forward with a hand in the center of my back.

Next to us, the building clatters all of her siding expectantly. A piece flips outward and whacks Oz in the side, poking him several times as it nudges him into Main Street.

I bark out a laugh, smiling at Petra. "Also, the town herself has some mighty strong opinions. You won't believe some of the things you'll see around here. She might toss drunkards into the street or slap Oz on the butt or any number of spicy behaviors."

Petra eyes the building nervously, but follows us.

Lemon points to her truck, its bed open and full of decorations from the storage shed out at Furyon's place. "This is gonna be fun!" she shouts.

Three hours later, at least one of us is having fun as Petra sits on Hadrian's shoulders, tacking the last of our twinkle lights into a hook on the side of the Welcome Inn. As I look around, a smile pulls to my face. Main Street looks absolutely gorgeous, and when dusk falls, it'll look even better. Sparkly glitter lights crisscross over the street, highlighting the train tracks that run up the middle.

"You know what, Hadrian?" I turn to him with a bright smile. "We should take Petra on Mabel. What a great way to see all of Pine Gulch."

He grins up at the young gargoyle, who's staring back at him like she's already in love.

Shit, girl, I think that makes two of us.

Realization courses through me. Is it possible to fall in love with someone in such a short amount of time?

Except it's not short, because I've been falling in love with Hadrian Alkazar for the better part of two decades, which is like a quarter of a human life.

"Today's not good for that, but I'm off tomorrow." He pats her on the knee. "You want to ride a train tomorrow? You can see all four corners of the haven plus the mountains and maybe the mustang herd if we're lucky."

Petra smiles down at me, wrapping her hands around Hadrian's long horns and yanking on them like they're joysticks. "Only if Auntie Bluebell and Uncle Jasper can come! Can you? Can you come?!"

Hadrian stares at me, then lets out a laugh. "I am not fully equipped to be a brother slash father, so please do come with us." He elbows Jasper in the side. "You too. You're on uncle duty."

Jasper shoves his hand in a bag of chips, retrieving a huge handful, which he promptly shoves in his mouth. "Only if you feed me. Long as there's food, I'm good."

I share a quick smile with Hadrian, but one thing is clear to me after spending this morning together—I'm in love with my best friend. It's not easy, and it's not gonna get any easier because hiding him sucks. The doubts in my mind aren't about him; they're just about the things that keep popping up between us. But I'm not sure that even matters anymore. I don't think I could deny Hadrian Alkazar if my life depended on it.

* * *

"How's Hadrian holding up with this whole sister thing?" Mom whispers to me as she hands me a bag of shredded cheese to top the giant tray of macaroni with. She glances out the window where my brothers are playing skyball with Petra in the back yard. Unfortunately for them, she's picked it up quickly and appears to be kicking their asses on account of her having wings and them being entirely human.

Until Jace touches the ground, and a vine snakes up fast, wrapping around Petra's ankle. She squeals and laughs, dropping the ball. Jack snatches it up and sprints out of view.

I sigh. "We haven't had much chance to talk about it where she couldn't hear, but I think he's still pretty shell-shocked. I mean...you know his folks well. Did you have any idea?"

Mom's eyes go wide as she purses her lips and shakes her head. "Honestly? We were all close before we had kids but once we had the twins, our priorities shifted. Theirs never really did, I don't think. It's not *that* surprising they didn't take the time to bring her here."

I suck at my teeth as I watch Petra barrel past the window, shrieking with Jack running after her, pumping his arms.

"They're kind of adorable, aren't they?" I muse as Petra spins and knocks Jack to the ground.

"Damn, that athletic gene runs in the family," Mama says, parting the blinds to get a better look. "She bounced right off his head like Hay used to do when he was a little nugget. You remember that?"

Oh boy do I. Because even at eight years old, I loved watching Hadrian play. Maybe it's the athleticism of a gargoyle in comparison to a human. I don't know. I just knew he was important to me then just like he is now.

"Is Hadrian coming tonight?" Mom grabs the bag of cheese from me and starts doing it herself.

I shrug. "Not sure what time practice ends. I just told him if he was late, I'd take Petra back to my place until he's done."

"Well," Mama says, "I know you'll be real helpful to him, not that you've got much free time."

"I sure don't," I mutter, snatching the cheese bag back to finish it myself.

She wraps an arm around my waist and presses her head to mine.

Forty-five minutes later, the boys are still outside with Petra, but the giant tray of mac and cheese bubbles happily in the oven. I put the finishing touches on a huge salad and head into our tall dining room to put it on the table. When I turn around, Petra's there with a smile and salad tongs in one hand.

She hands them to me. "Your mom said I should bring these in. Can I do anything else to help? I didn't realize you had already cooked, and I'm sorry I didn't come help you do it."

I shake my head. "Not a big deal, honey. I'm just glad you were having fun with the guys. They're awesome, right?"

Her dark lashes flutter against high purple cheekbones. "Do you think my brother will be here soon?"

I fiddle with one of the napkins. "You missing him?"

She nips at the edge of her finger and nods. "Yeah, I mean... I've been hearing stories about Hadrian for a while, you know? I feel like I know him even though he doesn't know anything about me."

Rubbing her shoulder, I offer what I hope is a comforting smile. "You've got plenty of time to learn all those special things about him too. And now that you're across the hall, you can visit me anytime, and I can tell you some really funny stories about your brother. We grew up together, you know."

Petra's eyes fall to my chest, and she smiles. "I can hear your heartbeat; it gets fast sometimes like the humans we lived with in the jungle. Do you mind if I touch it?"

I've met enough gargoyle children to be familiar with this compunction, and I don't want her to feel shunned, so I nod. "Yeah. Go ahead and thanks for asking."

She slides her tail up around my neck, the tip snaking just under the neckline of my tee. When she rests her spade over my heart, I smile at her. For a long moment, she stares at my chest. It stretches into a full minute and then two.

Moving slowly, she pulls her tail out of my neckline and curls it around her neck, then hangs on to it like a bath towel. "That was cool, I see why Hadrian likes that sound. I can tell he does, I mean."

My blood freezes. I hope she doesn't mean...

Jasper stomps into the kitchen and thumps Petra on the nose. "Your bro just called. They're about done with practice, and he's gonna come meet us."

Petra grins at him. "So should we wait until he gets here to eat?

"Hells no," Jack barks as he follows Jasper into the kitchen. "There is literally no reason on this planet that we'd delay dinner. Not even for skyball, and like we told you, the Tuckers are the Punishers' biggest fans."

Dinner's as raucous as ever with the Jays and my parents. Per usual, Jace is a quiet presence next to me, reading a book in his lap while picking at the macaroni.

I nudge him when I see the textbook he's holding. "Whatcha learning tonight?"

He looks up and smiles at me. "You see that vine I grabbed Petra with?"

I nod.

He winks at me. "I'm learning to pull them up out of the ground no matter how far away the nearest plant is. Basically, stretching my magic past what I can immediately see, which is surprisingly hard to do. Jasper can already do it, of course, but I'm learning fast."

"You're the best Tucker," I whisper to him, squeezing his hand.

He turns it over and rubs my fingers with his. "I know."

I snort as I pinch his wrist. His quiet wit is my favorite thing about any of my brothers. It's not cool to have a favorite, but Jace has always been mine. Maybe I should remember that next time I worry about how Jasper might respond to Hadrian and me dating.

Looking around the dinner table, I feel like things will work out. Mom and Dad are joking with Petra. Jack and Jasper are bickering with one another. But then the door opens, and quiet footfalls reach us.

My breath hitches when Hadrian appears in the doorway wearing a black-and-gold Punishers tee that highlights his enormous arms and shoulders. The coloring I did has worn off and he's back to that gorgeous purple hue. It must be an older tee; it's not one of the ones I had made, so it's tight...everywhere. Dark gray sweatpants do nothing to hide thick thigh muscles. When he reaches down and scratches at his hip, I can't stop staring at the thin sliver of purple skin visible between the top of his pants and the lifted shirt.

A smile ghosts his face.

Oh fuck him, he's doing that on purpose.

"Hey, brother!" Petra leaps out of her seat, slapping Jack on the head with her spade as she jumps into Hadrian's arms. She's obviously picked up the Tucker dynamic quickly.

He picks her up awkwardly, although her arms snake right around his neck, tail flopping happily. When she finishes her hug, he sets her down and runs a hand through his hair. Black waves hang around his ears and neck, and my fingers ache to reach up into that beautiful hair and tug that head back.

Hadrian's nostrils flare, and he looks over at me from beneath hooded brows. Petra returns to her seat next to me, patting the empty one next to her. "Here, brother. We saved you a spot."

"Not much mac left, though," Jasper says with a shrug. "Show up late, and that's how it goes."

"I gotchu," I mutter, leaving my seat and heading for the kitchen. I'd already made a plate for him and put it in the oven.

When I return and set the plate down, he looks up with a big smile. "Thanks, Bluebell. You're speakin' my love language with food."

I barely withhold a smirk. "You're welcome."

"Ewwwuh," Jasper shouts from across the table. "Don't you

two start." He tosses a dinner roll at Hadrian. "You know she's off-limits."

Cheeks blazing, I return to my seat as I struggle to get my mind off the way Hadrian talked to me last night. And this morning. The way I want him to talk to me all the time. It's weird sitting here in the room with my entire family with this secret occupying my heart.

"It's so nice that you all have one another," Petra says. Her comment stops all the side conversations.

My mom throws her hand over her heart. "Aww, sweetie, we're just so glad you're here with us now."

Petra nods but looks down at her hands clasped on the tabletop. "I never had friends in Brazil, not really. The group we lived with had a few children, but we weren't ever super close. It's hard being...different, you know? Mostly I was alone a lot after Mom died."

The table is utterly silent. I can't think of a single thing to say to that.

"You come to our ranch anytime, young lady," Dad says with a fierce look. "Once the Tuckers accept you, you're literally a family member for the rest of your life."

Jasper nods. "We've already got one little sister we love; a second one might help even out the vibe, ya know? Hadrian's pretty much our brother."

Oh gods. A second little *sister. Hadrian's pretty much our brother.*

I squeeze her arm as I stand, mumbling about hitting the restroom. My whole family's reassuring Petra as I head through the kitchen and to the back door.

A second little sister.

I need two minutes of space to wrestle with my emotions about all of this. It doesn't surprise me when footsteps echo after me. Except for when I turn around and find Jace standing there with his hands in his pockets and a knowing look on his face.

He steps closer. "You wanna tell me why you high-tailed it outta there like your hair was on fire when the Jays called Petra our second sister?"

I scowl at him, crossing my arms. "You always *were* too observant for your own good, you know that?"

He shrugs, glancing at the blue mountains off in the distance. "What can I say? If I wasn't the observant one on our jobs, who knows what would happen with the twins in charge."

When I say nothing else, he cocks his head to the side. He doesn't speak either, though, and he knows I hate silence. I'll fill a silence anytime.

"It's been a crazy few weeks," I hedge. "Buying the Bodice and discovering she hates being owned by me. Hadrian moving across the hall and Petra showing up. The Mead Cute Festival is in a couple days, and Lemon's opening the damn Keeper's house. It's just...there's *so* much going on, and sometimes I wish I could disappear for a few days and just wipe my slate clean, ya know?"

He eyes me with a soft smile. "Any particular part of that got you wound up more than anything else? I know the Jays have been asking a lot of you lately. I've been meaning to talk to you about that, by the way."

I wave away his concern. "Nah, it's just...all the things."

Reaching out, he slings an arm around my neck and pulls me close. Like always, the rich soap he uses fills my nostrils, and I smile. He's the only male Tucker with a fancy grooming plan that includes anything scented.

"Love you, Bloob," he says softly.

Just as I open my mouth to return the affection, my comm watch pings, and one of our renters' names hovers over the band.

Jace tugs my hair playfully before walking off. "Don't think I'm gonna forget about this conversation."

Sighing, I look up at the stars winking down on me as I direct the watch to answer.

"Bluebell? This is Angelina over at cottage two forty-nine.

We've got a leak, girl, and water is sprayin' all over the damn place! Can you help?!"

"On my way," I say as I head around the side of the ranch house to where my truck is parked in front.

Truly, there is no rest for the weary.

Hadrian

The following morning, I'm making pancakes with Petra's help. She slept in my nest again, and my back aches after another night on the sofa. I'm used to sleeping stretched out in the nest I had specially made at Hearth HQ. Although, based on how well Petra's sleeping in it, I have to wonder if she ever had a nest of her own.

A knock at the door interrupts my thoughts. Jasper shouts from the other side, "Let me in, asshole! I brought more food for your sister!"

Chuckling, I pick my way across the small apartment and yank the door open. Jasper stands on the other side, flashing me the middle finger as he dips past me and into the room.

"Hey, little one," he says to Petra. "Brought you donuts from Skylight Bakery across the street. Tell me you've experienced donuts?"

She shakes her head as Jasper and I join her in the kitchen. "No idea what a donut is, but I smell sugar, I think?"

He tosses the box of donuts on my island. "Girrrrrl, prepare to have your mind blown. Skylight makes about three hundred types of pastries, but the donuts are the absolute best. Go on and toss those pancakes in the garbage. Also make sure to save one for my sister. If she thinks I forgot her, she'll eagle screech and, ugh, I hate it."

Petra scoffs. "Throw food away? Are you kidding? I just learned to cook them!"

He looks at me. "Hey, don't you have an away game tomorrow?"

I nod, risking a look at Petra, who's staring between us with an observant look.

Jasper jerks a thumb at her. "What are you gonna do with the little one?"

She slaps him on the top of the head with her tail spade.

He laughs and swats at her swishing tail. "I'm just saying! Obviously you can come with us if there's not another plan."

"I don't have a plan," I admit. "I hadn't gotten that far. We were gonna tackle that today, right, Petra?"

"Right," she chirps as she dumps a half cup of pancake batter on the sizzling pan.

"I don't feel comfy leaving her in my hotel room, and she can't hang out on the sidelines without guidance. I'll just worry about her the whole time, and I won't be able to focus."

Petra scoops a spoonful of the batter and slips it into her mouth, licking it off the spoon as she looks between us.

"Gah!" Jasper shouts, grabbing the spoon from her. "Not raw, P! There are eggs in there if you did it right."

She shrugs. "I've eaten plenty of raw eggs. That's why I'm strong like Hadrian."

Jasper scrunches his nose but looks between us. "Listen, the Jays and I are headed to Mykel Shorthorn's ranch most of today and tomorrow. Let me take her with us. Mykel's got a young one about the same age, and they've got a bunch of horses too. We can teach her to ride."

"Ride what?" Petra takes another scoopful of pancake batter and bites it off the spoon.

"Horses," Jasper and I answer at the same time.

Petra's mouth drops open. "I've seen those in books! Oh my gods, I would loooove that."

I slip my tail to her hair and tug gently on the end of it. "You feel okay chillin' with the Tuckers overnight?"

She grins at Jasper. "You mean my *uncles*? Yeah, I think it'll be awesome."

Jasper stands and opens the donut box, snagging one before he turns for the door. "That's decided, then. Call me when you're ready to drop the kiddo off, and we'll take over from there."

I'm grateful for him for stepping up to help out with Petra, but I want him to do it for Bluebell too. It's a struggle to think of how to say that right now without sounding ungrateful though.

"I'll pack fun stuff!" Petra shouts at his retreating back, taking another bite of the pancake batter.

A burnt smell rises up from the stove, and I chuckle. "Your cakes are burnin', honey."

She yips and spins, grabbing the pancake with her long nails and tossing it onto a plate. Turning to me, she smiles and tucks her knees against her chest. "I'll miss you while you're gone, though. Sometime I'd like to see you play skyball. It seems fun."

I'm not sure what to say. Can I miss someone I barely know?

She rests her cheek on her forearm. "I know you didn't expect me. Neither did your mom or our dad. I was just in their way even though I tried not to be. Pretty sure they were excited when I said I wanted to come meet you. But I'll try not to be in your way, too."

My heart might not beat, but it cracks into a million pieces at the way she views herself within the Alkazar family unit. In that moment, I'd love nothing better than to throttle my parents for ever letting another child feel this way. It mirrors my childhood so entirely, I could cry.

Pulling Petra into my arms, I wrap my tail around her core so she's roped to me.

"Don't ever worry about that with me," I whisper into her

hair. "This might have been a surprise, but I will *always* be your brother, okay?"

"Okay," she mumbles, but she doesn't sound like she entirely believes me.

Pulling back, I flash her a bright smile. "Listen, let's play a game. Every day you tell me something I don't know about you, and I'll do the same. Before you know it, we'll know one another's' deepest, darkest secrets."

She looks up at me. "What about when Dad comes back?"

I tuck her dark hair behind her pointed ears. "Let's not worry about that just now, okay? They sent you to me for a reason. I wasn't ready for that, but have patience with me, okay?"

"And what about Bluebell?" she asks. "I like her, and you like her...right?"

"Yeah, I like her," I say. "She's been one of my best friends for my whole life. Her and the Jays. The Tuckers are kinda like my real parents, to be honest. I know them better than our mom and dad."

She shakes her head. "That's not what I mean. You *like* Bluebell, like, as a mate...right?"

I straighten, shocked. Running both hands through my hair, I debate what to say. Ultimately, I decide it's okay to trust Petra with this secret.

"Yeah," I say softly. "But we haven't told anyone yet, especially not her family. So...keep that secret between us, little one, until the time is right. This can be secret number one."

She smirks at me, holding her tail spade up for a high five.

I slap mine to it, chuckling. "How'd you even know?"

Petra laughs. "Your eyeballs get all squishy in the corners when you look at her."

Gods. Okay.

"Luckily, I'm good at secrets," she says in a satisfied-sounding tone. "Your secrets are *safe* with me."

Bluebell

Has it only been a day since Hadrian left for his away game? Petra's been hanging with the Jays and my parents, and I've been working nonstop. Shroud brought Vela by, going through the scavenger hunt from our haven welcome book. They're so adorable together and so obviously in love. She's assimilating into monster life so fast!

Downtown's looking great for the Mead Cute Festival. Lemon and Oz are bugging Sheriff Rygold to install the festive glamour later this afternoon. Only he can do that part since he's our stand-in Keeper.

I slept at my folks' last night to help with Petra, and I haven't even been home. It surprises me when I get back and open my door to find a folded slip of paper sitting on top of a box full of cookies.

My name is scrawled on the front in Hadrian's handwriting. Smiling, I unfold the pale blue sheet.

Little Witch,

I miss you already. Call me after the game if you get a free minute. I'll be done around eight p.m. tomorrow.

Yours, Hadrian
P.S. Enjoy the snacks

The note is short and sweet, and he must have left this yesterday, meaning that he'll be free at eight p.m. tonight. Glancing at my comm watch, I note that it's just past eight already. Rushing across my small living room, I head for the bedroom where I keep the communication disk that allows us to make interhaven calls.

Grabbing the disk, I toss it on the bed and direct it to call him.

He picks up on the first ring, his life-sized hologram rising tall from the disk. A smirk ghosts his face, and he's shirtless, wings held aloft at his back. Lifting his chin, he drops his gaze down my body and back up.

"You look beautiful, Blue. You just get home?"

I nod and slip onto the bed, dropping the disk at the foot so I can stare up at him.

"I did. Just found a nice little note suggesting I call."

His smirk grows. "Everything okay at home?"

"Petra's fine." I rest on the bevy of pillows against my headboard.

"I was concerned with more than Petra," he says. "Tell me about your day."

I sigh. "Do you really want to hear about my shift at Whiskey Business or any of the other shit I did today?"

"Yes, I do." He cocks his head to the side, tail twisting behind him. "And then I want to try something."

Gods, that sounds sexy. I nip my lip expectantly. I fill him in on what seemed like the most mundane of days, but he asks a million questions about every aspect of it, even questioning me about how the Bodice is today. Unfortunately, I didn't spend any time with her because Tiana is covering the shop for a few days.

"I still haven't figured out how to get on her good side," I admit.

He laughs. "Oh, I'm gonna help there. We're just going to

force her to tell us what she needs so we can provide it...together. I promised to help with that and haven't had much chance to, but once I get back, it's game on."

I groan. "A sports reference, really?"

He steps forward, his hologram enlarging. "You been thinking about me while I've been gone?" He reaches down and slips his hand inside his pants. "I've been thinking about you nonstop, Blue."

Oh gods. Are we really doing this? The sight of Hadrian staring at me like I'm his dessert while he's got a big hand inside his pants has me soaking my panties.

"Yeah," I admit. "I've been thinking about you too, Alk."

"Need a nickname," he demands. "And I need it now, baby. Try something, anything, to see if it fits."

"Alk doesn't sound good anymore?" I drag my fingertips along the hem of my shirt, pulling it up to flash a little skin. His eyes trail my movements.

"Baby, Mate, Mine, even the full Hadrian is perfect. Something, Bluebell, anything."

"Mate," I whisper. Is it too soon? It feels weirdly soon but also perfectly right to call him that. His eyes flash then go hooded, and he flares his wings wider, draping them over the edges of the bed.

"Say that again," he commands, stroking his cock inside his pants. "Again, Bluebell."

"I miss you, mate," I say softly. "I need you back home, big boy."

"Fuuck," he groans. "Need you to call me that when I'm buried inside that sweet wet pussy." He lets out another possessive growl. "Slip your hands between your thighs. Do it now."

Commanding, possessive Hadrian? I need that like I need air. Pulling my jeans open, I slide them slowly down my hips and pull one leg out, letting it fall wide. Slipping my fingers down, I pull my underwear to one side to reveal my slick pussy. Hadrian licks his lips, running a hand over his mouth as he stares.

"Baby, you're already wet for me, aren't you? Should we take care of that?"

I chuckle, dragging my fingers down my pussy lips and back up. "We haven't spent any time in a bed yet, come to think of it. Or a nest."

He stares at me for a long moment. "Bluebell…come here to me."

I smile, moving my fingertips to my clit. When I circle it, heat fires through me, nipples pebbling against the fabric of my tee. "Why don't you help me feel better, mate?"

He groans and shoves his pants down, revealing that beautifully thick, long cock. "I'm serious, come meet me," he says, lifting his chin defiantly as he strokes himself with both huge hands.

I shoot upright. "Wait…are you for real?"

He keeps stroking, a blush darkening his purple cheeks. "Yes. I'll send you the address. Come here. We can be wild and crazy and free of everything that weighs us down in Pine Gulch. It'll be like Santa Alaya, except now you know what you are to me, what's between us." He groans as precum drips from his hard cock.

A million reasons why this is inconvenient flicker through my mind. But then I watch him jacking off as he smiles at me, mouth dropped open to reveal those gorgeous white fangs.

"Be there as fast as I can," I say.

He pulls his hand out of his pants. "I'm not gonna come without you, baby. Write this address down. I'll be waiting, alright?"

The address is smack in the middle of Laporte, the New Orleans-based haven. I've never been there but always wanted to go. Hadrian clicks off so I can grab a bag. I guess I'll be there overnight. Will anyone miss me here?

Petra's safe with my folks and brothers. I'm not working at the bar tonight or tomorrow. I've already sent all of the Jays' invoices to their clients, and they're set for the week. The rest of the week is purposely slow so Jasper can finish practicing for his test. There's no reason I can't disappear for a night. No reason at all.

After throwing on dark jeans and a dark hoodie, I sling on a backpack and head out of the building. When I get to the door to the alleyway, the building opens it for me. Shocked at the kindness, I hike the pack higher and smile, looking around the small landing area.

"Umm, thank you? I appreciate that very much."

The building creaks and quakes, and the door shimmies back and forth. It's the friendliest sound I've ever heard the Bodice make at me, which is really saying something considering the events of the last week or so.

"I'm going to see Hadrian," I whisper. "He says we need to figure out how to make you feel comfy with me but that we'll do it together. I would really like that, if you can give me any hint at all about what you need."

She shimmies the door once more, almost like she's telling me to go again.

Smiling, I press a hand to the inside of the door. "Thank you, Bodice."

She waggles the closest siding, and the sound is friendly. Oh my gods, are we turning a corner? I can't believe it.

The building shimmies, the hallway quaking as a door upstairs slams open. I'm silent, waiting to see where she takes this. The door slams again, and then the stairs flatten, and a pair of handcuffs slide down the flat surface toward me.

Shocked, I drop to a knee and pick them up. Staring around the building, I bark out a shocked sound. "Is this for Hadrian?"

Another shimmy. An internal quake that honestly sounds like laughing.

Okay we've *definitely* turned some kind of corner. Tucking the handcuffs into my bag, I stroke the door to the alley as I thank her again.

A quarter hour later, I park my truck at the portal station. It's busy at this time of night with travelers coming to PG for the

Mead Cute Festival. Nobody pays me any mind as I step through the portal and disappear.

It takes me another thirty minutes to get to Laporte and make my way to Hadrian's address. When I get there and take the elevator to the opulent hotel's top floor, I take a moment to fluff my hair in the mirror-like surface of the elevator interior.

When the elevator doors open, Hadrian stands there wearing nothing but sweatpants and a smile.

"Hello there, little witch."

Hehe
Bluebell, come here
Ding
Hello there, little witch

Hadrian

Bluebell steps out of the elevator, pulling the hoodie over her head. Instead of the usual space buns, she's wearing her hair down long. It trails down over her breasts to the middle of her belly. A belly that's covered by clothing I can't wait to tear off her.

"You came," I manage. "I've been waiting, little one."

She slips both hands up my stomach, feeling her way along the chunky outlines of my abs. "You made a pretty compelling case, hot stuff." She pauses as I stare at her, raising a brow.

We burst into laughter at the same time, and she shakes her head. "Okay, that nickname did *not* work. Gonna have to try another one."

"Big boy was nice," I say. "Mate is good. But, yeah, I want something else too. I'm selfish. I want all of you, Bluebell."

She looks both ways down the hallway. "So, you got the entire top floor of the hotel again or what?"

Reaching down, I pull her up to straddle my waist.

"Nope, just a single room, but the rest of the team is spread all around the hotel. No one to hear us, no one to bother us." I stalk down the hall with her in my arms, pushing the door open with my foot. The room's as beautiful as they always are. The Punishers pay for the very best.

Bypassing the kitchen and living room, I walk to the giant nest in the middle of the bedroom. It's an unusual layout, but one I like. I can watch television while I'm falling asleep, when my mind won't turn off. Which happens more often than not.

Laying Bluebell in the center of the nest, I fall on top of her and slot my body between her thighs. "You look so pretty in this nest," I whisper, eyes dragging down her tiny form. I dwarf her like this. I'll always dwarf her, giant in comparison to her humanity.

Flaring my wings wide, I wince at the way my left one aches.

Bluebell shoots upright. "Hadrian, what's wrong?"

I fold the wing at my back, ignoring the pain that shoots along my topmost bone. "Just a little tackle during the game."

She rolls her eyes. "I'm literally a black witch. I can fix that." She slaps my belly. "Onto your stomach."

I know Bluebell, and she won't let this go. So I flip over and unfurl my right wing. Bluebell crawls onto my back and seats herself just above my ass.

"This might burn a little while I'm locating the source," she murmurs.

Closing my eyes, I focus on the sensation of her warm hands running up my spine to my wing. Her fingers tickle the edges of my topmost bone, and an uncomfortable heat follows her fingertips. I groan when she reaches the spot where the big minotaur tackled me.

"Hush, baby," she whispers, wrapping her hands around my bone.

My hard-on pokes into the nest's soft mattress, and I roll my hips to relieve some of the pressure. "'Baby' sounds good," I groan, rolling up onto my elbows, forehead pressed to the soft surface.

"Be good for me then, *baby*," she says in a confident, sexy voice.

Sparks of her magic flutter along my wing bones until the heat is almost too much for me to take. Somehow the pain just amps my lust and need. Maybe it was the earlier tease. Maybe it's just knowing we can do whatever we want for a single night...no one to interrupt us or need us for something. No one to burst in my door and demand my time.

"Bluebell," I moan. "Finish that and let me kiss you."

"Hush," she whispers, running her fingers along my wings. Up and down. Across and over and up again until I'm groaning into the soft sheets, clutching them in my fingers as I resist the urge to roll over and toss her down.

Take her.

Please her.

Keep her.

Feed her and do it all again.

I'd swear my heart is throbbing in my chest but I know it can't be...not until a mating bite happens. Still, that sensation of pounding inside me intensifies.

The refrains repeat in my mind as her soft, warm breath ghosts along the back of my wing. Magic slips beneath my skin, running like a faintly warm river along my bones and into the sore spot where that damn minotaur crashed into me.

"That's it," she murmurs. "Just relax, baby."

"More, please," I beg.

She huffs out a quiet laugh and slides upward until her hips are nestled at my lower back, her knees just beneath the lowest part of my wing. One hand moves to the middle of my back, and she uses that to prop herself up while her right hand feels further along my wing. Soft spells punctuate the air as she works her magic on the injury.

By the time she's done, I'm sweating and panting into the sheets, desperate for more. I know better than to interrupt Bluebell in the middle of her work, though. It's not like she hasn't healed injuries before. It's just never been like this, at a time where she came to me for something else entirely.

She grabs my wing and stretches it out, patting the middle of my back with her left hand. "Open your wing fully, big guy. How's that feel?"

"Big *boy*," I correct. "I like it when you call me that. I wanna be your big boy, Bluebell."

Her tone drops low with her next command. "Open that wing for me, big boy. I want to see how huge and pretty it is."

Gasping, I push onto my forearms so my back hits her chest, stretching my right wing out. She hums a happy sound and runs her right hand over the warm bones. Sparks of heat travel from my bones to my spine and down to my lower back.

"I think you need a little bit more work," she says in a throaty tone. "Flip over for me, Hadrian."

Brain running on lust-fueled fumes, I carefully roll to my back and hang my wings off the bed so I can stare up at her. Bluebell nips her lower lip as her eyes scan down my figure.

Bright blue eyes flick to mine, and her lips curl upward. "I'm gonna give you a little massage, and I want you to hold real still for me, alright?"

I lift a brow. "I'd stick around after games a whole lot longer if you were doing this every time."

She shrugs as she pushes my shirt up and undoes my jeans. Patting my hip, she looks back at me. "Hips up, help me get these off."

I follow direction dutifully, kicking the sweats down my thighs. My erection strains against the front of my briefs, a hard bar that makes it obvious how fucking attracted I am to her.

"This part would be awkward if you worked for the team but weren't mine," I say with a laugh, pointing to my cock.

"Or sexy," she counters. Leaning down, she draws her blue hair over one shoulder and closes her mouth around the tip of my dick, sucking softly. Heat shreds through me, and I hiss as I rock my hips to meet that sensual touch.

"Mmm," she hums as she drags her open mouth down my length, tracing each piercing with the tip of her tongue.

I watch with fascination as the woman I've loved from afar

laves at me like she can't get enough. It's every fantasy I've ever had, every fantasy I could ever summon—wrapped up right here. She's *here*. Finally.

"More," I moan. "Let me feel every inch of you, Bluebell."

She chuckles around a mouthful of fabric-covered cock, smiling as she bites at the underside of me, careful with the piercings. The way her movements tug at the bits of metal has me ready to come, dripping so hard, I'm soaking the front of my briefs. My abs flex beneath my skin as she pulls the waistband down, slowly revealing my cock.

Precum drips onto my stomach, my dick bouncing against my skin. It's like every ounce of desperation within me is channeling itself into the movement of my dick.

Bluebell brings both hands to it and wraps those thin fingers around it, squeezing tightly. Eyes locked to mine, she pulls her hands carefully down my dick and back up. Swirling her fingers over my crown, she gathers up the moisture there and uses it to jack me again.

Sparks fly from her fingertips and tickle downward as she massages me from tip to base. My hips move entirely of their own accord, helping her, desperate for more of her. I'm still not ready when she leans down and sucks the entire tip of my cock between those sweet blue lips.

I arch and fall back onto the sheets, right hand coming to the back of her head. Steady movements up and down take me deeper and deeper as I resist the urge to thrust hard and fast up into that sweet mouth.

"I'm losing control," I groan between gritted teeth. "Bluebell, stop. Don't stop. I can't think. Godsssssss."

She pulls off me and bends to place a kiss on the tip. "Sounds to me like you're a male on the edge, Mister Alkazar."

When she slides back down onto me, taking me nearly to the root, I growl.

"You keep doing that, baby, and I'm gonna pull you onto this dick and bite you. Gods, I want to bite you so damn hard."

She glances up at me with a saucy look. “So do it, big boy. I dare you.”

A dare?

A challenge?

Snarling, I shoot upward and flip us so she’s beneath me. Wearing too many clothes, but beneath me.

“You’re mine, Bluebell Tucker. I know it. You know it. And the reason we made that pact twenty years ago and I kept that bracelet is because I saved my claiming bite for you. But we both know that; ain’t that right?”

She leans down and bares her neck to me, dragging the slim column over my mouth. “Do it, then.” Her voice is roughshod, teasing.

“You’re pushing me,” I manage, biting the closest bit of skin and pulling it carefully. “I love the way you taste. Have I told you that today?”

“Not today,” she says with a little moan. “But you haven’t tasted that much of me today, Hadrian.”

Snarling with need, I pull her shirt off, toss it aside, and move to her pants next, removing the soft fabric to reveal a bright blue lace ensemble that matches the darkest part of her hair.

“You did this for me?” I roll her to her stomach and kiss the dimples above her ass. “It’s beautiful.”

“Mmm.” She pushes her ass up against my mouth.

Biting my way down the swell of her cheek, I pull the blue lace off with my teeth. Once it’s outta my way, I bring it to my nose and breathe in, closing my eyes.

“You smell so good, Bluebell.” Sucking the panties into my mouth, I moan at her taste. She was hot when she arrived, but these panties are soaked through with need. A need it’s my sole purpose to fill.

She winks at me over her shoulder. “I bet the real thing tastes even better, mate.”

Mate.

After tossing the panties aside, I pull her ass up and bury my mouth against her pucker, laving at the tight rim of muscle. She rocks hard against me with a needy groan that has my dick throbbing against my thigh. Moving down, I swirl my tongue against her opening. Sweet honey coats my nose and mouth as I bury myself as far inside her as I can go.

Her pussy clenches around my tongue, but I want her desperate. I want her out of her mind. Bringing my hand up, I rub her asshole with one finger while I slide my middle finger into her slit. She jolts and rocks away from me, then back hard, fucking herself on my fingers while I swirl my tongue over her clit. She's gonna come and squirt all over me, and I need it.

Snarling, I focus on eating hard, steady, methodically. Bluebell's thighs quiver against my skin as she starts moaning. The moans turn into cries, cries I've never heard from her because, last time, we had to be quiet. But we don't have to be quiet here.

"Hadrian! Oh gods! I'm so close, I'm—"

Bluebell

I'm close, so fucking close. Heat pools between my thighs as I struggle to focus on Hadrian. His fingers are everywhere, his mouth all over my clit. It's sensory overload, and I'm going to explode any moment.

Just as I hit the top of that beautiful rollercoaster of pleasure, he stops.

Zero contact.

Snarling, I glare over my shoulder. "What the fuck, Hadrian?!"

The look he shoots me is full of satisfaction as he leans forward and reaches a hand around to pinch my left nipple. He's cool against my back, that huge body overtaking me as he envelops us in the cocoon of his wings. Sharp fangs come to my shoulder and bite.

My demanding snarl turns into a plea for more as he drags sharp teeth along my neck and down my shoulder. His mouth is possessive, like he's owning every inch of me, teasing every bit of my skin with the promise of a claiming bite that'll start his heart and bind our souls together.

It's too much, and orgasm builds, rocking me as I chase that feeling with mounting desperation. My body's coiled tight like a snake as he thrusts against me.

"I'm not even inside you yet," he says with a soft chuckle, pulling my earlobe between his teeth. "Say my name, little witch."

That sexy little comment is the last straw, and bliss shatters through me, rippling through my core in waves that radiate over and over and over. I'm crashing against a shore, dashed against the hard planes of Hadrian's body. His mouth never leaves my neck, those fangs threatening to stake the claim he keeps promising me.

"Say it," he grunts.

His name mixes with the screams that erupt from my throat. For the first time, I let them out. They explode from me, echoing through the room as I let him hear every ounce of my pleasure. My voice breaks on the last scream, just before I slump to the sheets, sweat coating my body. Every muscle trembles as orgasm's aftershocks shoot through me in miniature bursts.

Hadrian laughs softly against my neck. "That was fucking beautiful, mate. Now let's do it again, but together. I wanted you to squirt, and I didn't get what I wanted."

I groan, arching my back and rubbing my ass against him. I need that magical mouth on my skin, those fangs tantalizing me with promise. The idea that he could bite me and keep me, that it's really so simple? It's intoxicating.

Hadrian's tail snakes up and loops around my neck, squeezing softly. It's like being collared, like I'm his pretty little pet, and it's fucking hot. He could control me any way he wanted to, and I'd be helpless against him.

Reaching between us, he notches his cock against my pussy and pushes softly, giving me just the first inch or two. "Tell me you're in deep with me," he growls into my ear. "Let me hear it, Bluebell."

"So deep," I groan. "I'm lost, Hay. Lost in you."

His rumbly snarl tells me everything I need to know. He's lost too.

"But why does it have to be so complicated? I don't want it to be."

The world crashes in around me despite the slow, intense pulsing of that magical ringed cock.

"*We* are not complicated," he corrects, slapping his tail spade against my chest. "Things *around* us are complicated, but what's between you and me is as natural as breathing. Tell me you agree."

"You're right," I manage as I shove backward, trying to impale myself on that gorgeous cock. The bars on the underneath almost seem to vibrate as he starts thrusting faster and deeper. His hips snap against my ass. But then that extra bit of bone vibrates against my clit. He stops thrusting long enough to circle his hips, grinding over my pussy as lightning radiates from my core.

"Again," he demands before biting my neck, harder this time. "Give it to me again, Bluebell. Another. And another. And another."

But an idea just came to me based on his comment from earlier about gametime healing.

"This is highly atypical, Mister Alkazar," I say breathlessly, looking over my shoulder. "I'm your team's healer, not your personal fucktoy."

He halts behind me, his cock halfway inside, and it flexes at my filthy words. Shit, maybe he's not int—

"Is that right, Miss Tucker," he says, falling forward and pressing my body to the mattress with his. He shoves inside me hard, *so* hard it nearly steals my breath. "And yet I find I can do whatever I want to you, isn't that right? Because you didn't deny me when I asked you to come to me."

Sweat beads across my brow. "It's unprofessional; we should stop."

He chuckles and the depth of his voice might as well be a finger pressed to my clit. Everything inside me lights up and tightens and I can't hold back a mewl.

"You touched *me*. You unleashed *me*," he says with a deep rumble. "I'm not stopping all night, little healer. I'm going to fuck you until you're boneless and then I'm going to do it again. We can keep this a dirty little secret from the team if you want, but *after* every game, you're mine."

"Only if you win," I snap.

Gods. It's role play but it's our real life, too, because I want to be the first thing he does after every game.

"You can't make me agree to that," I manage, bucking my hips to try to shove him off.

Not that I ever could.

He slings his tail back around my neck and uses his wings to hold me flat as he places a hand on the back of my head. I turn my face to the side so I don't suffocate on the damn mattress as he grips my left hip and pounds into me.

"Say we'll never stop," he demands, his voice rough and demanding. "Say that you can't get enough of me, little witch."

I'm so screwed. So totally screwed. Because I can't keep this play. Before I even know what happened I'm coming to the sound of Hadrian's satisfied, throaty laughter.

* * *

"You alright, Bluebell?"

Glancing to my right, I force a bright smile for Tiana. She's working all day, and I just came in to do inventory and shelve some packages that arrived this morning.

Has it only been two days since that magical night in Laporte?

I'm meeting Hadrian and Petra shortly to go over to the team breakfast. I've just got to dodge my family until then, which could be hard since my brothers don't have an appointment this morning. There's a very solid chance they'll be downtown.

"I made progress with the Bodice yesterday," I whisper, careful not to talk too loud in case the building decides she isn't into the progress anymore.

Tiana's brows lift. "Progress? How do you know?"

I look around. It's such a tentative progress.

"She opened the door for me." I nearly squeal with excitement.

Tiana grins and rubs my shoulder. "That's a definite improvement. See?! I told you things would be fine between you two."

The Bodice rumbles overhead, but it sounds happy enough to me.

"You feeling alright, sweetheart?" I look around, cautious not to touch the building knowing she doesn't like it when I do.

She rumbles again, and this time the sound is plaintive.

Tiana looks around. "I think she might want help, Bluebell. You should try."

"Them critters probably got back in."

Tiana and I whip around to find Rebekah, the Bodice's original owner, standing in the doorway with both hands on her thin hips. She smiles, her vampire fangs showing.

"Don't look so shocked to see me. Surely Hadrian told ya he called and I was on the way?"

Sputtering, I try to find the words to respond but fail to. He comm'd me a few times this morning but I was in meetings and not able to answer.

Tiana rounds the desk and crosses the floor, pulling Rebekah into her arms. "Bek, it is *good* to see you, honey. The Bodice ain't been the most welcoming."

Rebekah tsks and rubs the building's front door. "Sweet girl, what on earth? I left you in the hands of the most capable black witch I've ever met. How could that not be a match made in heaven?"

The Bodice lets out a string of awful-sounding, displeased noises.

Concern brews in my belly, but my magic sparks and sputters at my fingertips in response to the building's sad display.

"C'mere, Bloob," Rebekah says, waving me toward the front. "I'm so sorry I haven't been around. Just got back last night from two weeks in Santa Alaya with my grandbabies, and lords alive, it was so lovely. But I need you two to be happy together!"

When I join her, she takes my hand and slaps it on the wall. The Bodice rumbles, but the noise she lets out is less harrowing than in the past.

"Feel her," Rebekah croons. "Past the pain. Just let that flow over you. She's always been persnickety. I suspect we got a mix of that and something wrong going on."

Shoeboxes fly off the wall behind Rebekah, but the vampiress just laughs. "I see you, girl."

Magic courses through me as a sense of the building travels through my body. Something's bothering her...something physical. Something in the storeroom, almost like a sore tooth.

"Supply room," I murmur as I pinpoint the source of the pain.

Rebekah smiles at me. "She gets right bitchy when she's in pain, and that's how I always knew to call you to fix her in the past. She never really showed that in front of you, so I didn't think to mention it. I assumed y'all would sort that out naturally."

She jerks her head toward the back. "Let's head back there and see if we can fix this."

We cross the floor and pile into the storeroom. I feel around along the walls until I find a spot covered by boxes. When I move them aside, there's a scratching sound inside the wall.

Placing my hand on the wall, I gasp at the Bodice's pain. Magic flows from me and into the building, spreading along the plaster and deep into the brick behind it. Forcing my magic up along the cracks of achiness, I whisper a spell under my breath to fix what's wrong—termites.

They're one of the most agonizing things for a building, literally eating from the inside out, and while we don't see them often out here in Montana, when they do show up, they're a real pain in the ass.

"You're gonna need a few treatment sessions, pretty girl," I whisper.

To my surprise and relief, the Bodice shimmies happily, the

shoe boxes clattering on their shelves. It's the first normal response I've seen from her, and it makes my heart so damn full.

Tiana appears in the storeroom entrance. "Didn't you say you had somewhere to be this morning, Bluebell? It's almost nine."

"Oh shit!" I shout, darting past her. "Thank you for the reminder. See you later, T! And thank you, Rebekah! Dinner before you leave?"

"Bye, girl!" she hollers as I fly out the front door. "Find me later! And I'll keep coming around to help if you need it!"

Rushing around the corner and upstairs, I nearly run smack into Petra, who's standing in front of my door with a fist raised like she's about to knock. When I appear at the top of the stairs, she turns to me with a tentative smile.

Her hair's in something like space buns, but they look absolutely crazy.

"Bluebell, oh my gods, I'm so glad you're here." She points to her hair. "Hadrian tried to do my hair like yours, and it's the absolute worst. Can you fix it?"

I chuckle as I look at whatever he did to her hair. "Yeah," I say with a laugh, waving her toward Hadrian's open door. He appears in it, shrugging.

"Did my best, but it's so much harder putting someone else's hair up."

Petra scrunches her nose. "You've already got yours up in a bun. How much harder can it be?"

I push her toward one of the barstools and hop up onto the bar, thankful I've always got a ton of extra ponytail bands around my wrist. Petra glances up at me, snaking her tail around my neck to rest over my heart.

When I freeze, she blanches.

"Sorry, I didn't realize it's not super okay to just do that. Umm, do you mind if I leave my spade there?"

"It's fine," I say softly, glancing at Hadrian.

"I know your secret," she whispers with a half smile. "So if you want to hold hands in front of me or anything, it's okay!"

His expression's cautiously neutral, but he smiles softly at the way her tail's looped around me.

I'm surprised and unsure of how to respond, so I focus on her hair instead. Working quickly, I finger-comb it up into space buns that match mine. At the last minute, I wonder what sort of message it'll send to Hadrian's teammates if she and I match. Ultimately, I decide I'm going to put mine in a regular ponytail for the breakfast thing this morning.

"I'm gonna go change while you two wrap this up," Hadrian says with a smile. "Be back in a minute, okay?"

"Okay," Petra chirps.

When he disappears toward the bathroom, she smiles up at me. "You're his mate, right?"

Shocked, I work on the second space bun while I try to sort out what to say. That that's what this is between us, and it's not just regular two-decades-long attraction? Even though we haven't told anyone? I don't have doubts about Hadrian. It's the *reveal* that has me worried.

"I don't know about all that," I finally say, figuring that's the best answer for now.

"He does, though," she says, "and I can tell, too. Because of the way you look at each other."

Gulping around the lump in my throat, I debate even responding.

"I'm super glad," she says. "Because you're so nice. But Hadrian said we have to keep it a secret because everybody doesn't know yet. How come you don't want them to know?"

"It's complicated."

She cocks her head to the side. "How, though? Gargoyle mates are fated; nobody can deny that. Is it a human thing to not believe it?"

Oh lawd, I'm not even sure how to respond, so I'm endlessly grateful when Hadrian shows back up from the bathroom. He's got on a Punishers black-and-gold jersey and tight jeans, some of the ones I just had made for him.

"You two are a sight for sore eyes," he says. "You ready to go, girls?"

Something about him calling us girls warms places inside me I didn't even know needed warming. He smiles at me. "I'm thinking we should fly. You alright with that?"

I debate saying I should drive and they can fly, but I'd honestly rather be in his arms than anywhere else.

He waggles both dark brows. "It's literally just an excuse to have my hands on you."

"I want that," I say with a laugh. "I want everybody to *know* I want that."

His smile grows thoughtful as Petra and I head for the back of his apartment where we installed an oversized window for him to come and go from. He opens the window, and I stare at his huge biceps flexing beneath purple skin. Petra smirks at me, then rolls her eyes playfully when I pretend I wasn't looking.

Gods oh gods, if we keep this up, Jasper is gonna figure everything out in two seconds. And maybe that's fine, in the end.

I'm just not ready to have that conversation today. Although, maybe it would be good because then we could go on a date in public instead of slinking off to other havens to hang out together. This girl is not meant for secret dating. I'm the worst at secrets, which is why I had to immediately talk to Lemon and Oz.

Hadrian pushes the window open, and Petra hops out, dropping a few feet before flapping up and away. He turns to me and opens his arms. "Come here, baby."

It's on the tip of my tongue to tell him not to call me that in public, but damn, Petra already knows.

Sliding my arms around his neck, I allow him to nestle me around the waist, his big hands on my back and ass. He hops onto the window ledge, easy peasy, and then out into the air.

Which is about the time it occurs to me that anyone in the pumpkin and gourd garden or the flea market or hanging out at the auction house can potentially see us right now. Part of me wants it to happen simply because I can't and won't hide him forever. Maybe it's better to rip off the Band-Aid.

Shit, I can't even hide against Hadrian's big frame because I'm the only monster in town with royal blue hair.

Hadrian bullets straight up into the clouds, not slowing until we're up out of the misty chill. Petra flaps smoothly beside us as we head north toward Rip Shorthorn's ranch. Icy wind blowing off the mountain range has me shaking despite being in Hadrian's arms. He flaps faster, bulleting through the sky.

In just a few more cold minutes, we begin to descend out of the sky and back through the clouds. Sunlight filters through, warming me as the wind begins to slow.

Hadrian touches gently down and sets me on the ground, smiling as he drops me to my feet. The Shorthorn barn is behind us. Past that, faint sounds float toward us—children laughing, guys shouting. Playing skyball, if I had to guess based on the reason for the breakfast this morning.

"Hadrian!"

Rip Shorthorn emerges from the barn with his big arms held wide. He wears a big smile as he walks toward us, taking in me and Petra. If he's surprised to see either of us here, he doesn't show it.

When he joins us, he bends down and smiles at Petra. "Hello there, youngling. Hadrian tells me you gave him quite the surprise earlier this week. That musta been kind of fun."

Petra laughs, tail swishing from side to side. "Yeah, I mean, I've known about him my whole life, so it was definitely easier for me. Poor Hadrian. Hope it hasn't affected his skyball skills."

Shorthorn chuckles. "Your big brother's a true pro, little one. Separates his personal life from the game. We're just glad you're here."

Petra slings her tail around my waist, pulling herself close to me. I stare between her and Rip Shorthorn, who watches the movement of her tail with apparent interest. A smirk pulls his fuzzy lips slightly upward.

"Must be my turn for a surprise, Miss Tucker," he says to me. "Didn't expect to see you here."

I don't even know what to say to that, but Hadrian comes to my rescue. "Bluebell's my best friend, Coach."

He gives us a disbelieving, affectionate smile. "Mhm. This haven is full of love lately. Been a while since I've seen so many folks I admire find one another. Happy for you both, for sure. If you're lucky, maybe you'll have what I have with my Pollyanna. Seven calves and seventeen grandcalves later, and I think I'm the luckiest male in the world."

"Every one of them is a sweetie too," I compliment. I've known the Shorthorn family my whole life. I've just never seen Rip in this sort of scenario.

Rip jerks his head toward the barn. "Y'all come on through. Pollyanna's cooking breakfast outside, and the team's playing two-touch tag." He smiles at Petra. "Tons of other kiddos here too. At least half our players are already mated with families. You might make a couple friends, young one."

Petra cheers and takes off toward the barn, leaving us behind.

"Kids are so adaptable," Shorthorn murmurs as we watch her go. "She's sticking with you for a while, right?"

Hadrian nods. "Seems like it."

If Shorthorn has thoughts about that, he doesn't share them.

"Shall we?" I ask, anxious to get to the pancakes now that the scent is wafting toward us.

We head through the enormous barn—the site of at least four or five haven-wide parties each year—and out the back into the big field between the barn and the ranch house. A giant outdoor kitchen situated at the back of the barn is the site of a pancake breakfast for the ages. At least half the team sits with their mates and children, digging into piles of luscious-looking golden pancakes.

Rip's mate, Pollyanna, directs two of her grown sons at a long, flat griddle. They refill the plates on the tables as we find an open spot at a long table.

I recognize every player here and most of their mates as well. What are the chances of this *not* getting back to Jasper? Although, I don't think he hangs out too terribly much with the mated players, so our secret is probably safe for a little while longer.

One of the players looks up with a smile. "Ah, so you must be the reason I can never get Hadrian to come out with us after games."

My brows rise, and I bark out a laugh, lifting both hands in supplication. "Not me. We're just friends."

Wrong. Wrong. Wrong. It feels so incredibly wrong to say that.

Hadrian pulls a seat out for me. "I brought two surprises today—my best friend, Bluebell, and my surprise sister, Petra. Figured I didn't want to show up empty-handed, and my buddy Jasper's on a job today."

That's a lie. Jasper is most definitely *not* working today, but I suppose it suits the flimsy story we're telling.

The other player, Zakaria Longhorn, beams at us as he shoves a plate of pancakes across the table. "Alright then, Hadrian's sister and Bluebell, of course. Eat up, y'all. The dancing starts at nine thirty."

"Dancing?" I hand the pancake plate to Petra, who snatches one and shoves it right in her mouth before slapping four more on her plate. "I don't do dancing. I've got two left feet."

Hadrian looks under the table. "Yuck. You do? I never noticed that."

He winks when I scoff at him.

Petra glances under the table, looking genuinely concerned. "Wait, are you for real, Bluebell?"

We all laugh as she disappears under the table and yanks my shoes off, examining my feet for a full minute before I can convince her to come back out.

Half an hour later, music comes on from overhead speakers, blaring out over the field and the outdoor kitchen. Petra's gone, playing touch skyball with the other younglings. Now and again, she appears next to the griddle with another young gargoyle. They steal a pancake and dart away, all raucous laughter and swishing tails.

Flashing a smile at Hadrian, I wave at Petra. "She fit in pretty fast, hmm?"

"Like it was meant to be," Hadrian says softly.

I look over at him, because it sure doesn't sound like he's talking about his little sister.

Purple eyes scan my face, and he smiles. "Dance with me, little witch?"

My mouth goes dry as he stretches a hand toward me, palm upturned. It sits there for a moment, waiting. Glancing around at the monsters who surround us, I realize nobody is even paying us any mind. Hadrian's open hand is still there like the sweetest representation of *everything*.

Fuck it. Jasper's gonna find out sooner than later.

Curling my fingers into his, I return the smile as he pulls me to a stand. I'm *so* aware of the other monsters as he guides me toward the dance floor. A dozen or so couples swirl around the parquet surface.

"Look at me," Hadrian commands.

I snap my eyes to his at the demand in his tone.

He pulls me against his far larger body, lifting my hand up to his chest. One of his hands rests on top of mine, and the other comes to my waist, sliding partially up my back. "I need that focus on *only* me," he croons. "Let me lead, Bluebell."

Everything around us fades as bright purple eyes stare into mine. He never looks away as he spins us around the dance floor, swaying to the rhythm of the music. One song becomes two, then three, then five until we're laughing and flirting, and what anyone else thinks is the farthest concern from my mind.

The music picks up pace, moving from a slow song to something jazzier. Pulling me to the edge of the dance floor, Hadrian leans back against a wooden column, slotting me between his big thighs. He tangles a hand in my hair and brings his forehead to mine. "I wanna kiss you, little witch."

My lips part at the possession in his tone. I want that kiss. No matter the cost.

Popping onto my tiptoes, I slant my mouth over his. He sighs against my lips, rumbling as his mouth opens. A soft, cool tongue slips along my lower lip as he tastes me gently, tenderly.

Both hands come to my arms and hold me tightly against him as his kiss grows harder and more heated.

"I knew you loved him," Petra says from somewhere by our side.

Shocked, I leap backward as Hadrian chuckles, the sexy moment broken.

"I guess it's not that big of a secret anymore, huh?" she continues on, tail swinging from side to side as she grins at us. "I can't wait to tell absolutely everyone!"

She pushes off the ground and takes off toward the ceiling beams as I hiss her name and grab at her feet, barely missing her.

"Don't worry," Hadrian says. "She'll keep the secret until we're ready, baby."

But the thing is, I *am* ready. I don't think I can hide Hadrian much longer. It's not fair.

Hadrian

I can't keep her a secret. I don't want to, and, just, I can't. At the team breakfast this morning, all I wanted to do was call her my mate in front of everyone. That kiss? I'd have deepened it, taken it so much further if Petra hadn't shown up. Being with the girls and my team felt right in a way that's been missing from my life. If I'm honest, I've never had family like what I'm building now. Petra even made a few friends and we organized a couple of playdates.

These roots I'm putting down in Pine Gulch don't look quite like I imagined, but I don't care because it's even better.

"No, dude, you don't put the cinnamon coating on the apple pie beforehand. That's so weird!" Jack slaps Jasper on the back of the head, cinnamon crumbles falling from his hands all over the pie.

I'm dating your sister. I love her.

I'm barely withholding the words as the twins bicker back and forth about cinnamon and sugar.

Tucker family dinner has always been my favorite night of the week, but right now it feels like we're here too much. What I want is to be at home with Bluebell, hiding away from the world and lavishing my love on her. The typical gargoyle mating traditions are hard to do when one can't publicly express his love.

Not that that stopped me earlier.

Bluebell shoots me a warning look, a desperate plea not to announce our secret just now.

"We're doing it my way, dude," Jasper barks, grabbing the cinnamon and covering the pie with it. He sticks it in the oven with a victorious smirk.

Jack tosses a dinner roll at Jasper's head. I catch it before it hits him, smirking at him as I throw it back at Jack. It bounces off his head, and Jasper and Petra burst into peals of laughter.

Next to me in the kitchen, Bluebell's tense and quiet. That's not necessarily anything new for her at family dinner. She's usually thinking about her insane to-do list. But I suspect this has more to do with us trying to hide our romance from the five other people in the room with us.

She needs something to relax.

I pull out her chair and wave her into it. Her brothers follow, taking their seats. It takes a few minutes for everyone to find their chairs and start passing the food around.

Unfurling my tail from my thigh, I slip it over the top of Bluebell's thigh and nestle it in the seam of her pussy. She jolts and masks a clearing of her throat as a cough. The Jays keep poking fun at Jack for his crush on someone, so nobody's paying attention to us. I use my spade to nudge Bluebell's jeans button open then slide her zipper quietly down.

She reaches down and grabs my spade, shoving me away, but I grin and move it back up. Across the table, Petra grabs two bread rolls and tosses them at Jasper. Both hit him in the head, and chaos breaks out around the table.

"Food fight!" Petra shouts.

Elena and Bill bark for everyone to stop, but their warnings are lost in the chaos.

Jack hollers to high heaven and grabs a tray of bread rolls, dropping one in Jasper's water. When it splashes over the side and onto his book, Jasper snarls at his twin.

Elena nudges Petra. "Come with me a second, honey. I got something to even up this fight."

Petra whoops and follows Elena out of the room.

I push my spade inside Bluebell's jeans, reaching beneath the table to pull her right knee out, giving myself space to tease her. She jerks a second time when I touch her pussy with my spade, rubbing it up and down with quiet, low vibrations. She rocks her hips, once, twice, then grabs a bread roll and stuffs it in her mouth, moaning softly.

A dinner roll flies past my head. I duck and slide my tail lower, curling it into a cone and slipping the tip inside her pussy. She grips the edge of the table, knuckles going white as she coats me in slick honey.

Smiling, I grab a tray of lasagna and offer it to her with a smile. "Want more, Bluebell?" My smile is teasing.

"Fuck yes," she says softly, cheeks dark pink and mouth dropped open.

I set the lasagna down and cut another piece as I fuck her slowly, quietly with my spade. It's so hot, doing this when we shouldn't. After cutting another piece of lasagna, I slide it onto her plate and top it with shredded parmesan.

She grabs her fork but grips it so hard, I think it might bend in half. Stabbing the fork in, she spears a huge piece and stuffs it into her mouth.

"Bluebell, honey, are you alright?" Her father's brows lift as he stares at Bluebell from across the table.

I don't stop my delicious, entirely inappropriate movements, angling my spade so I can fuck her and rub her clit at the same time.

"Just, mmph, hungry," Bluebell mutters around a mouthful of dinner. "Lasagna's my fave, you know."

"Okay, sweetheart, just slow down so you don't choke," Bill warns.

Bluebell's thighs quiver as she starts to tighten around my tail. She's gonna come all over the place, and nothing could please me more than for that to happen. I'm thankful human senses aren't anywhere near as good as monsters'. Nobody will know what's going on.

Bliss hits her, and she reaches beneath the table and grabs my tail, squeezing it so hard, I nearly come from the dominance of the move. As she shatters around me, I force another bite of lasagna, struggling to hold an impending orgasm at bay. Everything about her pleasure sparks mine. She flutters chaotically around me until ecstasy fades, then she slumps in the chair and picks at her lasagna.

Nobody seems to have noticed a thing. The Jays are still arguing and Elena and Petra haven't returned. Next to me, Bluebell's a soaked mess, leaking sweet honey all over my tail. After withdrawing it carefully from her channel, I move it back to my thigh and wrap it around. I'd love nothing better than to suck her off my skin, but that's going too far.

Still, a dark, deviant part of my gargoyle nature is half considering doing it.

"You get enough to eat, Hadrian?" Elena asks as she returns.

I grin at her. "I'll eat anything you make, Mama Tucker. You know that. Seconds. Thirds. Not sure I can ever get enough."

Bluebell makes a choked sound as I beam at her mother. Oh, yes, a little deviance is suiting me *just* fine.

Elena turns to Jace, tucking his hair behind his ear as she asks him something about his day.

Bluebell leans close to me. "You for real right now?"

I give her a saucy look. "No idea what you're talking about. Wanna enlighten me?"

Growling, she reaches down and carefully and quietly zips up her jeans. Then she grabs my plate and hers and heads for the kitchen.

"He might not've been done, Bloob," Jasper shouts at her retreating back.

"Oh, he's done!" she shouts back.

He gives me a quizzical look, but I just shrug and keep smiling. I can't say what I want to say.

Just then, Petra swoops back into the room with two water pistols and starts shooting all three Jays. Chaos erupts as they scramble to get outta her way. Jace rolls his eyes and ducks beneath the table. The twins jump up and dash from the dining room with my sister hot on their tails.

Hours later, Petra's asleep on the Tuckers' living room sofa. Elena and Bill are snuggled up in their oversized recliner watching a game show, and Jace has disappeared to his room. The twins, Bluebell and me are sitting around the dining room table playing gin rummy. Per usual, Bluebell's kicking our asses.

Jack slaps my shoulder. "Hey, y'all wanna go skinny dipping? I invited a couple of girls to meet us in five minutes."

Jasper snorts. "What if we'd said no, asshole?"

Jack matches the saucy sound. "When have you ever said no to skinny dipping with girls?" He flashes me an amused look. "Sorry, Bloob. I didn't invite any men for you, and we're all your brothers, so come if you want, but I can't promise I'll be on any sort of good behavior."

She laughs. "No surprise there. I'll come just to keep you out of too much trouble, unless you don't want me to."

Jasper tugs on one of her space buns. "Long as you don't mind seeing a bunch of big-ass dicks."

She scrunches her nose. "Appealing as you make that sound, I'm good."

"Come, it'll be fun," I encourage her. "I can hide their dicks with my wings so you don't have to see 'em. Plenty of coverage for those disappointing little things."

She looks between us.

"You should come; we haven't done this in a while," Jasper says. "Maybe bring a bathing suit though. It's my job to protect you and I don't need any of them monster dudes getting ideas, just in case some of them are into bitty titties."

She scoffs. "That's rude. I have to look at your nuts, but you don't wanna see my boobs? Boobs are—"

"Oh gods," Jack says with an eye roll. "She's about to launch into some Mother Earth stuff."

"Maybe you should listen for once." I reach out and slap him with my wing tip. "She's right."

Jasper snorts. "This protective gargoyle thing is cute and all, but this is Bloob, and she can take care of herself." He tosses a dinner roll at her but she neatly dodges it, completely ignoring him otherwise. "Anyways," he continues, "as the eldest Tucker it's my job to protect her."

"Maybe she shouldn't have to take care of herself," I bark before realizing my tone is entirely too aggressive for his joke.

Jasper goes silent, brows rising as he stares at me. He's probably trying to figure out if I'm being serious or not.

The sound of tires rumbling up the Tuckers' drive saves me from saying anything else. Jack leaps out of his chair and rushes to the door, grabbing his coat and flying out without saying another word. One of the girls must be the one Jasper keeps teasing him about having a thing for. Jasper grins and follows, waggling his brows at his mother as he walks out the door.

Bluebell looks at me. "You'd think they were eighteen and not going on thirty-five."

"It's a proven fact human men don't mature until at least their mid-thirties," Mama Tucker chirps from her spot nestled against her husband's chest. "You sure you two want to go with them? I swear you were both born old souls, and skinny dipping doesn't seem up your alley."

"It's not," I admit. *Not with the Jays, anyhow.* "But we've kept the Jays out of more trouble than I can even admit to you, Mama Tucker."

She places a hand over one ear. "Gods, I don't even want to hear about it."

Bluebell sighs as she stands, grabbing her coat from the back of the chair. "Guess we'd better go keep an eye on them."

I trail her silently outside, where Jasper and Jack are talking to four pixie females in a truck.

"Oh boy," Bluebell says.

"Let's go, lollygaggers," Jack shouts as he slides into the passenger seat. Jasper hops into the driver's seat and waves two pixies over so they're smashed between the brothers. Two more slide into the back and wave at us.

"You two coming or what?" one of the pixies hollers from the back seat, leaning halfway out. I think she might already be drunk.

We mostly manage to get into the car without incident...until I try to fold my wings into the back seat.

"Nice wings," one of the pixies teases. "You're a big boy, though, so you might want to hang out of the window a little bit."

Bluebell glances up at me, nostrils flaring at hearing someone else call me a big boy.

"Move over!" the other pixie shouts from the middle of the back seat.

"Fuck this," I mutter, hopping out of the truck. "I'll sit in the bed."

"I'm coming with you." Bluebell follows me and leaps up into the truck bed.

"Dude, make sure my sister doesn't fall out!" Jasper shouts from inside the truck.

As if I'd let that happen.

Joining her, I slump against the window. Before she even has a chance to get settled, Jasper takes off up the driveway, throwing gravel. Bluebell bounces forward, almost falling over the side of the truck until I grab her and yank her back against my chest.

"What the fuck, Jasper?" she shouts at the back window. Inside, the pixies and her brothers laugh raucously. The only light is the faint one from the headlights in front of the truck. Nobody can see us back here, much less hear us.

That means I've got an opportunity.

"C'mere, baby," I murmur in her ear, nestling her close against me as I wrap my arms around her. Sliding my spade up to her lips, I run it over the plump lower one. "How do you taste, Bluebell?"

She sinks hard against me, digging her fingers into my thighs as we bounce loudly over dirt roads. The next thing I feel is her hot, wet tongue sliding along the edge of my spade. Heat shoots through me in a never-ending barrage of lightning bolts. Bluebell's fingers trail up the length of my tail to my spade then curl around the base below it. She sucks hungrily at me as she moves her hips in my lap.

The hard-on I'm sporting could punch a hole through walls. Resting my head against the window, I risk a glance inside the cab. It's dark, although the Jays and the pixies are being loud as hells inside. With my better vision, I can see them, but the Jays won't be able to see shit back here, much less hear us.

Leaning forward, I release a needy groan in Bluebell's ear. "You keep doing this to me, and I'm gonna embarrass myself right here with you in my lap."

She cries out and rocks harder, bouncing up and down as she leans against me and grips one of my horns in her hand. She shoves my spade up her shirt, pressing it against a taut breast, and I'm lost. Lost to the heady sense of knowing she's so entirely mine. It doesn't matter what Jasper or anyone else has to say about it. I'm telling him the moment I can.

Wrapping my wings around us, I cocoon us in darkness to shield her from the wind and Jasper's godsawful driving. We hit a pothole and bounce up off the truck bed, but all it does is ram my dick against her ass.

Snarling, I wrap a hand around her throat to keep her steady against me. My hips move entirely of their own accord as I pound over and over. She's moaning in my lap, grinding against me as her hand tightens on my horn.

"I'm about to come, little witch," I admit into her ear, kissing a trail down the side of her neck. "So fucking hard, teasing you like this." Moving one hand to her hips, I guide her on and off my lap as I slide the other hand inside her jeans and stroke soft circles over her clit.

She jolts and arches against me, body locking up tight. I can't even help it, sinking my teeth lightly into her neck. I imagine it's a claiming bite, that I'm putting all of my intention and obsession into it. One day, when she lets me claim her, it'll create an unbreakable bond between us because she'll pour her intention into it too.

She comes all over my fingers, and I drink her scent in until it fills me so completely, I can't fathom where she ends and I begin. Bluebell snarls and turns, threading her fingers around my neck as she rides my lap harder. She reaches down between us and grips my cock, stroking up and down my length.

"For the love of all that's holy, stop," I moan, letting my head fall against the truck window.

"You deserve this little tease for that stunt you pulled at dinner, big boy," she whispers into my mouth. "You thought that was funny, didn't you? Not to mention that pixie calling you big boy made me want to flip tables. I didn't realize quite how possessive I was feeling over you."

When I chuckle, she drops down and yanks my pants open. Before I can process the move, she dips low and sucks my cock into that hot, sinful mouth. A guttural cry rumbles from my throat as I struggle around the idea that at any moment, someone could turn around. I'm relatively sure they can't see, but that little niggle of worry has my cock pulsing with need.

"Bluebell, fuuuuck," I moan.

She slides as far down as she can, my length hitting the back of her throat and going further. She moans like she can't get enough of me, of doing this, and that alone spurs me closer to orgasm. The truck hits another bump, and she bounces another few inches down my cock. Choking, she slips off and looks up at me.

"Careful, little witch," I murmur, staring into her stunning eyes.

We take a sharp left. I *know* that left. We're almost to Jack's favorite skinny dipping spot.

"Time to put our clothes back on," I murmur, smiling at Bluebell.

She doesn't answer, just bends low and tugs one of my piercings between her lips. Heat shreds my self control as I grip her shoulders and attempt to pull her off my length. She pops up with a saucy look.

"Only to take them right back off," she says with a laugh, sinking against my wing and the side of the truck.

"I wanna keep teasing you," she whispers, knowing I can hear her over the sound of the wind. I leave my wing behind her to shield her from the worst of it, hanging on to the edge of the truck bed as we bounce over the last mile or two to the edge of the gulch.

When we get there, Jasper throws the truck into park so fast, Bluebell nearly bounces back into my arms. Snarling, I bang on the window. "Jasper, chill the fuck out, dude!"

I throw Bluebell a frustrated look. "He always drive like this when you're in the truck?"

She snickers. "You feeling protective, big *boy*?"

"You fucking bet I am," I mutter, watching as she leaps out of the truck bed.

The rest of the monsters pile out, too, but it's all I can do not to stare at her.

Off in the distance, the mustang herd's whinnies echo up out of the night.

"Aww, they're out, awesome!" shouts one of the pixies as she slings an arm around Jack's neck and drags him toward the gulch.

Jasper grabs two of the other girls' hands and follows, hooting and hollering.

I want to grab Bluebell's hand and hold it, but I don't want her to have to pull it from mine when we get close enough for them to see us again.

Leaning in close to her, I drag my fangs up her neck to her ear. “We can’t touch in front of them, not yet, so maybe we should make this a fun tease, little mate. What do you think?”

Her eyes flash in the moonlight, and she grins. “Love that idea.”

For a moment, nobody exists outside Bluebell and me. It’s just the two of us, the rocky riverbank and the cold, waiting water.

Tires screech as more cars pull up. A half dozen of the Punishers hop and fly out, rushing toward the riverbanks with partners in tow.

“Oh shit,” Bluebell whisper-hisses. “What are we gonna do?”

“I almost hope someone says something,” I admit. “I don’t think they will, though, so let’s just enjoy ourselves?”

She glances in the direction of the river, frowning as she seems to debate what I said. Finally, she smiles up at me. “It’s gonna come out sooner or later, right?”

“Let me distract you,” I offer.

A fire crackles by the shore. One of my buddies from the team drops onto a fallen log and pulls a guitar from his back. The first strumming sounds seem to relax Bluebell. Some of the players smile at her as we walk toward the water, but thankfully nobody mentions that kiss from the team breakfast this morning.

Mustangs splash at the far end of the river, content to watch us from afar. Jasper and Jack are already naked and in the water, howling about how frigid it is.

I pull my shirt over my head, then kick the pants off. I’m dying to know if Bluebell’s staring at my half-hard cock, but I settle for the assumption that she is. Closing my eyes, I roll my shoulders and walk to the water. I turn and back in, shooting her a wink as she stares at me, eyes wide.

Someone splashes me from behind, the freezing water sending a chill down my skin. Bluebell pulls her shirt and bra off in one big swoop then drops them to the ground in a pile with my stuff.

My breath hitches as she pushes her jeans slowly down, revealing slim thighs, that godsdamn tattoo, and the soft thatch of dark pubic hair.

"Fuck," I mutter, getting harder as I devour her naked figure cloaked in moonlight.

"Alkazar, we got smores whenever you're done playing around!" one of the players shouts from the shore.

Bluebell dashes into the water, screaming at the temperature as she wraps both hands around her body.

"C'mon, Bloob," Jasper shouts. "Just get them bitties all the way in, and I swear it won't be so bad!"

She laughs as we sluice through the water to meet Jack, Jasper and their dates. Slapping me on the shoulder, she jerks her head toward the riverbank. "I'm gonna need that fire and those smores in, like, four seconds because this is a miserable level of cold."

"Aww, it's not that bad," I say.

She barks out a laugh. "Yeah it's like, twenty degrees closer to your body temperature than mine. I bet this feels just fine for you!"

I roll to my back and float, back-paddling closer to her. "Yep and I could just disappear beneath the surface and swim around for hours. Don't even need to take a breath."

"Stop showing off, Alk!" Jasper shouts. "And put that thing away!"

Bluebell and I share a look just before he lurches out of the water, tackling her into it. They disappear beneath the surface, and I force myself not drag her up into my arms. Moments later they emerge—Bluebell with an angry screech and Jasper with raucous laughter.

"Oh my gods, I'm gonna frickin' *kill* you, Jasper Alan Tucker!" she shouts. Water streams down her hair.

I shoot her an understanding look.

Laughing, she shoves him toward his date. "Get the hells away from me, you big asshole!"

As he falls into the water, the pixie girl diving on top of him with a whoop, Bluebell looks up at me. "You ready for smores, Mister Helpful? Because I literally cannot take this water for a moment longer."

Stepping closer, I put a hand in the middle of her naked back, leaning in close. "I'll feed you whatever you want, Miss Tucker, anything at all."

Bluebell

"Bluebell, honey, you alright?" Mama bumps my hip as she tosses a handful of chocolate chips into her waffle batter. To her right, the entire griddle is covered in sizzling, snapping bacon. I'm *still* cold from last night's dip. Fucking Jasper.

I look over at her with a smile. "Yeah, Mama, just thinking about Jasper's test tomorrow and all the stuff I've got to get done in the meantime. Mead Cute Festival's a day away, and I'd love to do something to surprise him for when he passes, ya know?"

Mama sucks at her teeth. "Listen, baby, I got to talk to you, alright?"

My blood freezes, and I spin to fully face her, eyes wide. "Are you okay? Is Daddy alright? What's going on?"

She grips my upper arms and shakes her head. "No, baby girl, nothing like that."

I breathe out a huge sigh of relief. "At your age, you should know better than to ever utter 'we need to talk,' Mama." Yanking my to-do list out of my back pocket, I wave it in her face. "Look at this shit I need to get done today. Can this convo wait, assuming nobody's dying?"

She smiles at me. "That to-do list can wait, Bluebell Delia Tucker. Give some of that to your brothers, anyhow. Probably

Jace because, if I'm honest, Jack and Jasper are not the ones. Although, I do think they'd rise to the occasion if you were willing to trust them."

When I lift a brow, she gives me an understanding look. "You might as well be my firstborn with how serious you take things, honey. I know it's hard for you to let go because you don't want to fix things when the boys don't do it your way. But why don't you start with Jace, okay? I been suggesting you do this for a while but I'm gonna start demanding, honey. I can see you're stressed."

"Mkay, sounds goods," I chirp, knowing there's no way in hells I'm gonna pass the to-do list off at this point. "Good talk, Mama."

"I wanted to talk to you about Hadrian," she says. "And your relationship."

Sputtering, I throw a hand over my heart, looking around for any sign of the Jays. "Hush your mouth, and what are you talking about?!"

My father traipses into the kitchen with a big smile. "We talking about how you and that boy are in love?"

My mouth drops open as I stare between them in utter shock.

Mom smiles softly at me. "You can't hide love, Bluebell. It shines from both of you like a light."

"Stop," I beg them.

Dad slides an arm around Mama's waist, grinning at her. "You owe me fifty bucks, Elena."

She elbows him. "Guess I do, you old coot."

Lifting both hands, I scowl at my parents. "What in the world are you two talking about right now? There is nothing going on between him and me."

"Lies," my dad says. "Your mama and I knew it would come to this one day, honey. Y'all always been so close. Why do you think when we redid the house, we made everything extra tall? None of us have wings, Bluebell. We just knew that boy belonged here." He takes a sip of his coffee and looks at me over the rim. "You gonna break the news to Jasper one o' these days? I assume you've just been waiting 'cause you know he's protective over you. We probably did you a bit of a disservice in that 'cause we were always tellin' him to watch out for you."

I shake my head, dumbfounded at this fricking turn of events. "Yeah, we didn't want to say it before his test. We didn't want to give him any reason not to be in a good headspace. And honestly, if he's gonna protect something, I'd rather it be my time."

"Smart," Dad says. "We're never gonna rush you, sweetheart," he goes on, "but you should tell him soon because I'm tired of pretending y'all aren't making googly eyes at one another, and Jace knows. Just a matter of time before the other Jays figure it out, and it would be better to be up front."

"Noted," I manage, grabbing a spatula to remove the now burning bacon from the griddle. What the hells am I gonna do with this information?

We fall into an uneasy silence. Well, it's uneasy for me, but my parents act like they didn't just drop a bomb on my damn head. Do I need to call Hadrian and warn him? Part of me is just relieved to have the news officially out in the open to *someone* in my family.

The front door slams open and hits the wall, and my mother rolls her eyes. "If that boy could figure out how to work a door without putting holes in my house, I would dearly fuckin' appreciate it."

"Language, Elena!" my dad shouts as Jack and Jasper pile into the kitchen.

Jack's got Jasper in a headlock, and they roughhouse to the ground. I pile the bacon onto a plate and step over their writhing bodies to set it on the kitchen table.

They look up at me from their spot on the ground. Jasper beams like a kid in the candy store.

"Good thing you're here, sis. I got a huge to-do list for you, and I was gonna tackle most of it myself, but with the test tomorrow, I'm not sure I'll have time."

I look at my parents, but my mother wears a neutral smile.

No, she's waiting for me to just stand up for myself and tell the Jays I'm not their secretary. And I should, I really should. But today is not the day. Doesn't mean I can't lay some groundwork, though.

"Give it to me, and I'll tackle what I *can*," I say grudgingly. My level of resentment at having to do so much for my brothers is gonna bubble over if I can't offload some of this shit. I've got my own problems, not least of which is managing the fallout when we tell Jasper about Hadrian and me.

I shoot Jasper a warning look. "I'm hellsa busy today with a coffee date with Lemon and some folks from monster HQ *and* a shift at the Bodice. So I've got to help in between all of that. I'm not promising to do it all, alright?"

He winks at me. "Heard, sis. I color-coded the list by priority."

I'm not sure I've ever wanted to smack my brother quite this hard.

Reaching into his back pocket, he withdraws a handwritten to-do list and slips it into my shirt pocket. "Thanks, Bloob. You're the best."

"I'm heading out," I grumble, spinning and turning for the door even as my mother encourages me to come back. I'm not hungry anymore, though.

I fume the entire way back to downtown, although I'm cooled off a bit by the time I get there. Parking in front of Brew-HaHa Beans, I sigh as I glance in the mirror. Tiny stress lines frame the edges of my eyes, and the elevens between my brows seem like they're permanently etched. Sighing, I run a hand through my blue waves and debate whether I even look presentable for this morning's coffee thing.

Resting my forehead against the steering wheel, I reminisce about last night. Everything felt right in Hadrian's arms. But in the light of day, we're hiding again, and I'm honestly tired of it. Part of me thinks it would be better to just call Jasper now and spill the beans. He's a grown-ass man. He can deal with it.

Except he's still a little bit of a man-child, and I truly don't think he'll handle it well at all. Which is why Hadrian and I had decided not to tell him until after his test, even though it's stressing us both out.

Groaning at the sheer *inefficiency* of this entire scenario, I exit the truck and head into BrewHaHa. But when I get inside, the minotaur female behind the counter smiles at me.

"Bluebell Tucker. Got a message from Lemon for ya." She winks at me as she clears her throat. "Bitch, bring us some lattes. They should be waiting for you. Come down to the Keeper's place." She shakes her head. "That Lemon sure has shaken things up around here, hasn't she?"

"You can say that again," I mutter.

She pushes a tray of lattes over the counter toward me. "There you go, sweetie. I knew you'd be on time, so I premade 'em."

Thanking her, I grab the tray and head out of the coffee shop, debating if I should stop into Skylight Bakery and grab a bunch of scones too. Then again, if Lemon wanted scones, she'd have sent me over there as well. It only takes me about five minutes to walk the length of Main Street and round the corner to the decrepit Keeper's mansion on the left.

Except today, my mouth drops open at seeing the mansion's front entryway gleaming with health.

Lemon stands just inside the gate, making grabby hands at the tray of lattes. "You got my message, perfect! I was entertaining the headquarters people. Also look how *amazing* she looks! I just had her painted by a friend of mine from back home, and she *allowed* it."

"How do you do it, Lemon?" I look at her as she slides her free arm around my waist.

She shrugs and guides me up the brick walkway toward the open front doors. "I just can't water myself down, ya know? I kinda tried when I first got here, but unfortunately, it's just not possible." Flipping her hair, she winks at me, dragging her crimson eyes down my body. "Also, you look delicious today, Bloob. How are things going with our favorite skyball hottie?"

"Well," I mutter. "Jace knows, my parents know, I'm guessing Bryony and her sister know, although they haven't splashed us across the *Gulch Gossip* front page yet. Petra, his surprise little sister, *also* knows, and, oh, I went to the Punishers' family breakfast yesterday with them, where he introduced me as his best friend."

But proceeded to kiss me in front of everyone, including Petra.

Bluebell's eyes spring wide. "Best friend, huh? How'd you feel about that?"

I sigh. "Like it's what we agreed to until after Jasper's test, but I literally cannot wait to just let the cat out of the bag? Secret hottie boyfriends sound fun and all, but the practical application in a nosy small town is just a big pain in my asshole."

She barks out a laugh. "You've got a way with words, Bluebell Tucker. Which is why I need you here on this panel with the folks from Hearth HQ."

Moving her hand from my waist, she sails through the mansion's open front doors. My mouth drops open in shock yet again at seeing the entryway tile beautifully restored. The walls are now covered in stunning black beetle wallpaper and a shiny chandelier dances down from the ceiling, casting shards of bright, warm light on us.

"Holy shit, Lem," I mutter as I stare at the stunning home. "This place has been decrepit for, like, fifty years."

The house groans angrily, and I lift both hands, nearly spilling the lattes. "Sorry, beautiful girl. You'd just never let anyone in, and I'm aghast at how stunning you look. Absolutely radiant."

Lemon presses her hand to the nearest doorway, rubbing the building lovingly. "I think she'd let you do your thing now, if I asked her to. Maybe not today because I know you've got a lot going on. But when things slow down for you."

"When hells freeze over?" I loop my arm through hers, laughing as we enter the formal dining room. It used to be full of holes with the flooring ripped to shit, but now it's as stunning as the front entryway. Double elk horn chandeliers hang from the ceiling. But no sooner have I noticed those than I notice the witches sitting at the far end of the table.

A tall, stunning redhead sits at the head of the table. To her right, a shorter blond witch plays with a ball of blue magic, tossing it back and forth between her hands.

"Oh my gods, the Hectors?" I hiss to Lemon. The two women now rule monster headquarters along with Morgan Hector's father-in-law, Betmal of House Zeniphon. The same Betmal who had a hand in our brand-new haven welcome books. I'd have dearly loved to be a fly on the wall when those three staged a peaceful coup to replace the vampiress who previously ran the haven system. So much drama...they could've been a television show.

Lemon nods, pulling me all the way into the room. Around the table sit Furyon, Lemon's mate; Varek Shorthorn, our local would-be land developer; Sheriff Rygold; Betty from the burger bar; Merit and Bryony; and Cairn from the shifter pack. They look like they've been here for ages.

"Sorry if I'm late." I lift the tray of lattes.

Lemon grabs another and heads to the other end of the table, setting it in front of Furyon with a seductive smile. Smiling at the redhead, she points to the woman. "Morgan, why don't y'all introduce yourselves, and then we'll do the same from our side. We're so excited to talk to you."

That's a stretch. While we might appreciate being hidden away from the human world, Pine Gulch has always preferred to fly under the radar. Not that Hearth HQ has ever completely ignored us—unfortunately for all the Keepers who've tried to put down roots here.

The redhead looks around the table and waves at us. "Hey, y'all. I'm Morgan Hector of House Zeniphon."

"And I'm Lou Hector," the blonde says, blue sparks disappearing into her fingertips. "Yeah, I'm the blue witch," she says with a laugh. “Not hiding! Us blues don’t have to hide anymore now that we’re in charge. Damn, it’s nice to not be hunted by that bitch who used to be in charge.”

“Nice to meet you and all, but can I ask why you’re here?” I bark out before realizing I should have considered holding my tongue.

Morgan looks down the table at me. “Straight to the point, I like that. We’re...aware Pine Gulch doesn't have the best history with monster headquarters. Shit, I don’t think any of us did. We sure didn’t in Ever. But we’d like to change that.”

Now that I opened my big mouth, I might as well keep going. Looking back at her, I lift my chin. “What if we don’t want y’all meddling here?”

She snorts out a laugh. “Are you quoting *Firefly* or just randomly cool?”

The ghost of a smile tips my lips skyward. I’m a huge *Firefly* stan. Cowboys in space? Resistance? Humans with weird powers? Sign me up.

She returns the smirk as she lifts both hands. “Listen. Hearth HQ has sent more than a dozen Keepers here in the last ten years. Some have lasted a while, but none longer than a few years, and most have lasted only a short time. But you have this beautiful house, which is obviously meant for a Keeper. We’d like to hear your thoughts on why that is. Sounds like you don’t necessarily care for HQ to meddle, is that right? And what about the ophiotaurii clan? I don’t see them represented here today...”

Oof, she’s right about that. The monster motorcycle club has a mostly bad reputation in town.

Varek lifts a beefy forefinger. “If I may, Miss Hector. It’s more that—and I’ve learned this the hard way—Pine Gulch is beautiful, but we can be stuck in our ways too. Gulchers don’t love change.”

Discomfort rumbles through me. I’m one of many Gulchers who doesn’t love Varek’s vision of PG’s future—a “neighborhood" of mini ranches on the outskirts of town. Who wants that? Not me. Give me solitude any day of the week.

"I take it you agree?" Lou asks from down at the end of the table. "You're making a face."

I resist the urge to laugh. "He's not wrong. Honestly, if PG could function entirely outside the haven system but still be protected from thralls and the like, we probably would."

Morgan cocks her head to the side. "You don't see a benefit to being connected to headquarters?"

Everyone's silent, like nobody wants to say what we're probably all thinking.

She looks down, reaching into her bag and withdrawing a thick notebook. Its edges are curled up like it's been read a thousand times. Sliding it to the center of the table, she looks at each of us.

"This document was penned by your own Sipan Varian, the Gulch's first Keeper back in the day. And, apparently, it's been collecting dust in Evenia's private library ever since then."

Lou takes over. "I came across it when I was going through trying to figure out what all that bitch kept secret while she was in charge." She blanches, slapping a hand over her face. "Ugh, sorry. I just really hated her a lot, and I think most other people did too. Monsters, I mean."

Suddenly, I decide I like this witch. She reminds me of me.

"What's in the document?" I gesture for someone to send it toward me, and Varek slides it down the shiny burled wood table.

Lou smiles. "Sipan had big plans for Pine Gulch, and they included involvement from Hearth HQ. Lots of cool gardens and growth. He didn't seem to intend for Pine Gulch to hide away from the rest of the monster world. Not that you're exactly hidden because you've got so many great events. But he had a lotta plans and ran out of time to do them all."

"Why didn't it happen?" That question comes from Furyon.

Morgan shrugs. "Knowing my mother-in-law like I do, I'm guessing she didn't like his ideas, so she buried them. But what we came here to find out is if these ideas, or any others, are something you *want* to do for your home. Because, if they are, we can help. We aren't here to impose our view of what Pine Gulch should be. We want to help you make it the best version you want. You live here. We don't."

She shrugs. "Headquarters has lots of money at its disposal, funds created specifically for each haven. Yours hasn't been used since Sipan's time, specifically because no other Keeper got far enough into any project to warrant it. You could literally use it for anything you wanted to build here..."

Lou looks at me as I thumb quickly through Sipan's book. It's full of drawings. I never knew Sipan—he died in a potions accident long before I was born—but some of the old timers have talked about how wonderful he was and how much the gulch loved him.

"We don't need an answer today," Morgan continues. "Truly, we aren't here to lord some master plan over you, we're not. We want to help if we can. I do believe you'd be better off with a Keeper, primarily because it's been made clear to us that Sheriff Rygold doesn't intend to do that job forever."

"You got that fuckin' right," the big, scarred gargoyle grumbles. "This job's gonna be the death of me, and if you keep treatin' me with magic so I can even *do* the job, who knows what my face'll look like."

"We don't want you being forced to do a job you don't want," Morgan says, her tone suddenly serious. "I've seen that happen to...someone else, and we don't want it for you or anyone else." She looks around the table. "I'm going to stop sending Keepers to you until you've had a chance to look through Sipan's book. I think there might be a future where a Keeper naturally shows up, but maybe we need to focus on some of the other projects first. For now, keep his original copy; I've got a copy back home. I'd love it if y'all can get back to us in the next couple weeks to let us know if you're interested in any of what he saw as the future of Pine Gulch."

"PG or the Gulch," I correct softly, staring at a gorgeous drawing of an elegant bar hovering over the edge of the gulf. It's got a great view. Down below, chunky mustangs happily munch the grass that grows out of our riverbank.

"What?"

I smile up at her. "That's how we know you're not locals. So if you wanna start being accepted a little bit more, we're PG or the Gulch. And we call ourselves Gulchers."

"Gulchers," Morgan says with a grin. "I love the sound of that."

The next hour is full of invigorating conversations about the types of things we might want for the Gulch. Morgan and Lou share some of the high-level projects they read about in Sipan's document.

It's thrilling, it really is.

But some part of me just feels like I'm gonna end up with more shit on my to-do list, and I'm not sure I want that.

Hadrian

"Downtown looks *amazing*," Petra says excitedly. She claps her hands as she slides her tail around my wrist. If I'd known her when she was younger, she'd have ridden around on my shoulder and wrapped her tail around my neck, resting the spade over my heart.

Sorrow fills me that I missed out on her entire life so far.

I suppose Dad missed out on it too. Technically we all did.

I had the benefit of growing up in Pine Gulch and experiencing this town and so many of her beautiful festivals. It's part of what I love about living here.

I reach for her hand and thread it through the crook of my elbow. "Okay, little sis. You're not old enough to drink mead, but there's a non-alcoholic version you can enjoy tonight. Part of what happens during the Mead Cute Festival is a whiskey and mead trail that starts at the Welcome Inn and ends at the Auction House. It's the first step in the festival with a huge dance that happens tomorrow." I smile down at her. "You want to walk the trail with me?"

She looks shyly up at me. "What about Bluebell? It seems like we should do this with her. She's been working on this event ever since I came to town."

Sadness fills me. I tackled some of her to-dos this morning.

Deliver flowers to each business on Main Street. Check.

Paste flyers about the dance in every business window and drop extra flyers off at the wraith hotel and the portal station. Check.

Set up the Bodice's table with a custom mead ordered for the occasion. Check.

But there was a lot I just couldn't do without her guidance.

"I'd love nothing better than to do this with her, Petra, but we're still keeping this a secret for another couple of days, right?"

She shakes her head. "I hate that you don't feel like you can tell anyone what you are to one another. How is that gonna work? Is Uncle Jasper going to freak out?"

"Yep," I answer honestly. "I think he will. And it'll take me some time to convince him it's all gonna be fine."

"What secret are you gonna tell me today?" She bumps her hip with mine. "I'll tell you mine. I prayed that when you met me, you'd be cool, and I'm lucky it worked out that way."

Pulling her close, I noogie the top of her head. "I'll tell you a secret too. I always wished I had a little sister, but I didn't think my folks would ever do it. I always felt like I was in the way of their research and I didn't think they'd want more children. But now I have you and not them, and it's pretty cool."

Her eyes go wide and fill with tears. "For real? You wished for me too?"

"Yeah," I admit. "I didn't know you'd be this cool though. I'm pretty glad about that." For a long moment, I stare into purple eyes that mirror mine, shocked at how quickly I've acclimated to having this small person in my life.

"I'm pretty sure I love you," I say with a soft laugh. "Even though you've only been here a short while. How crazy is that?"

She hops up into my arms, throwing hers around my shoulders. "I always loved you, even before I knew you. But thank you, brother."

I wrap my arms around her and hug her close. Time slows as I infuse care and connection into the hug. When we break, she wipes a tear away as she slides back down to the ground.

"Well, should we start at the Welcome Inn, then?"

The Inn waves her shutters at us in a clear invitation. Laughing, I look down Main Street. Every building is welcoming, doors flung open wide. Happy creaks and groans ring out.

It's almost like PG herself is in a better mood than usual, and that's a beautiful thing.

Petra loops her hand back through my arm and pulls me toward the two-story hotel. The front entrance is wreathed in a short pumpkin tunnel covered in dozens of varieties of green and orange pumpkins. Long tables beneath the Welcome's front windows are full of mead and fall-themed desserts. Helpers pass out drinks, and I guide Petra to the nearest table.

A minotaur male smiles at us. I recognize him from around town, although I don't know his name. "Hi, little one," he says kindly to Petra. "Pumpkin hot chocolate for you?"

A tiny gnome hops up onto the table and lifts a cinnamon roll toward her. "And don't forget to try the pumpkin cinnamon rolls. They're mini, like us, and it's a gnome specialty!"

"Oh my gods," Petra exclaims excitedly. "A gnome. I've never met a gnome! Thank you so much. I'd love to try the hot chocolate and the dessert."

She takes them both with more effusive thanks. After that, we visit BrewHaHa Beans, Skylight Bakery, Whiskey Business and then hop back over to the Buxom Bodice. I'm disappointed not to find Bluebell there, but I knew she had a full day and a meeting with Lemon and some reps from Hearth HQ. How she continually lands herself on every committee and organizing group is a surprise to me, but somehow she does it.

It's one of the many things I want to help guard her against. I want her spending her time precisely where she wants to, and not with her brothers or whoever else just because they expect her to. My woman has been running so hard for so long, and I didn't realize just how much it drained her until I lived across the hallway.

"Hadrian?"

I spin in place to find a gargoyle male standing there with a younger gargoyle on his shoulder. The younger one hops up and down while holding on to the male's horn.

The male smiles at me, reaching out with one hand. "You probably don't remember me. I'm Alo, and this is my son, Iggy. We're from Ever. You spent a little time with us during that exhibition game while we were convincing Manorin to stick around as our coach."

Realization courses through me, and I grab his hand to shake it. "That's right! And you did steal him. I came here hoping *he'd* be here, but Ever snatched him right out from under us."

He chuckles, purple eyes dropping to Petra.

"Ah, this is my sister, Petra," I offer.

"I'm nine," Petra chirps, staring up at the younger gargoyle. "How old are you?"

"Seven." He hops off his father's shoulder to hover in the air with a big smile. "Do you want to go play somewhere? I don't like pumpkin-flavored stuff, and Dad says everything is gonna taste like that, and also I'm already *so* bored."

Petra laughs and looks up at me. "Is that alright with you? I can take him to the pumpkin maze. It's super cool." She winks at the younger male. "I also just got here, but I promise nothing tastes like pumpkin, it's just *full* of pumpkins. And gourds."

I look between her and Alo. "If it's okay with his father, it's okay with me. Just keep in touch, okay?"

Petra lifts her arm, pointing to the comm watch. "Aye aye, Capitán."

An aqua-winged pixie skips up to Alo and throws her arms around him, smiling up at him like he's the best thing in the entire world. His eyes soften at the corners when he looks down at her.

She rests a hand on her swollen belly, rubbing it.

Pregnant, she's pregnant.

"Actually I think I'll follow them around for a minute, if you don't mind."

"You don't have to do that," I start but she waves me off and points to her belly. "This baby is growing so dang fast and the walking will do me wonders. I'll keep an eye on your little one too, no worries!"

I look between the adults. "Are you absolutely sure?"

The younglings look at us for just a moment before Iggy grabs Petra's hand and yanks her up into the sky. "C'mon! Mir will hang with us and she's so cool, she's my mom now!"

The younglings dart off and Mir sighs. She reaches up and pecks Alo on the cheek, then turns toward the alleyway, lumbering after them with one hand on her lower back. Once they disappear down the alleyway between the Welcome Inn and Whiskey Business, I turn to the other male. "How long you in town for?"

"Couple of days," the big gargoyle says with a smile. "My mate wanted Iggy to experience everything Pine Gulch has to offer, but we'll head home after that."

I watch her walk slowly down the alleyway. "You sure we shouldn't follow her? I feel bad that she's watching the kiddos."

Alo blows out a breath. "Oh I learned not to correct my pregnant mate about the first day or two after we found out. She would be highly miffed if we followed her now. And you don't wanna be on the bad side of a pregnant pixie, I can promise you that."

My mouth dries as I think about how fucking fun it would be to see Bluebell like that, her stomach all huge and rounded with our child. We haven't even discussed children since we started dating, although I know it's something she wants eventually.

The need to sink my fangs into her, to claim her, to have us belong to one another the way these two do? I'm salivating at the idea of it.

He watches her go, a soft look in his eyes. It's so striking to see such an obviously predatory monster so...taken. So sweet. I want that so badly I can taste it. Once his mate is gone from view, he glances at me again. "I'm gonna head up the street and find my uncle but it was good seeing you, man. Hope we kick your ass next time we play, but I'm not holding my breath."

Chuckling, I shake his hand.

Now all I want to do is find Bluebell. I hope she's done with her meeting because, like always, I can't wait to see her.

After saying goodbye to him, I head down Main Street. Lemon and Furyon are standing with Sheriff Rygold, meads in hand. Oz has his back to Lemon as he flirts with two male pixies, one of whom has his hands all over Oz's chest. Maybe he'll finally get laid, since it seems to be his chief complaint lately.

My gaze drifts back and forth as locals and visitors alike partake in the beauty of downtown PG. The town herself is in a great mood, waggling shutters and flapping window sashes at passersby. Even the Bodice is ready for the day, my flowers brightening up her front window. Her door is thrown wide open, and even from the street, I can see she's full inside.

"Fancy seeing you here."

Warmth and desire curl through me as I turn to find Bluebell standing there with two meads in hand. She hands one to me as she takes a sip of hers.

"Long-ass day, but I am *finally* done with my to-do list," she mutters.

Bite. Claim. Cherish. Protect.

The need to wrap her in my wings, sit her on my cock, and bite my way up that slim neck overwhelms me. My focus narrows, tail swishing as I lift my wings just slightly. My chest heaves as my body tightens.

Bluebell cocks her head to the side, giving me a quick once-over as a blush trails over her high cheekbones. "Hay, you alright? You look...tense."

"I am," I whisper as I take a step closer to her. Can't touch her in public. Don't want to hide her. I'm so fucking done with this. "Come upstairs with me for a minute? I need to talk to you."

"Of course." She sets the mead down on a tall round table. "Everything okay?"

Grabbing her hand, I pull her toward the alleyway between our building and the next. I open the door, flaring my nostrils as she slips through. Her footsteps disappear up the stairs as I grip the doorframe and try not to lose absolute control.

Gargoyles aren't meant to love in hiding. Our love is loud and public and centered on snacks and extreme affection. We practically make falling in love a sport. Loving Bluebell behind the scenes feels like I'm not doing my job, not doing our love justice.

After rushing up the stairs, I follow her down the hall. Yanking my door open, I pull her through and lock it behind us.

"What's going on?" She plants a hand on her hips and waves at my body. "You look like you're freaking out." Her beautiful eyes spring wide as she scans my face. "Oh my gods, did something happen?"

I shake my head. "Baby, I just...I saw you there, and all I wanted to do was shout about how fucking much I love you."

She gasps, but a smile quickly overtakes it. "You do? You love me?"

I wrap both wings around her and pull her until she hits my chest. Reaching down, I lift her into my arms, tucking her legs around my core. Forehead pressed to hers, I brush my lips against her soft mouth. "I love you, Bluebell Tucker. I will *always* love you until the gods take me from this earth. And even then, among the stars, I'll still love you."

I part from her long enough to fist her long braid around my hand. "And I want to claim you, feel you in my chest, feel my heartbeat sync to yours. I want you inside me so deeply, nobody can tear us apart."

Her lips pull upward into a sensual smile as she stares into my eyes. "I want that too, Hadrian. I've thought about it for literal decades, wondered what it would feel like to have that bond with you, something even deeper than the friendship we already shared."

She jerks her head toward my nest. "So what are we even waiting for, mate? Let's do it now."

Groaning, I stalk to the nest and fall on top of her in the soft sheets, careful not to flatten her as I flare my wings and grip holes in the walls to hold myself steady.

Pulling my shirt apart, I toss it aside. Bringing her hands to my stomach, I guide them to the top of my jeans. A feral smile overtakes me as I watch her fumble with the button, pulling it open.

"I'm gonna take you so hard," I murmur as I watch her shove my jeans down my hips. "And you're gonna take me, Bluebell of House Alkazar. Then you'll feel me, all of me."

"I can't wait," she says with a demanding little noise. "I'm done hiding you, Hadrian Alkazar."

You look tense
I am
Was shout about how fucking much I love you
I saw you there and all I wanted to do...
You do? You love Me?
Hadrian...
So what are we waiting for to mate?
Claim me now...
Gasp

Bluebell

He's right. There's no reason to wait. We've hidden our love long enough, and Jasper's gonna find out in less than twenty-four hours.

Hadrian uses his grip on the wall to pull himself slightly off the nest, just enough that he can shove his jeans all the way down. His thick cock springs free of the fabric, bobbing against his muscular thigh. My mouth waters, knowing that fabulous dick is mine for all of eternity.

Mine. All mine.

"So..." I waggle my brows at him. "I need to bite you, right?"

He nods and drops down, placing a beefy thigh on either side of my body. "Me first, baby, and then you seal the deal with your bite." He pulls back enough to shoot me a serious look. "It's all about intention, little witch. My intention to belong to you and yours to belong to me."

He brings his mouth to mine so we're breathing the same air. "I'd have done this on our first date, if I'm honest."

Heat flares between my thighs, my body tightening in anticipation of him.

"I can't wait to hear your heartbeat," I whisper.

"You'll feel more than that," he says with a sexy little growl, leaning to drag his open mouth up my chest to the spot where my neck and shoulder meet. "Here." He bites softly at the spot. "Right here is where I'm gonna bite you, little mate."

Groaning, I arch my neck to give him full access. I cant my head to the side, moaning when he slicks his cool tongue up my skin.

"Fuck, Hadrian." I sling both arms around his neck, loving how frankly *enormous* he feels on top of me.

"You're wearing too many clothes, little one," he croons against my skin. Moving quickly, he pulls himself off me, hovering above like a sexy devil as he stares down at me. He makes quick work of the clothing, shredding my shirt and yanking my jeans down my thighs. After slipping a dark claw beneath my panties, he drags it carefully along my pussy.

Heat swirls through me, and I moan as he dips his claw just inside. He's gentle with that deadly touch.

Until he spears his claw through the fabric and shreds it too. Underwear ruined, he pulls them from me and lifts them to his nose, sucking in a deep, ragged breath.

"Wet," he says with a sexy moan. "Soaked through, mate. How hot are you for this?" Reaching down, he strokes his length, coaxing pre-cum from the tip.

We let out matching moans as he drips the sticky substance onto my lower belly. I reach down and gather it up onto my fingertips, then bring it to my mouth. Sucking my fingers clean, my eyes roll back into my head.

"So good." I lap at my fingers, desperate for more of him.

Hadrian drops lower and brings his thighs around my face. Gripping his cock, he drags the tip along my lower lip. "Open up, baby."

Like a good girl, I open wide and stick my tongue out.

He rubs the tip all over my tongue too, pre-cum coating it as a dark purple flush crawls over his cheeks and down his chest. His horns flex and straighten, rising tall above his head.

Shifting upward, I pull the tip of his dick into my mouth,

hollowing my cheeks around it. He cries out, back arching as he brings both hands to his head. He's desperate, wound tight, ready to explode.

I suck his tip, laving at the pinched skin on the underside, tickling my tongue down every piercing as his gasping cries grow louder and louder. When he sounds like he's ready to combust, I fall against the edge of the nest and smirk up at him.

"You're teasing me," he bites out, purple eyes glittering. He leans forward, the leathery skin of his wings snapping tight as he moves low. Guiding his cock against my pussy lips, he thrusts once, hard, sinking to the hilt as I gasp.

"Gods! Oh fuck!" I let my knees fall wide, pumping my hips rhythmically as I force my overfull pussy to relax around my big mate.

He surges forward and rolls us, bringing his lips to my ear. "Use me, baby; ride this fat cock until you're ready to come, and when you are, I'll bite you."

It's too much. Too hot. Too full. And still I need more.

Rolling my hips, I grind my pussy against Hadrian's body, loving how insanely full of him I am. How is it possible I can take all of him? I have no idea. But I do, moaning with desperation as he bites a slow path up my chest to my neck.

Just knowing what he's about to do is enough to push me to the brink. Soft bites grow ever more insistent as he begins to vibrate the thin bit of cartilage that sticks out over his cock. The rhythmic vibrations against my clit have me thrusting hard and fast against him, chasing that relief. I scrape my nails down his chest, practically begging to come.

With a sexy groan, he slips his tail between my ass cheeks and prods at my back hole. It's featherlight pressure and it's still enough to have my ass clenching in expectation of him.

"I'm so close," he growls. "So damn close, baby."

Rocking forward, I bend low enough to lick a flat path over his small, peaked nipple. He jolts and shudders, gripping my hips hard as a ragged groan leaves him.

"Do it again," he commands, his tone nearly as pleading as I was feeling just seconds ago. Knowing my magic produces a sort of zing on his skin, I drag my fingers along his abs, pushing magic into his belly as I lave at his nipple.

"Now," he roars, the baritone depth of his voice pulling goosebumps to the surface of my skin as magic sparks all around us.

Shifting forward, he clamps his mouth around that sacred spot, fangs sinking into my flesh. The pinch of pain has a howl echoing from my throat, but it falls into a scream as bliss erupts between my thighs. My body clenches around him, pulsating rhythmically as he roars into the bite.

Something snaps in my chest, arching my back as he drags a scream of pleasure from my overwrought body. Hadrian cries out again, the sound desperate as he pumps my pussy full of cum. It spills out of me, dripping down my ass and thighs as his thrusts grow erratic and wild.

I'm barely clinging to sanity as bliss fades, aftershocks rocking me when he carefully pulls his fangs from the wound.

Amethyst eyes come to mine, and he rubs a hand over his mouth. "Baby, talk to me. You okay?"

My chest heaves as I struggle to find the words. Shaking my head, I stare at him in utter awe. "No, mate, I'm not okay. I'm so much better than that. You're mine, and no one can ever take that from us now."

His serious expression fades to satisfaction, and he nuzzles my nose with his. "You need to bite me to complete the bond, sweetheart."

I jerk my hips, demanding he roll onto his back. He unhooks his claws from the wall and tucks his wings behind him, settling against the headboard.

One brow lifts when I stop moving. "Yes, Mrs. Alkazar? Did you need something?"

I slide onto his lap, nestling his still-dripping cock against my belly. Rocking up and down it, I tease his mouth with mine.

"So if I don't bite you right now, what happens, *Mister* Alkazar?"

"I'll be in agony," he says with a sexy, breathless moan. "Total and complete agony, baby. I'll follow you around like Ginger with Oz until you bless me with our bond."

I rock up and down his length again with a playful shrug. "I dunno, Hadrian. Sounds kinda fun to me. There's something appealing about the mental image of you chasing me around like you can't get enough."

He grips my throat, big thumb pressing to my lower lip. "If you need me on my knees, trailing after you with a leash and collar on, just say the word, mate. Whatever you want, it is my pleasure and *privilege* to provide. Whatever, I'm serious about that."

Reaching down, I slot his cock between my thighs and sit down, clenching as I go.

Hadrian gasps and grunts, reaching up to grip a small cutout in the headboard wall. "Fuck, Bluebell. You're gonna kill me with that sweet pussy."

"What a way to go, though," I murmur as I lean forward and lick a stripe up the muscular column of his throat. "Mine," I growl. "This fucking body is all mine, do you understand me? No one else's."

"Yours," he says, gripping my ass with his left hand as he starts shunting his hips again. I'm barely off the high from that last orgasm, and the bond is a swirling maelstrom of heat in my chest. But it's a demanding heat. It seeks more. It needs completion.

I wanted to tease him, to drag this sexy thing out a little longer.

But I can't.

I won't.

Not when we've already had to hide one another for far too long and for stupid reasons. Worrying about our friendship? That was a valid worry. But as I stare at the male awaiting my teeth, eyes closed as his lips pull into a satisfied smile, I know I'm not gonna wait a single moment longer.

Surging forward, I sink my flat teeth into his skin, tugging at it as I infuse every shred of intention and power I can into the bite.

Hadrian screams, a guttural, primal sound that shakes the walls of the nest. In my chest, that thing between us snaps tight and sparkles, and he's fucking *there.*

Another orgasm obliterates rational thought, giant rolling waves of pleasure radiating from my core. I don't let the bite go, terrified to lose that sense of him, all those emotions swirling in him that I can *feel* now.

"Baby," he gasps out. "You won't lose me. Never."

Oh gods, he can feel that worry now.

Pulling my teeth from his skin, I admire the way dark blood wells beneath the surface. The tiniest crescent indentions mar his skin. Frowning, I pull back. "I don't think that's even gonna scar. Damn, I bit as hard as I could."

He chuckles and pulls me close, kissing my lips tenderly. When we part, he breathes hard against my mouth. "Baby, it's jus—"

His body jerks, wings flaring up into a protective position. His body shakes as he grits his teeth and cries out. It's a pained sound that has me running my hands up his throat and along his jawline, my magic sparking from my fingertips.

"Hadrian, baby, talk to me!" I shout.

But then that pained sound morphs into pure pleasure as his eyes roll into his head. His hips jerk with another orgasm, and the pressure of him stuffing me full has bliss shattering through me. The welling bites at my neck throb with piercing emotion.

His.

Mine.

A sense of possession so primal and strong, I can barely breathe around the strength of it. Gasping for air, I lean forward and press my ear to his chest.

Thwomp.

Thwomp.

Thwomp.

His heartbeat speeds up slightly, catching up to mine until they're thumping along at exactly the same cadence. Even the muscles of his heart know he belongs to me.

The new bond is like a physical highway for emotion back and forth. It's so fucking beautiful, I don't know how I existed as a being without knowing this level of comfort. Of safety. Of just having someone ten thousand percent in my corner.

Any worry I ever had about our relationship, even the silliest ones that just stemmed from this bullshit with my brother, those are gone as I listen in amazement to the steady thud of our joined heartbeats.

"Mine," I whisper into his skin. "You are all mine, Hadrian Alkazar."

Hadrian

I can remember my grandmother once telling me that there was nothing in the world like the first moments after a mating bond snaps into place. She was right, of course, because as I stroke Bluebell's hair and stare into those beautiful blue eyes, I can't fathom *not* having this.

A heartbeat? That sound I've obsessed over my entire life? I produce it on my own now, and it's synced in time with hers. Only ever hers.

It's not like I doubted she was mine, once I started allowing myself to consider it. But this? It's a whole different level of knowing. It's surety in the most astounding of ways. Every cell in my body exists to be near her, to be part of her, to create life with her.

To love.

Bluebell smiles at me, her fingertips skating up my jawline to my horn. As she plays with the base, heat sears through me like flame.

More? How can I possibly be ready for more? I've never come so much as the last quarter hour.

"Mate," she says, her voice throaty and sounding well used. "I'm not ready to leave this nest, not at all." She rubs at her chest.

"But we're gonna miss the entire dance if we don't head downstairs. You okay with that?"

I know why she's asking, because I can feel how torn she is in her heart. She's on the organizing committee, and she's debating how to tell me she feels compelled to be present despite what we just did. I get it, because I get *her* so very deeply.

"We need to put in an appearance." I roll her onto her side. "Even if it's just for a little while."

She smiles. "Guess you're basically a mind reader now, huh?"

I smile. "Something like that. But so are you, little mate."

Her smile overtakes her face. "It's such a non-human thing that's gonna take some time to get used to."

I chuckle. "Wait until we tell your family, and I can love you in the open. I'm gonna be all over you all the time."

"Good," she huffs. "The more I think about it, the more irritated I am that we put our own feelings aside just because of Jasper. Like...how dumb?"

"It's more than that," I offer. "I mean, it's that, of course, but it's a deep respect for all of our friendships. It's a worry about losing something that's been so steady and constant. I get it, and I was worried too, even though the rational part of my brain wants to say fuck it, he'll deal." A laugh burbles from me, although it's wry. "He'll deal tomorrow, so we're almost there."

She rolls off me with an adorable grumble. "Don't remind me. I need to stock up on tequila for both our places, because we're gonna need it after he finds out."

We've hashed this topic out so much that I can't find anything to add, so I watch in silence as she pulls her clothing back on. She's covered in cum, and we probably both need a shower, but I love that she doesn't bother to hide the evidence of what we just did. There's something supremely satisfying about that.

Half an hour later, I'm anything *but* satisfied. Bluebell flits from group to group, checking on monsters and doing an all-around bang-up job as part of the committee. I've already busied myself for a half hour checking on Petra and Iggy. They're having a great time playing chase in the pumpkin maze with Iggy's mom.

Me? I'm drowning in our combined emotions and desperate to lavish affection and adoration on her. We just completed the bond; I want to stand up on a stage and shout it out to all of Main Street.

She can feel it too, blue eyes flicking to me as she stands with Lemon and Oz. Her breath hitches, and I feel that too, even from across the street. Leaving her friends, she picks her way through the crowd to rejoin me, rubbing at her chest. Long blue hair covers the swollen spot on her neck where I bit her.

"Hay—I—let's get outta here," she whispers. "Surely this is enough showing my face, right? I need you."

"Fuck yes," I growl out, reaching for her hand just as Jasper and Jack appear from the crowd. For the first time in the years I've known him, Jasper looks...harried. Black brows are bunched together, his mouth dropping open when he sees Bluebell.

"Bloob, thank fuck I found you. I've comm'd you three times!" He lifts both arms in exasperation as she spins to face him.

Jack glances from Jasper to me to Bluebell and back again. My tail starts lashing of its own accord at the inherent demand in Jasper's tone. In the brand-new bond, concern and irritation swirl from Bluebell to me.

Jasper huffs out an irritated sound. "Did you get my stuff done yet? I don't have any more time today. I've been prepping all morning, and I didn't even eat lunch."

Bluebell's mouth drops open. "No, I haven't done your shit yet, Jasper. I literally just walked out of a meeting thirty minutes ago. I didn't eat breakfast *or* lunch, and I've only had one coffee. Your shit is gonna have to wait an hour or two, but I'll get it done la—"

"No!" he snaps. "I was counting on you, Bluebell. I can't *tackle* this shit today, and you—"

"Will get it done after I have a damn drink," she says reasonably.

The bond swirls with anger, although I can see she's trying to temper his response. Balling my fists, I resist the urge to push him away from her. My mating bond throbs, my need to protect making me see red.

Moving my hands to Jasper's chest, I urge him to look at me. "I'll help her as soon as she has a moment to decompress."

He shoves my hand away. "No, dude. I need to be able to count on her. This is what she does for our business. This is her part in it and—"

"I'm not technically on the Tucker Greens payroll," she says with more bite in her tone. "I help you so you don't *have* to, but you don't pay me, and it has to come after my other responsibilities. That's always been true. But I'll get it done later, like I said." Her voice is full of clear warning, dark blue brows furrowed in anger.

"Let me grab you a drink," I offer, hoping to defuse the situation before I start yelling. I don't like the way Jasper's looking expectantly at her, like he might launch into an even more ridiculous tirade. "Or we can head back to Tucker ranch and help you in your final—"

"Dude," Jasper snaps. "Stop, alright? Today of all days, just stop."

Frustration rises in me, and I ball my fists.

Today of all fucking days? The day I claimed my mate and kept it a fucking secret to protect *his* mental wellbeing?

I think fucking not. I'm done protecting Jasper Tucker, third-level mastery test be damned.

"I don't want to start arguing right here," I say in the coolest tone I can muster, "but you need to step away from this and focus on your test tomorrow. Bluebell and I will help you *later,* but her schedule does not revolve around you."

Jasper turns to me with a fierce look, stepping into my space despite me standing a full head taller. "Whose fucking side are you on, Hadrian?" He slaps both hands to my chest and shoves.

I see his move coming a mile away, so I lean in, and when he pushes, I don't move an inch. "Step away, Jasper," I snarl.

Jack grabs Jasper's forearm and tugs, but Jasper's mouth drops open. "Or what, asshole?"

"Stop acting like a petulant child," I hiss. "You're a grown-ass man, and you need to start acting like it. I don't care how big of a day tomorrow is for you, *you're* being a godsdamned jackass."

The bond coils tight in my chest, apprehension taking over both our irritation.

His eyes spring wide, mouth dropping open. Just as quickly, fury overtakes his features, and he cocks back, ready to hit me.

I duck him easily, but his momentum carries him forward, and he crashes against me, then falls to my left. He swung too hard, and the force takes him all the way toward Bluebell. I grab and hang on to his shirt, but he lands on her right arm, knocking the mead all over her neck and chest.

Roaring, I yank him up off the ground and thrust my face into his. "Calm down," I snap, even though we're drawing a crowd. I'm barely maintaining control of what's now rage at how he's treating my mate.

"Put him down, Alk!" Bluebell shouts, but I'm too fucking hyped.

"She promised to help!" Jasper struggles, clawing against my hands and forearms.

"It's not gonna be right now though, so are you gonna walk away?" I snap as I set him down.

He glares at me but turns. At the last second, I realize he's *not* fucking done, not by a long shot. Flaring my wings wide, I lift my hands and stop him as he swings a second time.

"Leave her alone!" I roar, lifting my daggerlike wingtips up and above us in an attack position.

Bluebell gasps, and Jasper's eyes go wide. I drop my wings carefully at my back as he looks at me in shock.

"Dude, fuck...I...why do you even care? This is between her and me."

Swinging my left wing around her, I pull her to my side and tuck her against me as red overtakes my vision. Not only is he being a general asshole, but he's expecting too much, causing a scene and hurting her feelings. He's taking advantage, and I'm here to make sure no one takes advantage of her ever again.

The mating bite throbs so hard, I'm about to drop to both knees.

"Leave my godsdamned mate alone," I snarl. "Or you and I *will* have problems despite our friendship."

Bluebell swivels her gaze up to mine, and Jasper and Jack look at each other, then back at me. All three look shocked. Surprise tears along our bond.

"Your *what*?" Jasper gasps. "You're fucking kidding me right now. She can't be your mate. She's my *sister*. She's practically *your* sister. We grew up together, Hadrian. What the fuck are you talking about?!"

He's shouting now, and any moment, Bryony or Merit or both are liable to start snapping photographs of this altercation.

Bluebell scratches at her mating bite. Jasper's eyes drop to her hand. Then his eyes spring wide. He grabs her hand and yanks it away from her neck.

"Just focus on tomorrow, Jasper," Bluebell says cautiously, even as he scans the obvious indentations. "We don't have to talk about this now."

"Come on, Jazzy." Jack pulls Jasper away from us. His eyes are as wide as Jasper's as he stares at the swollen spot where I claimed her.

"Are you fucking kidding me, dude?" Jasper shouts. "You're my best friend! How could you?!"

"Because we want to," I say simply. "Because we're fated, Jasper, and nobody, not even you, can come between that kind of connection. We'd have told you sooner if we weren't worried about you being a complete fucking asshole like you're being right now!"

Bluebell gasps again and takes a step away from me. "Hadrian, stop, please."

This is getting so, so, so out of hand. I turn to Bluebell with an imploring look. "We were trying to give him space, baby, but—"

"No," Jasper barks. "Absolutely not. Dude, this can't be. You fucking bit my sister?"

Bluebell reaches for him, but the moment she rests her hands on his shoulders, he yanks out of her grip, glaring at her.

"We were gonna tell you after your test," she says softly. "This doesn't change anything, Jazzy. I'm still your sister, and he's still—"

"I don't want to hear this." Jasper turns and pushes through the crowd.

She calls out after him, but he doesn't stop. Mouth dropped open, she looks up at me with tears in her eyes. "You had to tell him right now? We knew this is how he'd react, Hay." She throws both hands on her head, spinning away from me. "Fuuuuuuck."

Our bond snaps around her utter desolation and fear.

"Bluebell," I implore, pulling her toward me. "Please. I—"

"I need a minute," she snaps, eyes wide as she backs away from me and Jack. "Just give me a second to process this, okay?"

"I'll take Jasper home," Jack says cautiously. Green eyes flick between us, his expression carefully neutral. "See you guys—well, I'm not sure when."

She turns and runs toward the Buxom Bodice, disappearing inside without a backward glance.

"Fuck!" I shout into the sky, beyond frustrated.

"This ain't great timing, friend," Jack says quietly.

Snarling, I look between him and the Bodice. I fucked up by telling him that way after she and I were on the same page about it.

Shiiiiiiit. What if she can't forgive me?

Bluebell

Sitting alone in the Bodice storeroom, I'm thinking I overreacted a tiny bit. Jasper was being *such* an ass. I can hardly blame Hadrian for protecting me—it's such a gargoyle instinct, he probably couldn't turn it off even if he wanted to.

In our bond, frustration and regret tinge everything, tension forcing pressure in my chest. Part of me is actually relieved now that the truth is out, despite the drama.

"Little witch?" Hadrian's voice echoes from somewhere in the front of the building.

The Bodice clatters the display hooks on the wall, leading him to where I'm hiding in a corner of the storeroom.

When Hadrian sees me there, he slides onto his knees and puts his hands on my thighs. "Baby, I'm so sorry. I didn't mean to tell him like that, but the way he was pushing you wasn't okay."

I sigh. "I'd have preferred to stick to our timeline, but honestly, it was gonna come out sooner or later. I just hope it doesn't fuck up his mind for the test tomorrow. He gets *so* in his head about things...you know how he is."

Hadrian glances down, stroking my thighs. "He does, and I feel bad about that. But at some point, he and the other Jays have to stop taking advantage of you. That's what they're doing...You realize that, right? I'm upset about it, on your behalf, of course."

He shoots me a half smile. "Maybe it can fuck him just a little bit?"

"It was always going to come to this," I mutter. "I've been so bitter about how much I *think* I have to help them. Mama even told me I should try trusting them to do this, and she's right. Maybe not Jasper—he's not organized—but Jace."

"Agreed," Hadrian says quietly. "They could probably do it if you helped teach them. You don't *have* to hold them together, baby, even though you're so very good at it."

"I am, aren't I?" I flash him a halfhearted smile.

"You're soft," he says in a lower tone. "The opposite of me. There's a tender side to you, Bluebell, a side that needs support and protection. I'm a winged destroyer, a blunt weapon, hard in every way. And sometimes you need me to be that wall between you and the rest of the world. I want you to actually have *time* to slow down, baby." He pats my thigh. "I've seen that ridiculous to-do list a time or two."

"Slowing down sounds really nice," I whisper. "I think I just held on because I was good at it, and I didn't trust them to do it well. But they can figure it out, right?"

Hadrian nods. "We can't talk to Jasper right now...but we'll talk to him soon, after the test tomorrow."

I shake my head. "I'm not even sure we *should* show up to support him."

"We should," Hadrian says. "He's my best friend and your brother, and even though he was a dick tonight, we should still be there for him. Everything will be alright, I promise."

Petra pops up behind Hadrian, and I scream at her sudden appearance.

Hadrian jerks and spins around, wrapping a wing around me and yanking me close. When he sees it's his sister, he slumps with a relieved sigh. "Petra, what the hells? I thought you were with Iggy?"

"He flew off with the gnomes," she says with a shrug. "I heard shouting, and I followed you in here. Guess the cat's out of the bag, huh? Like the humans say?"

"Yeah," I say with a laugh. "The cat is very much out of the bag."

"Glad I don't have to keep that secret anymore," she mutters. Then she smiles up at me from Hadrian's arms. "Hay and I tell each other a secret every day so we can keep getting to know each other. Do you want to do the same thing with us? Maybe it'll take your mind off Uncle Jasper."

I look between them with a soft smile. "Yeah, Petra, I'd love that. And maybe let's don't call him uncle anymore, that doesn't really fit, does it?"

"Oh, I guess not." She shakes her head.

"Hello!" Oz shouts as he and Lemon swan into the storeroom. "I heard most of the shenanigans since you did them in the middle of godsdamned Main Street, but go ahead and let Uncle Ozifer and Auntie Lemon in on the secrets too. We're besties; you can't leave us in the dark!"

He drops gracefully to the ground next to Hadrian, and Lemon follows him, tucking her legs to the side like a lady with manners. Wearing those damn hot pink sparkle boots she loves so much. Ginger follows them in and sits between Oz and Petra.

I groan as I stare at the four monsters in front of me. This is turning into a whole...*thing*.

"The secret's out!" Petra says with a waggle of her dark purple brows. "Uncle Jasper threw a fit, Auntie Bluebell came here to hide, and, well, we're kinda dealing with things. Oops!" She throws a hand over her mouth. "Not Auntie and Uncle. Just Jasper."

Oz's mouth drops open, and Lemon smacks her lips with a knowing nod.

"What she said." I wave at the young gargoyle as she tucks herself against my mate.

Petra shrugs. "So are we gonna share some secrets or what? I can go first!"

We all chuckle at her childish exuberance, but if I'm honest, she's pulling me out of my funk. "Go on, girl. Hit us with a big secret."

She crosses her arms. "I think I have a crush on Iggy, that new kid who's visiting."

Lemon and Oz let out matching gasps.

Hadrian looks over at her, brows lifting high. "That didn't take long."

Petra shrugs, examining her dark nails. "You know how it is, brother. When you know you know."

"And love abounds!" Oz says with a snap of the fingers on both hands. "Love that for you, little thang. Here's my secret." He looks around our gathered group with a devilish smile. "I'm finally working on my business plan so I can open an honest-to-gods salon on Main." He chuckles. "And I do mean salon, not saloon. We've got enough of those, surely."

Lemon rests her head on his shoulder. "Thank gods, Oz, because what I really need is a place to get my tips done. I don't want to keep going home to New York."

It's on the tip of my tongue to tell her I can easily change her hair with my black magic, but she shakes her head at me, smiling.

"Don't even offer, sweetie. I know how long that to-do list is in your back pocket. I wouldn't even ask you on my death bed. I felt bad enough sending you for lattes one time."

Hadrian and I share a laugh because she's right. I literally do not need anything else to do.

"So what about you, Lemon?" Petra reaches over, sliding her tail spade up Lemon's arm and over to her heart.

My bestie smiles at us. "Are y'all ready?"

"We're hanging on your every damn word," Oz squeals, clapping his hands.

She shoots a superior look at our group. "I bought plain brown cowboy boots, y'all. I haven't even shown them to—"

"Godsssssss," I moan as I sink against Petra and Hadrian. "That doesn't fucking count."

Lemon slaps my thigh. "Bluebell Delia! That's a big *deal* for me!"

"And there goes a secret I didn't need getting out." I look at Petra. "Delia's my middle name, and I absolutely hate it." She scoffs at Lemon and Oz. "How did y'all even know that?"

"I think it's beautiful," Petra says with a huge smile that shows all of her teeth.

"Me too," Lemon whispers. "Just like you, bestie."

And just like that, some of the tightness in my chest fades. It's gonna be fine. This is all gonna be fine. I've got my monsters here with me, and we *will* get past this.

Hadrian

I didn't sleep a wink last night, not even with Bluebell tucked against me in my nest. I'm sure it didn't help that Petra was snoring on the sofa, and since my apartment's one big room, I could hear every stuttered intake of breath...all night.

What I really wanted was time alone with my mate—we've got to figure out some better sleeping arrangements. I'm thankful the ranch has multiple bedrooms, and Petra can pick from any of the available ones. My timeline for completing renovations on the house needs to move up.

Fast.

I follow Petra, who's got her arm looped through Bluebell's, as we walk into the skyball stadium where Jasper's master's test will take place. Anxiety prickles across my skin, sending waves of uncomfortable heat along my wing bones. Those nerves poke along the bond, too, and I hate that Bluebell can feel it. Worry over his mindset is the reason we didn't tell him sooner, and it didn't work out well anyhow.

All I know is, I'm certain that *not* showing up would be even worse.

When we appear in the stands, his parents and the other Jays look up with concern on their faces. Jace waves us over, but the rest of the Tuckers look a little shell-shocked, especially when they note Petra holding on to Bluebell. I risk a glance at the field to find Jasper standing there with the test proctors, glaring daggers our way. I shoot him a quick smile, then look back at his family.

Taking our seats, we make small talk, but it's awkward as hells despite how delighted Petra seems to be to see her "uncles."

When my sister stops talking the Jays' ears off, I tap Jack on the shoulder with my wing. "How was he last night?"

Jack shakes his head, running both hands through his black waves. "Drunk mess most of the night. Wouldn't talk to any of us. He just went out to that old tree fort we built when we were kids and sat there 'til this morning. He rolled in for breakfast, but he's barely spoken two words."

Oz, Lemon, and Furyon appear then and find spots next to us in the bleachers.

Jack waves at them and then shoots me a half-hearted smile. "How come you didn't just tell us? We've always thought of you as our brother, but we'd have...tried to understand. I would, at least."

I frown. "We would have, but we didn't want to spring it on Jasper before this." I wave at where Jasper's talking to the proctors on the field.

"That didn't exactly work out," Jack mutters.

"Hush, it's starting," Bluebell says quietly, hands clasped in her lap as she leans onto her thighs.

"What's gonna happen?" Petra asks loudly.

Just then, one of the proctors, a big troll male, presses his fingers to his ear and begins to speak, his voice echoing loudly toward us.

"Welcome to Jasper Alan Tucker's third-level mastery of green engineering final presentation. This is the last step toward officially proclaiming Mister Tucker as a Master-Level Green Witch. In order to pass this series of tests, he will need to grow a field of local cacti, including at least prickly pear and spinystar. The second test is to grow the plants to a great size. He'll then be required to transmogrify them into anything of his choosing, remembering any particular local celebrations or events where such magic could be used. The final two tests are surprises chosen by the proctors at the time, so details were not provided ahead."

He smiles over his shoulder at Jasper, lifting his arms wide. "Let us begin with the first three bits of the test, and then we will announce the final two sections."

I've never been to a masters-level green magic presentation before, although I've seen Jasper use his magic hundreds of times. Some of these skills are things I know he's struggled with, although I know he's been preparing for this day.

The proctor returns to Jasper, and the three speak together for a moment. Both proctors shake Jasper's hand, and then he steps away from them, closing his eyes as he steps his legs apart and looks at the ground. My heart is in my throat as he opens his hands and flips them so his palms face the ground.

"Come on, Jazzy," Elena mutters.

Next to me, Bluebell's stiff and silent, eyes focused on her brother.

The ground in front of us begins to shimmy and shake, and a smile tips Jasper's lips upward. Cracks streak across the dirt in every which direction, and pale green appears. Slowly but steadily the spots of green become small mounds, then larger mounds until miniature cacti appear. They grow larger and larger as Jasper remains focused on the earth at his feet.

I suspect we're all holding our breath as the cacti shoot up and unfurl, spreading their arms out until they're perfectly formed.

"Halt," calls out the troll proctor. "Well done, Mister Tucker."

Jasper looks over at us with a smile, but when he sees me, it falls, and he looks away.

"First test is a success," the second proctor, a troll female, calls out. "Let the record show one of five is complete."

The male troll marks something on a small notepad in his left hand.

Fuck, I'm nervous for Jasper even though he rocked that. I don't like being at odds with him.

"Now, Mister Tucker, please grow the cacti field to three times its normal size."

Jasper steps forward and places a hand carefully on the cactus closest to him, watching the plant. In the space between us, the cacti begin to bubble and grow until they're stretching tall and wide, bumping into one another as they creak and groan.

When they're at least three times their original size, the troll proctor calls for a halt again. The second test is marked as a pass.

The female proctor presses against her ear again so that when she speaks, we hear it over the field of cacti. "For the third section of the test, Mister Tucker will transmogrify the cacti into something relevant to Pine Gulch as a haven. Points will be awarded for successful transmogrification as well as creativity."

Jasper steps forward and walks into the middle of the field, picking his way carefully around them and avoiding the longest of the spines. Once he's surrounded, he begins speaking under his breath again, palms facing the ground once more.

Once again, the cactus bubble and burgeon, growing taller and wider. Whatever they're doing happens more slowly this time, and I start to worry that it's not working.

"It's a mustang," Bluebell says softly, pointing toward the cactus closest to us.

The moment she says it, I realize it's true. Each of the plants is growing taller and elongating. They take shape slowly but surely, tendrils and leaves forming into forelocks and manes and tails and long, beautiful limbs. Some of the horse shapes are standing, some are rearing, and it's then I realize just how masterful this artwork is.

At the edge of the field stands a big stallion, watchful over the herd just as he is with our local herd of mustangs. The smallest "mustangs" representing the foals are toward the center of the herd with the mares protectively around them. It's just like how they behave in the wild.

My throbbing heart is in my throat as the entirety of the cactus field finishes growing into the shape of mustangs.

Jasper smiles and steps toward the proctors, who ask him questions, although we can't hear from this far away. He points to several of the animals, smiling as he goes back and forth with the proctors.

After a few minutes of conversation, the male proctor presses his ear button and announces, "Test three has been passed with flying colors. This is one of the more stunning creations we've seen of late! Let the record show that Mister Tucker has passed three of the five tests. Only two remain, and these two are surprises—one from me and one from my co-proctor."

He gestures toward the second proctor, who steps forward with a smile. "For the fourth test, I'd like Mister Tucker to create a list of the forty-two species of plant within range of his green magic. I compiled my list earlier today. In order to pass this test, he will need to identify all forty-two varieties."

Jasper's mouth drops open, and he looks between the proctors, huffing out a disbelieving laugh. The male claps him on the shoulder with an encouraging nod.

"You've got this, Jazzy," Jack shouts. "Rock it, dude!"

Normally I'd shout for him too, but I'm worried about distracting him.

Jasper drops to his knees on the ground and places both hands on the dirt. Curling his fingers into it, he calls out species as he identifies them. "Butterfly weed, quaking aspen, columbine, lupine, blanket flower, frost aster."

The Tuckers start cheering, and I join them as he gets all the way to forty identifications. Chokecherry and bitterroot take him a few minutes to get, but when he murmurs the last plant, the female proctor shouts, "Well done, Mister Tucker! All forty-two identified, and rather quickly too! Excellent job!"

I breathe a sigh of relief as I risk a glance at Bluebell. She smiles softly up at me.

When I look back at the field, Jasper's staring at us, smile gone.

The male proctor claps him on the back again. "For the fifth and final test, I chose a practical application of green magic. Mister Tucker, it is possible to tell something of the life of a plant by using our magic to enhance our inner wisdom and sense of that plant. For example, you might ascertain that a plant was recently treated with a certain chemical or that it's not regularly getting enough water."

Jasper smiles, but he's thumping his fingers on his sides, a sure sign he's nervous. This should be relatively easy for him because he does some form of this all day each day, reading the state of plant life. He's got this.

The proctor reaches into his pocket and retrieves a small, spindly plant, handing it to Jasper. "This is an air plant. Just this morning, I did something to it, and I'd like you to tell me what it was."

Jasper's mouth drops open, brows bunching. The proctor clicks off the button on his ear so we don't hear their conversation. Jasper appears to ask some questions that the male proctor answers. After a few long moments, Bluebell places a hand over her mouth and stares at him.

I lean down and ask, "Is that super hard?"

Jace looks over Bluebell at me. "Really hard, yeah. It's easy enough to tell if a plant needs water. Figuring out something that was done to it? It's not a skill we use often because, while it's practical, it's almost more like detective work. Plus, this plant isn't in dirt. Air plant roots are only for attaching them to other things, so it's very atypical."

I turn back to Jasper, but he's staring at the air plant in his palms, his expression focused and intent.

Five minutes later, the proctor asks him something. Jasper shakes his head, and the second proctor joins the two males.

Red stains Jasper's cheeks as he runs a hand through his dark hair. For the first time since he started this fifth test, he looks up at us. He's obviously frustrated, brows angled and his stance tense. He frowns at me then looks back at the plant.

Five more minutes later and he shakes his head, turning to the proctor. Once more, the proctors encourage him.

Ten minutes after that, he closes his eyes and lets his head fall back. The proctors share an uneasy look. When he hands the air plant back to the male proctor, my heart leaps into my throat.

The proctor looks almost stricken as he depresses the button in his ear for the final time. "Let the record show that Mister Tucker did not complete the fifth and final test of the masters certification. As always, there is no limit to the number of times one can apply, although the test can only be proctored once per year." He nods at Jasper, then at us. "Best of luck next year, Mister Tucker, should you choose to apply."

Jasper balls his fists and stares over the field of mustang-shaped cacti at us. Without a word, he turns away and stalks toward the exit.

"Well fuck," Mama Tucker mutters, slumping back into her chair.

"Shiiiiiiit," Jack says.

"I'm gonna go talk to him," I say quietly, scratching Bluebell's shoulder as I stand.

Petra looks up at me. "You sure that's a good idea, brother? Jasper seems really pissed off."

I head off in the direction he disappeared, jogging to catch up to him. Twitching my ears to listen, I hear the click of a truck door opening. Flapping up into the sky, I zoom in that direction, finding him sliding into the driver's seat of his truck. When I land just outside his door, he shakes his head.

Rapping the closed window with my knuckles, I pray he'll give me a minute to speak.

He stares out the windshield, shaking his head, but after a moment, he rolls the window down and looks up at me. "What do you want, Hadrian? To tell me a little more about what an asshole I am?"

"No," I say truthfully. "I don't ever want to discuss that with you. I wanted to check on you after...what happened back there."

He blows out a sigh. "Dude, I don't wanna talk about that. I fucked up. I wasn't ready for that...It's not a common thing for us to do, and I just..." He looks up at me with a frown. "I'm mad at you. I don't want to talk to you right now." It's like he forgot for a second that he's pissed at me.

"Listen," I say softly, leaning onto my forearms on his window ledge. "It hasn't been going on for long, and we only waited because we didn't want it to affect your test today. I was going to tell you literally tomorrow, although that obviously didn't work out, but I love her, Jaz. I've loved her for a very, very long time, and I tried not to. I really did. She's my mate, and I can't change that, even if you don't want to hear about it."

He scrunches up his nose. "I just can't stop picturing all the times we've spent together, wondering if there was more to it that I didn't see. My job as her brother is to protect her, and I know you too well. I've been there for thirty years of your life, Hay. What if you break her fucking heart?"

I stand with a sigh. "I'd break it by denying her, Jazzy. And I won't do that. I'm concerned with you and what you need after today's test. Can I help?"

"Help? I don't think so," he snaps, putting his truck in reverse.

He backs out before I can say anything else. I try not to let frustration fill me as red dirt clouds mark his path away from me.

Ten minutes pass while I consider if I should go after him again. But my best friend is dramatic at times and easy to anger. I love him, but we're opposites in that way.

"Best thing you can do is give him time."

I turn to find Bluebell standing there with her hands in her back pockets. Wind blowing off the mountains rustles her hair across her face, highlighting those beautiful blue freckles I love.

"What do you propose we do?" I cross the distance between us until I'm close enough to draw blue bangs behind her ears. "To fill the time until he forgives us."

The bond is tight with love and resignation. Jasper has to come around on his own timeline, and we can't hang around waiting for it.

She smiles. "Petra left with my family. Said she needed some time with the Jays." She shrugs. "I'm thinking maybe you and I should go work on the ranch for a bit. Not sure I'm ever going to love sleeping in one big open room with your sister, despite her adorableness."

I nod and reach down, pulling Bluebell slowly up into my arms. "Noted, mate. You alright with flying?"

"Yeah." She reaches up and strokes her warm fingers along my jawline. "I'd love nothing better than to be in your arms right now."

Dipping low, I brush my cheek along her neck and shoulders, her scent blooming across my senses. "I want that too," I murmur. "Just to hold you, baby."

Flying with her in my arms and not worrying about being seen brings me more joy than almost anything else. I drop out of the sky onto my front porch, not ready to let her out of my embrace.

"This place is looking better and better," she murmurs.

"Slowly but surely." I jog forward to open the front door.

Bluebell sails through, stroking her fingertips along the doorframe as she steps inside.

"I've got an idea." I take her hand and slide it up my shirt to rest it over my thudding heart.

"Oh yeah?" She nips her lower lip. "I like your ideas, Hadrian. You're so...creative."

"Mmm." I rub her hand in circles over my pecs, loving how utterly warm and soft she is. "I've been working on carving my family's memories into the three walls of my nest, per gargoyle tradition. But I'd like you and I to add one of ours. And sometime next week, I'd like Petra to help me add her too."

Bluebell smiles up at me. "That's actually a really beautiful idea, Hadrian, and I'd be honored to carve your nest."

"Our nest," I correct, pulling her closer to me. "Our nest, little mate."

Bluebell

Hadrian guides me across the open living space and to the left of the kitchen, down a small hall to the primary bedroom. I've seen it before, of course, but last time I was here, Petra was too.

My concern and anguish over the drama between Jasper and me still weigh on my heart, but he's gonna have to figure this out for himself. I allowed him to take advantage of my time for years, and it had to come to a head. More than anything, at this point, I feel relief over our situation, even if it's tinged with sorrow.

I cast that aside at the sensation of Hadrian's big fingers tightening around mine.

Tonight, we're utterly alone, and that sends a deliciously warm sensation through my core.

"You smell good like this, wanting." Hadrian tugs me into the bedroom. Placing both hands on my chest, he pushes me backward onto the giant round mattress.

I hit it and snuggle in with a smile, stretching my arms as I curl my fingers into the soft sheets. "Ah, the magic of a gargoyle nest. This has got to be the most comfortable place in the entire world."

He falls on top of me, bracketing me between both huge arms as he uses his knees to press my thighs wide. "It's been a rough few days, little mate," he murmurs, dragging his nose up the front of my neck. "Let's take the edge off before we're confronted with reality again tomorrow."

"Break from reality? I could use that," I manage as he places a line of heavy kisses down my chest to the hemline of my shirt. Twisting the fabric in his fingers, he tears through it with those black claws, yanking and pulling until he reveals my upper body.

"No bra, Miss Tucker?" Dark brows lift in mock surprise. He presses forward and takes my left nipple into his mouth, hollowing his cheeks around the peaked bud.

I cry out and arch into him as the pleasurable tickle of his tongue sends shards of heat streaking through my core to my pussy. I'm wet for him immediately.

"Mmm," he hums around the bite. "Maybe we should have a little fun before we do the carving."

When I wriggle against him, he chuckles and pulls away with a saucy look. "Actually, I'm thinking you need a little teasing, and you know how much I love to edge you."

I slap him and slide off the bed, noticing a book next to the carving tools. When I grab it and lift it he sighs.

"If you can believe it, Jasper ordered that for me and it showed up this morning."

I'm shocked, honestly, at the foresight it would take for my brother to plan a gift. But it proves one thing—he's definitely capable of it.

Moving on, because I can't think about him right mow.

Hadrian takes the book from me, sets it down, and grabs two carving tools from a small table next to the nest and hands me one with a smile that lights up the room. "What should we carve first, little mate?"

"I've been thinking about that, actually." I lean over and kiss a spot I love on his giant shoulder. "What about when we had our fake wedding and exchanged our bracelets?"

He laughs. "You mean the one you promptly got rid of while I kept mine for literal decades?"

I punch his beefy arm, threatening violence with the look on my face. "Yeah," I finally admit. "That's the one."

He nods. "I love that. You carve me, and I'll carve you." Leaning over the bed, he grabs something from beneath. When he emerges, he tosses a plastic box onto the nest. "And I got a kit for us to make new bracelets because I obviously can't let you out of this house without one."

Barking out a laugh, I grab the box and look at the array of brightly colored flat beads. I nip my lip and smile at him. "Should we make one for Petra too? I miss her, even though I'm glad to have this time with you."

"Definitely," he says, fangs glimmering in the low light as he takes the box and sets it on the nestside table. He thumps the carving tool still in my hand. "Memories first, though."

Nerves fill me, and I look at him. "What if I don't do this right, and our room looks stupid?"

He strokes my hair away from my face with an understanding smile. "My little overachiever, huh?"

"I'm serious, Alk!"

He pulls me against him. "If you carve me and I look like a gremlin with one giant eyeball, I'm still gonna love it because you put it there. Plus, when we have Petra do this, imagine what kind of talent she's gonna have. She's never even been to a school. It's gonna get crazy in here."

I shrug. "That's true." I'm mostly musing aloud as I lift the tool to the pale wood and dig in.

Ten minutes later, my carved Hadrian does look kinda silly, but his version of me isn't a whole lot better. Still, the artwork brings tears to my eyes.

He and I stand with our hands interlocked, smiling at one another. Even in the carving, he dwarfs me. My brothers stand in a half circle around us, witnesses to that promise we made as children.

"It's beautiful," I whisper when he puts the finishing touches on my braid.

"Yes, you are." He tosses the tool onto the table and pulls me into his arms. "Pleasure first, but then we can make bracelets and eat the cloud cake I bought from Skylight. It's chocolate and strawberry, your favorite."

He makes short work of my clothes using his wings and tail. Spreading my thighs with his, he smiles as he places my body just where he wants it.

"I love manhandling you," he says with a saucy smile. "Putting my little mate where I need her, where I want her."

I brush my lips over his as his hands roam down my back to my ass. "And what do you want from me right now, big boy?"

He shudders at the nickname, squeezing my butt as his tail sneaks between my thighs, rubbing circles over my clit. "Your ass, Bluebell. I want your ass tonight. Then I want to wash every inch of you in our shower and do it all over again."

Reaching behind us with one wing, he grabs a black cowboy hat off the wall by the bedroom door. Slotting it over his horns, he grins sexily at me as he pulls it onto his head. "How you feel about ridin' this big cowboy's dick, little human?"

Sitting up, I reach behind me and grip his cock, stroking it hard. "You don't have any chaps, Hadrian?"

He laughs and drags big claws down the center of my chest. "Don't need a stitch of clothing getting in my way." He leans back, exposing the muscular column of his throat. "Bite me, baby. Give me those teeth."

Snarling, I lean forward and sink my teeth into his skin, pulling hard at it. He bucks beneath me, groaning as he brings a hand to my hair to fist it tight. My big mate wriggles his tail, and a cap clicks open. Cold gel splatters against my ass as I move my bites to the lower part of his neck.

Hadrian's spade slathers the lube over my pucker. Then he leans up into my space, curling his lips back to reveal beautiful twin fangs. "Ride me, cowgirl."

Groaning, I sit upright and grab my ass cheeks, holding myself open. Hadrian rolls his hips carefully, teasing inside me. Once he's partway in, I relax, opening for him as he splits me wide around that gorgeous cock. My body clings tight to his, dragging him deeper as sweat beads at the base of my back.

He licks up my neck and chest, swirling his tongue over my throat. "You need more, little mate? Tell me. Let me hear everything you want."

I fall forward onto his huge chest. "I need you everywhere, mate. Inside, everywhere you can be."

He reaches down and strokes my clit. "You telling me that pussy's too empty, Bluebell? That having this big dick in your ass isn't enough?"

His filthy words just serve to light me up, and I rock up and down his length, loving how he fills me.

"Yes," I murmur. "Please, baby."

He lets out a self-satisfied chuckle and brings his tail between my thighs, sliding the spade down and curling it into a tight cone. He slips it in and out of my pussy, slowly at first.

"Hadrian..." I gasp, throwing my head back as I focus on how he feels. I'm stuffed so full, I can barely think around him. And it's always like this, overwhelming in the best of ways.

Mine.

All mine.

* * *

"How you feeling today, Bloob?" Oz dips a spoon into the bowl of potato salad I just made, lifting it to his mouth.

Petra leans over and snatches the spoon then shoves it between her lips. Amethyst eyes roll into her head as she chews happily.

"My gods, so delicious. I've never had potatoes before, but these are so gooooooood."

Oz tsks. "Yeah, and that was the perfect bite, little girl. I was so ready to enjoy that. Didn't they teach you manners in the...wherever you grew up?"

She snorts out a laugh. "Yeah, but I get the feeling our manners aren't the same as haven manners. Either way, I'm the kid, so you're always supposed to feed me first. That's our rule."

Lemon shoves the bowl of potato salad closer to Petra, who dives greedily in. She looks up at me with a smile. "So, we ready for the Mead Cute dance tonight?"

"Yes." I slide a tray of turkey sandwiches over my island to them. "The decorations are up, downtown looks awesome, and when I worked a shift at the Bodice this morning, she was super nice to me. It's been a great day so far."

Lemon places her hand on mine. "Have you talked to your brother?"

I shake my head and pull my hand away, looking up at her. "We intended to celebrate his success tonight at Mead Cute, so it's bittersweet. His failure feels like it's our fault because we fought with him. It's exactly what we were trying to avoid, ya know?"

Petra waves at my comm watch. "You've tried calling him, right?"

"Buncha times," I admit. "He hasn't answered."

Oz smiles brightly. "Speaking of *fun* things, where's Hadrian?"

"Practice," Petra chirps. "Wanna hang with us until everything begins?"

For the next few hours, we just chill at my place, and it's the first time in a long time I didn't have anything else to do. Well, I did, but Hadrian encouraged me to relax before tonight's festivities. I can't say I'm great at relaxing, but I think I did a better-than-average job.

He'd be proud.

Now I'm standing in the middle of Main Street. Every business's doors are flung wide open, and music from the end of the street echoes off stone and brick, bouncing around and filling the air.

Petra's in the middle of Main, hovering a few feet off the ground as she dances with Oz. They're cackling together like they're best friends. Lemon left to find her mate, and I'm just waiting on Hadrian to be done.

As if I summoned him by thought, he drops out of the sky and lands in front of me with a seductive smile. Tucking his wings away, he shuffles the tips together. "Hey, little mate. You're looking lovely this evening."

I step forward until my upper body hits his. I'm not hiding him anymore. I never wanted to, but now I absolutely refuse to. Off to my right, I vaguely catalog Merit and Bryony watching us, but I don't care about that either. Let them splash us across the cover of the *Gulch Gossip*. I'll frame the article and put it in our living room whenever we move out to the ranch. Now that I think about it, we did offer them an interview and I know they'll want to take Hadrian up on it.

Hadrian runs both hands up my back and into my hair. "May I have this dance, Bluebell Delia?"

Smiling, I sink against him and start swaying to the music. The world around us falls away as Hadrian looks at me like I'm the only female on earth. We start slowly, but as the songs change, Hadrian moves us masterfully between other couples, covering ground. He was always such a good dancer. Our bond is loose and sated, pleasantly warm like an inside hug.

But then the next song that comes on is slow, and we stop in front of the Bodice.

Hadrian jerks his head to the left. "You notice the flowers in her window?"

When I look where he gestured, my mouth drops open at seeing a giant bouquet of flowers in all shades of blue. "When did you drop those off? Those were *not* there this morning."

He grins, one hand sliding to the crack of my ass. "Few minutes before I found you. I wanted to sweet-talk her for a few minutes, tell her how proud I am of the corner you two have turned. And then I saw you standing there, and I just had to watch you for a minute or two."

"Creepy," I say with a saucy smile. "So creepy."

He laughs. "It'll never be creepy for me to stare at how fucking beautiful you are. Did you relax earlier?" One of his dark brows lifts.

"I did!" I shout, slapping his chest. "Ask Lemon or Oz or Petra; they were there! We had breakfast at Betty's to celebrate Ginger bonding to Oz. He's officially got a pit hell now."

"An official bonded pit hell," he hedges, spinning me away from the Bodice and back into the center of the street. "Wow."

Another slow song comes on, and we dance in time to the beat. Whispers surround us, accompanied by the stares of monsters I've known my whole life. But I find I don't really care.

A hand taps on Hadrian's shoulder, and we stop, turning in place.

Jasper stands there, a cautious look on his face. "Can I cut in, Hadrian? I'd like to talk to my sister."

I freeze, but Hadrian takes my hand and lifts it to his mouth, kissing the back of it tenderly as he glances back at me. "Are you alright with that, mate?"

I guess we're not holding back. "Yes," I say confidently, looking from him to my brother.

Hadrian takes my hand and offers it to Jasper, who takes it in his and tugs me gently to him.

"I'll be at the Bodice," Hadrian says to me. "If you need anything."

Jasper watches him go, frowning at Hadrian's huge retreating back.

I hold my tongue, I'm sure it won't help to say he shouldn't scowl at his best friend. Not for loving me.

He turns to me with a sorrowful look, sucking at his teeth as he starts guiding me in a slow circle to the music beat. I'm silent, looking away when he doesn't immediately speak. Hadrian's off to one side, standing in front of the Bodice, who waggles her sign at me.

"I'm sorry, Bloob," Jasper says. "I was a fucking asshole when I found out about you and Hay. I guess I had a weird mixture of protectiveness over you and jealousy over him. He's always been my best friend, and sometimes I felt like you were stealing him." He rolls his eyes. "What a dumb thing to feel for a grown-ass man. But the stress of the test just made all that feel so much worse to me."

Green eyes focus on me, his brows forming a concerned vee. "Those are stupid excuses, little sis, but it's what was happening in my brain."

"I don't want to come between your friendship," I admit. "He and I were fated from the beginning, and nothing will change that. I love him with my whole heart, and I've been hiding it for a long time. But I can also believe that you and he are fated friends, Jazzy."

He stares at me in silence for another minute, then smiles. "I want you to be happy, Bluebell, and I shouldn't have put all that Tucker Greens shit on you. I was freaking out, but it's not an excuse. Hadrian was right to call me out on it, and I'm just sorry I've been bugging you about it for literal years. I'm *so* sorry."

I wrap my arms around his neck and smile. "Part of this is on me too, Jasper. I never let go; I just wasn't willing to. But I should have trusted the Jays to manage your own business."

"We need to learn for sure," he says with a quick huff, "but Jace is probably the best one to start with until Jack and I can get our shit together. I mean, Jace has already said he's taking over all the bookkeeping and appointment stuff. We had a big family conversation about it this morning."

"Without me?" I stare at him in shock.

"You're not part of the business, Bluebell," he says softly. "And I don't mean we don't want you to be. I just mean that we run it, and so we need to *run* it. I'd love for you to walk us through how you handle it all, sometime when it fits into your schedule."

"Okay." I fall silent as I think about how grateful I am that he's coming around.

"Mostly I'm really sorry," he says again. "Can you forgive me?"

I grin up at him. "I'll think about it and let you know."

He laughs, but it's half-hearted as he spins me in a circle in time with the music.

"I suppose I deserve that. I'll apologize to Hadrian too, of course. But I wanted to talk to you first. Family above everything, right? Isn't that the Tucker family motto?"

"We don't have a motto," I say with a laugh. "But that's a good one as long as you consider Hadrian an honorary Tucker."

He snorts. "Yeah, in like, not the way I initially imagined it. I'm still going to have to make the mental switch from actual brother to brother-in-law. That's rough."

"And yet I believe in you," I say as he spins me again. "Also, I'm sorry about your test. I feel like we screwed that up for you, but we didn't want to not support you, either."

He pulls me close, guiding me along with a slightly faster song. "That test was my responsibility, Bloob. I wasn't ready, and I didn't pass. That's really all there is to it. A good green witch has to be able to do all those things under much harder conditions than I faced. It's okay, I'll try again. Maybe not next year, but eventually."

I can't think of anything to say to that, but I pat his muscular shoulder just as Petra zooms over with a gargoyle child in tow. They flap in the air to our left as she pokes Jasper with her tail spade.

"Jasper, I'm so glad you came around. This is Iggy; he's in town for a couple of days with his dad, who's the sheriff's nephew! How cool is that? It's such a small world even though it isn't really!"

Jasper laughs and grabs her tail, twirling her in the air. The young male gargoyle flaps along, letting out a cheerful whoop. Hadrian appears to my right, sliding a hand up between my shoulder blades.

Jasper stops playing with the kids and flashes Hadrian an unsteady smile. "Man, I'm so s—"

Hadrian yanks Jasper to his chest, clapping him on the back. "You'll always be my best friend," my mate says. "Nothing's changing that, not even when we disagree."

"Awkward," Iggy chirps, causing Petra to burst into laughter.

Hadrian and Jasper part.

"Okay, are we friends again?" Petra shouts, darting between everyone and alighting on Hadrian's big shoulder. Except, as tall as she is, she can barely cling on and ends up hanging off his side with one hand on his horn and her tail wrapped firmly around his neck.

He's halfway choking to death as the younger male gargoyle flits between us and starts playfully attacking her with his spade. Petra shrieks, then uses her leverage on Hadrian's shoulder to bullet up into the air. Iggy follows her with a war cry that nearly pierces my eardrums. Hadrian, Jasper and I look between one another, laughing.

"Kids make everything better," my brother says.

"They do," Hadrian says softly, smiling at me.

Jasper throws his hands in the air. "Oh fuck, please don't start with that! I'll have to really internalize that you're romantically involved if there are children. Give me, like, a month to come to terms with this." He waves between us.

"I'm not ready for kids, don't worry," I assure him. Then I look at Hadrian. "But one day, for sure."

"One day," he says with another seductive smile.

Hadrian

The Bodice's front door opens, the bell chiming as Lemon and Oz enter. Ginger, Oz's red-coated pit hell, slinks through the doorway after him, a shadow at his feet. Her eyes never leave him, although once they're inside, her focus moves to me and Bluebell.

Ah, so this is the difference when one of the dogs bonds. She's wary of others in a way she wasn't before—protective of Oz now that she's claimed him as hers.

Fascinating.

I flash the trio a smile. "What are you doing here bright and early?"

Lemon lifts a to-go tray of coffee from BrewHaHa Beans.

"Thank gods you're here!" Bluebell jogs from the back room. "This shipment is absolutely wild, and I'm redoing the storeroom organization."

Lemon squees and hops up and down. "Ahhhh! You know how much I love organizing projects!"

Oz flashes me a grimace. Ginger whines at his feet, eyes firmly on the two females.

"Shit," Bluebell says, "I'm just glad the Bodice finally agreed to let me do something about the storeroom. Rebekah's organization style does not suit me in the slightest."

The Bodice flips a piece of wood paneling out and slaps Bluebell's ass, knocking her forward a step.

I chuckle at the newly playful dynamic between my girls. Suddenly, I'm wishing we were alone this morning. We don't get as much free time as I'd like, but the perks of having a little sister are that our home is filled with nonstop laughter.

Petra's staying with us for the foreseeable future. If I'm honest, I think Bluebell and I would both be devastated if she wanted to move on and go elsewhere.

Lemon follows Bluebell into the back of the building. Oz halts next to me, Ginger at his feet with her eyes firmly locked onto me.

His focus drops to my chest, soft wrinkles appearing at the edges of his eyes. "Your heartbeat...I can hear it." He smiles up at me in apparent wonder. "What's it like, the bond?"

Smiling, I grab his hand and place it on my chest. His brows lift at the steady, loud thumping.

"Never gets old," I say. "It just feels...right. It's a sense of knowing I can't explain because there's nothing else like it." My smile broadens. "Even now, she's there in the bond. It's so fucking cool."

He snorts and pulls his hand away. "As long as she doesn't mess with you when you're on the field, though, am I right?" His trademark joking tone masks hurt, I can tell.

"It'll happen for you one day too. I know it will."

Oz smiles but waves the comment away. "Oh, I've sworn off men entirely. There's literally no point. A man does not exist in this world who could convince me to date again."

He disappears toward the back with Ginger trailing behind him even though she keeps a wary eye on me.

Stroking the countertop, I consider how much things have changed in a few short weeks. I was happy in Pine Gulch, I really was. But this? As Bluebell pulls at me through the bond—her need for me like tangible fingers in mine—*this* is heaven on earth.

. . .

THE END

++

Oz is next and OH BOY, his happily-ever-after is as *wild* as you'd imagine it to be. Think fake marriage, drama with an ex and the sexiest half-troll bull rider you ever saw!

PREORDER HERE

Books by Hazel Mack

PINE GULCH EVER AFTER MONSTER COWBOY ROMCOM

Small town monster romcoms with a Wild West vibe

Live Love Lasso

Buckle Up, Buttercup

Another Man's Treasure - Coming August 2026!

HAVEN EVER AFTER MONSTER ROMCOM

Cozy romcom from a hidden New England monster haven with swoon and a whole lot of spice

Getting It On With Gargoyles

Tangling With Trolls

Partying With Pixies

Waltzing With Witches

Wrestling With Werewolves

Victory For Vampires

Slaying With Sylphs

Making Out With Mermaids

Misbehaving With Minotaurs

COMING IN 2027!

Calling All Angels, published by Orbit Books

www.ingramcontent.com/pod-product-compliance
Lightning Source LLC
LaVergne TN
LVHW010638110826
845149LV00014B/2881

* 9 7 8 1 9 5 7 8 7 3 6 5 7 *